Letters

to *Rosy*

MURDER, REVENGE, AND INFIDELITY
REVEALED FROM A TORTMENTED PAST

BY
C. ELLENE BARTLETT

REVIEWS & PRAISE FOR

Letters to Rosy

"Letters to Rosy is an interesting tale of two women… with more twists and turns than a mountain road, but it all comes together by the end in this story of romance, mystery and crime… What a beautiful cover on this book!"
—Linda Brandau
BookVisions

"I loved the author's style of writing, it flows well, and definitely captures and holds your attention to every written word. There is no lack of suspense in this novel, right up to the end…
I thoroughly enjoyed this intriguing novel! "
—Jill
Frugal Plus

"Bartlett took what seemed to be random threads and wove them together into a delightful mystery."
—Debra Gaynor
Book Reviews By Debra

"I couldn't put the story down. What a wonderful book with so much suspense and humor all mixed in."
— Julie Moderson
Bestsellerworld.com

"This isn't your typical story and it's not your typical compilation of letters. It's a story about friendship, mystery, kidnappings, forbidden love, obsession, and more. By the time, I finished this book I had tears in my eyes. This book is five out of five postage stamps."
—C. Carter Martina
CC-Chronicles

DEDICATION

These letters are strictly fiction, and any resemblance to place(s), incident(s), or person(s) is purely coincidental.

I dedicate this book to my husband, Donald Blatchford, who inspired and encouraged me to keep writing until I felt it was finished.

I extend my deep gratitude to John Drexler of Bradenton, Fla., who suggested I write in the epistolary style.

To my good friend Sue Newton, who read the pages and expressed her enthusiasm by urging me to continue, I extend my thanks for her being there.

To my son James E. Black, I profess my love and appreciation just because he is my son.

Last, but not least, my love and appreciation to my daughter Deborah D. Benedict, who read the story numerous times, and being an avid reader, enjoyed the story and encouraged me to get it published.

First published by Dog Ear Publishing
4010 W. 86th Street, Ste H
Indianapolis, IN 46268
www.dogearpublishing.net

ISBN: 978-159858-760-9

This book is printed on acid-free paper.

Printed in the United States of America

CAST OF CHARACTERS

KEN MITCHELL: Easygoing, self-confident, and determined to ease the impact of his one major error committed long ago.

MARSHA STOW MITCHELL: Ken's wife, so pure at heart and so vulnerable to the weakness of her mind.

SASHA: Ken & Marsha's adopted daughter vanished from her sickbed in a feverish stupor.

ERIC VON HUSSEN: A very wealthy, handsome, successful, sophisticated writer has an air of mystery about him.

ANGELICA VON HUSSEN: Eric adopted her and she became the shining star in the Von Hussen household.

ERMA VON HUSSEN: Devoted mother of Eric - her wisdom and strong will camouflaged her own heartache for the happiness of Eric and Angelica.

JACCO (JAMES COLLON): Eric's childhood friend and lifelong companion. The love of Eric's family replaced the lack of love Jacco received from his remaining family after his mother and father died in an accident.

BRIDGET R. BARTEAU: A seafaring companion to Ken. She lived her life in luxury with no clue that she had narrowly escaped a life of poverty, possibly even death.

RUDOLF VON SEEGAN: He was a beaten man, stripped of his beloved children during a horrendous war; endeavored to rebuild his life.

DR. BENJAMIN HOWARD: Was a physician and friend to everyone. He took an oath to heal, not only through medicine but also by healing the whole person.

BUD AND PATSY BROWN: Too young for retirement, found a home on the Mitchell farm, a perfect place for them to thrive and bring their aging years to fruition.

MENDY SUE ARNOLD: Strong willed, wife of Trevor Arnold. Daughter of wealthy parents and has a leadership personality and uses it to the fullest, sometimes vengeful and always loyal to her most trusted friends.

TREVOR HOWARD ARNOLD: Handsome, debonair, successful, the brother of Elaina and Deborah and is married to Mendy. He realized much too late what an impact his moments of weakness had on so many lives.

MISTY ARNOLD: To be so young and to witness so much, leaves her in a state of denial.

ELAINA ARNOLD: She let her guard down as an FBI agent and her sister Deborah slips through her fingers.

DEBORAH ARNOLD: She grew up as an outcast by her siblings. She endeavors to be a pain in the butt for everyone.

JEFFERY WARREN: Teen jealousy drove him to kill a cat belonging to a girl he wanted desperately. Insanity invades his very soul because of retaliation in high school, to avenge the death of the cat, destroyed his dream of becoming a professional athlete. His madness drives him to achieve greatness beyond the wildest imagination.

BERNHARD WARREN: Weaker than his brother Jeffery, he became Jeffery's assistant and confidante. As children, both had escaped the atrocities of World War II.

NATHAN GIRROD: Born into a family of police officers is an investigator with the Atlanta Police Department. He is obsessed with finding the missing Mendy and Misty alive.

PROLOGUE

After all these years, why in hell am I thinking of Ken Mitchell? That bastard! How dare he drag his friends into his terrible plight to find his missing daughter?

Terrible memories are rushing back. My mind is overflowing with fury.

I try to calm my anxieties by admiring the beauty of my garden and appreciate the privilege to be able to sit here in my rocker and enjoy the many varieties of foliage snuggling close, so many beautiful colors huddled in one place. I sense they are trying to tell me something. What is it? Even the branches on the trees, heavy with leaves, reach toward me stirring precious memories long forgotten. These memories will soon fade and the horrors of yesteryear will surface, horrors I would rather forget. . . forget? Thanks to Ken Mitchell, it is not possible.

Suddenly an angry voice blasts into my consciousness; "Rene DuBois, you are an old lady... much too old! Clear out those recesses of your mind and make space for what lies ahead. If circumstances still haunt the tunnels of your mind, you must erase these horrors and move on."

My attention is riveted. A second, more resolute, voice insists that I listen and act. I wait with anticipation for the next instruction; yet nothing comes...total silence. That moment frozen in time draws my attention to a single rose nestled in a nearby flowerbed. Its lovely crimson petals beckon to me. A name from the past, clear as the morning dew, springs to my lips. Softly I whisper "Rosy!"

Roselee Payton, Rosy we called her, is one of three devoted friends of our youth. Mendy Sue Parker and I completed the trio.

I have lost contact with Mendy but I feel certain that Rosy knows where she is and we will be a trio once again even if it is via the post. Now with renewed confidence I can begin my "Letters to Rosy."

Letter #1

1 March 2002

To My Dear Friend Rosy,

Even though our paths have gone in different directions, I cherish the friendship we once had as young girls. The words I now write to you are a segment taken from the memories stored deep into my soul. I feel you will understand the reason I have not shared this story with anyone, until now.

It is imperative that you learn the facts about Ken Mitchell. He harbored such wonderful plans for a bright future. Being young did have its disadvantages with testosterone rising in a 16-year-old.

Ken and I met much later in life and we became very close. I was amazed to learn we both had shared life in Bartsville but, alas, at different times.

Ken married Marsha Stowe, a longtime resident of Bartsville. The adoption of Sasha, a beautiful, six-year-old, raven-haired little girl, was the fulfillment of their childless marriage. The little girl went missing and Marsha was so devastated that insanity consumed her.

Ken gave up on life after his little girl disappeared and Marsha was taken away to an institution.

His days consisted of roaming the woods hoping for a clue that would lead him to Sasha, or sitting on the porch daydreaming of what could have been. His health suffered and neither food nor a bath was on his agenda. It was his intention to waste away into oblivion and feel no more pain.

Rosy, I have written my recollection of the facts on separate paper and have enclosed a portion in this writing. As they progress, I will send them along to you. I trust this letter finds you in good health.
Yours,
Rene

ONE

Marsha

Marsha stared in disbelief at the empty bed where her sick little girl had lain just moments ago. The body imprint of the six-year-old was still visible on the cloud-white sheet. Marsha knew instantly that her precious Sasha was gone forever. She tilted her head back and screamed as her hands pulled her arms toward the heavens. Something snapped in her already weak mind.

"Where is my baby?" She shrieked satanically. She turned instinctively and headed back to the dining room where her husband, Ken, her mother, Rita, and Bertha, Rita's only living sister were finishing their lunch.

Ken was already on his feet when he heard the first scream from Sasha's bedroom. He collided with Marsha in the hallway. She began to smash her fists into his chest, repeatedly screaming, "Where is my baby?" Her hysteria frightened Ken as he attempted to hold her in his arms.

"Rita," he yelled, "Call Dr. Howard. Bertha, check on Sasha. Marsha is out of control." Ken used all the strength he could muster to get his wife into the bedroom. Though he was a muscular man who regularly exercised and was in very good health, she was getting the best of him.

Rita hurried into the bedroom and gasped at what she was witnessing. Ken was on top of Marsha trying with all his strength to subdue the tiny woman, but he had a tiger by the tail and did not know what to do with it.

"Dr. Howard is on the way," stated Rita.

"I called Sheriff Murphy, too. Sasha is nowhere in the house. Bertha is looking outside."

Too many questions were running through Ken's mind. He could not let go of Marsha.

It seemed an interminable time before Dr. Howard arrived. He entered the bedroom and knew instantly what to do. He gave Marsha a sedative and after a few moments, Ken felt he could release her. She settled down and Ken fell on the other side of the bed releasing a sigh of relief.

"What in hell happened here, Doc? She lost it."

"Ken, she's gone far beyond my field of expertise. I suggest we call the Grady Memorial Hospital in Atlanta. They will find out what's happening with her." The doctor said.

"I think you are right. Go ahead and make the call, I have to find Sasha. Doc, she is so sick. How would she be able to get out of bed and wander off without making a sound or any of us noticing?"

Dr. Howard thought for a moment then explained.

"Delirium is an affliction we don't know much about. It's similar to being drunk to the point of not being able to sort out what is real and what is not. One is looking for something but can't determine what it is."

"It's so sad, isn't it Doc?" Ken replied, and then left the room to join the sheriff.

TWO

Ken Mitchell

Shortly after his 16th birthday, Ken Mitchell was uprooted from his friends and the one place, Washington DC, where he had spent his entire life. His father had accepted a post in France as the ambassador.

Ken was devastated when his father made the announcement. His immediate thought was that he would never see his friends again and when, or if, he returned, life in Washington would not be the same as he had left it.

His new home in Paris was not as he expected. He was excited and wished to explore this new and fascinating place. He covered every inch of ground the estate had to offer and found multitudes of strange shapes and forms he could spend hours investigating. However, in the early days of his new life, there was a tight reign on the comings and goings of the adventurous lad, but young men have a way of eluding authority.

Mr. Mitchell, Ken's father, intended to groom his son for the political world and hopefully follow in his footsteps. Ken had a different picture of what path he would take and it was not politics. He said it often enough to his father, "I would make a lousy politician" and the fight would begin. Mr. Mitchell had little patience with his son but was confident that his own plan would come out on top.

Ken loved books, books, and more books. His driven determination to enter the fascinating field of book publishing led him into many conferences with his counselors at school. Their advice to him was to do extensive studying to achieve his goal.

When not spending precious time with his exploring, he worked hard and made excellent grades.

His father was not aware of the plans embedded in his son's mind and he was convinced his plan was progressing splendidly.

The bombshell exploded, so to speak, as Ken rushed into the room where his father and mother were spending a quiet evening doing their own individual things. He halted abruptly in front of his father and defiantly stated,

"Father, mother, I have been seeing this French girl for some months now and tonight she informed me that she is pregnant with my child. We want to get married before the child's birth." He was quite adamant about defending his honor and that of the girl. His heart was racing and he took a step backward to wait for the inevitable reaction from his father.

For the first time ever, Mr. Mitchell was speechless, his gaze so intense that Ken became highly agitated. Saying not a word, Mr. Mitchell lost his cool, slammed his book upon the table and stalked out, clearly thoroughly disgusted with his son.

Mrs. Mitchell turned on Ken, which she usually did not, and demanded he relinquish the name of the girl in question. From her tone of voice, he knew she really meant business and he spilled everything he knew.

Mrs. Mitchell was more disappointed in her son than angry. He told her that he and the girl had informed her parents of the situation. They contacted the Mitchells a few days later and being proud French people of upstanding reputations, informed the Mitchells of their intent to take their daughter away and put the baby up for adoption. There were no other options for Ken or the girl.

Ken's father was overjoyed with the decision and agreed this plan was best for both the girl and his son. Ken protested but had no choice but to go along with the decision.

Ken was in contact with the girl throughout her pregnancy and knew when the birth of the baby happened. The baby was placed for adoption in an orphanage, in Atlanta, Georgia.

Ken graduated, with honors, from high school in France. His father's term as ambassador had not ended when the time arrived for him to return to the states to attend college. His father protested. However, Ken had come of age and Mr. Mitchell had to accept that fact, and of course, Mrs. Mitchell cried a lot.

Ken matured rather rapidly after the episode with the French girl. He kept his pants zipped during his college years and studying was always his first priority.

He was in his fourth year at Harvard when his parents returned to the states and settled near the college. His graduation was a huge event in the lives of his family and the friends in their social circle.

The dean at the university informed Ken of an open position in Atlanta, Georgia at the Saturn Publishing Company. He jumped at the opportunity and applied immediately. His parents were not pleased that he accepted the position in the south, but knowing their son and his strong will, wished him well.

He sacrificed his social life, worked hard, and climbed the ladder of success to become an editor with a substantial salary. His financial position was where he wanted it to be. His family was extremely proud of him and never discussed politics again.

Ken insisted on living on his own without having to rely on his father to keep a judgmental eye on him. Therefore, in the beginning, he rented a small apartment near his office.

It was early evening when Ken returned home from work, much too early to eat dinner, so he decided he would take a walk to relax. He closed his door behind him, and surveying his surroundings, released a long sigh.

"God, what a day I've had."

His thoughts were totally on his workday and he did not realize he was almost running. His destination was a popular park just around the corner, about three blocks down the street from his apartment.

As he turned the corner a bit too fast, he came face-to-face with a beautiful woman and her mother, he assumed. Ken had to put his arms around her in order to stop without falling. Both Ken and the woman were surprised and Ken didn't know what to do or say. After they had regained their balance, the three started laughing at once.

"If you will release me sir, I will introduce myself," she said.

"Oh! Pardon me!" he said apologetically, "I wasn't paying attention."

He let go of her and said, "I'm Ken Mitchell, I live just down the street."

"Well, Ken Mitchell I'm glad you ran into me. I'm Marsha Stowe and this is my mother, Rita Nubella."

"I'm so glad to meet you both. The park is just down the block; care to join me for a walk?" He asked politely.

"I have a better idea." Marsha replied. "There is a little coffee shop across the street. That was our destination before you ran into me. Would you join us?" She chuckled as she asked.

"I accept and it will be my treat ladies. It's the least I can do to redeem myself." His red face had returned to its natural color.

A little thrill went through his body as he took Marsha's arm and started across the street.

Immediately, Ken realized that he wanted to see this woman again.

Ken, Marsha, and Mrs. Nubella entered the coffee shop and found a seat. Questioning conversation began with Ken.

"Where do you ladies live here in Atlanta?"

"We don't," was Marsha's reply. "We are here just for the day. We will be going home when we finish our coffee."

"And, where is home, if I am permitted to ask?"

"In Bartsville, it's just outside the limits of Atlanta about 25 miles or so. It's a small town but we love it."

Marsha had a twinkle in her eyes as she talked to Ken. She wanted to know more about this handsome gentleman. She felt she had to get right to the point. She might never see him again. She boldly asked, "Is there a Mrs. Ken Mitchell?"

Ken was surprised at her direct question.

"Oh no, there is no Mrs. Mitchell. I haven't had the time to do much dating since I graduated from college. I've been too preoccupied with my work. I wanted to be sure that I am all set before I take a wife and start a family.

"I graduated from Harvard last year. The position at Saturn came open and I grabbed the opportunity and moved to Atlanta. My father wanted me to go into politics as he is. We fought and I won, with the help of my mother, God love her." He seemed proud of himself.

"That is enough about me. What's your story?" He thought if she could be bold, so could he. "Is there a Mr. in your life or someone special?"

"Heavens no, I haven't been so fortunate to meet my Mr. Right." She gave him a sly look and said to her mother, "we must get going. It's getting late." She turned to Ken.

"Mr. Ken Mitchell, it's been a pleasant meeting. I do hope you will run me down again soon." They all laughed.

"That's to be sure. May I call you some time?" He asked.

"That would be nice. Here, I will give you my number and perhaps we can get together later, good-bye Mr. Ken Mitchell and do have a pleasant evening." Marsha shook his hand and she and Mrs. Nubella left the coffee shop.

Ken stared after them. He was in a world of his own and his thoughts were of Marsha. Smiling to himself, he sat down on a bench outside the diner to evaluate what had just happened.

For the next few days, he could not get Marsha out of his mind. He called her one evening and they talked for hours. Marsha felt the same about Ken and the two were married three months later. Ken gave up his bachelor apartment and purchased a large farm in Bartsville so Marsha could be near her mother and aunt.

After many tries and failures to conceive a child, the couple agreed to adopt. Ken already knew where to find the perfect child for them. He spent a small fortune over the years for the privilege of claiming his daughter some day soon and the day had finally arrived.

Marsha and Ken left the orphanage hand-in-hand, little Sasha between them. *Now*, Ken thought, *my life is complete. I have the career I want, a wife I love very much, and my own little Sasha.*

At six years old, Sasha seemed so grown up according to Ken. His chest swelled with pride when he introduced her to anyone...

THREE

Murphy

Sheriff Claude Murphy and one deputy were the only law enforcement in Bartsville. The trust placed in him by the residents was unquestionable. His playmates gave their friend the name "Murphy," because they did not like Claude. The name took hold and it continued throughout his life. Bartsville was his birthplace. He grew up there, graduated from high school, attended the Clayton County Law Enforcement Academy, finished his two years in the army as an MP, and then returned to Bartsville and became the sheriff.

Murphy stood with his deputy wondering where to start first. He had not had a disappearance of any kind, but he knew he had to do it right. He saw Ken exit the back door and heading in his direction.

"Hi Murphy," Ken extended his greeting. "Sasha is missing. We cannot find her anywhere. Marsha is so upset we had to call Dr. Howard.

He is with her now. I think we will have to send her to the hospital in Atlanta. Doc can't handle her."

"Where do we start to find Sasha?" Ken asked. "Murphy, she's sick and very weak, we have to hurry and find her."

"Let's start in her bedroom and then go from there." Murphy stated. In an extremely professional manner, he started toward the house. Ken followed him into the house and, knowing the layout from his many visits, Murphy hastened to Sasha's bedroom. He examined everything, from the doorway to the window that had been raised about three inches. The only observation of interest was the little girl's pink slippers at the bedside and her robe folded neatly over the back of a chair.

Murphy found nothing suspicious that would influence him to conclude a kidnapping had taken place. However, the family was in the dining room during that time and a clear view into the hall, leading from Sasha's room, was obstructed and possibly an abductor could have passed unnoticed.

"We need some volunteers to start combing the surrounding area. She might have wandered off in a daze, if she was delirious from a fever," Murphy stated.

He sent the deputy back into town to recruit volunteers to help canvass the grounds around the house and the wooded area behind the family property and to get Henry Stevens and his tracking hounds to come back with him. Meanwhile, Murphy and Ken started the search. He left a message with Rita to direct the deputy and the volunteers into the woods when they arrived...

FOUR

The Search

Henry Stevens had the best tracking dogs in the county. That was a known fact. Henry was proud of his hound dogs and often boasted. Even though he was the butt of the dog jokes around town, he didn't care and laughed also.

The search team was anxiously awaiting the arrival of Henry and his infamous dogs. An excited Henry finally arrived and freed the dogs from the truck. They knew by instinct that it was time to go to work.

Henry asked Rita for something belonging to Sasha so the dogs could get her scent. She brought out a doll and one of Sasha's shoes. When they got the scent of the items, they went wild, circling the house, barn, and the immediate area. They found the main scent and started for the woods dragging Henry along with them. The search party followed. The path they were following led them deep into the woods heading to the river.

Ken and the sheriff had gone ahead. They spotted a couple of playful otters on the bank that slid gracefully into the water when the men approached. That was all the movement detected.

Ken spotted something familiar near a clump of brush. He picked it up, tears began to swell in his eyes...he fell to his knees on the muddy creek bank as he clutched a mint green bedroom slipper close to his chest.

"Where are you Sasha?" He asked repeatedly.

Nowhere in this dense dark forest could he sense a presence of his precious missing child. The slipper he held so tightly was not hers. With tears still stinging his eyes, he handed the item to Murphy and said, "This is one of Marsha's slippers." Sasha must have gotten out of bed, put on Marsha's slippers and wandered outside, not aware of where she was or where she was going."

Henry and his hounds came thundering into the clearing just behind where Ken and Murphy were standing. They were almost knocked to the ground. The dogs were tracking hot and heavy until they approached the river. The barking ceased and the dogs lay down panting. The deputy and the others approached. They had searched visually along the way, but did not find any clue to the missing child.

Henry announced that they could do nothing more. The trail was cold and the dogs lost the scent. Darkness was fast approaching and the sheriff ended the search for the night.

Ken resisted Murphy's plea to stop the search. He felt Sasha might be hurt and could not yell for help. Once again, he started looking around like a lunatic, but Murphy finally convinced him there was nothing further they could accomplish, as it was just too dark.

However, to soothe his friend, he asked Henry to have his dogs sniff the slipper they had found and cover the area once again. But alas, the trail was cold and the dogs were not responding.

Murphy took Ken's arm and led him through the woods toward the farm, only then did Ken realize and accept that the search could not continue in the dark.

As the team neared the farm, its lights were a welcome beacon for the exhausted men.

They gathered in the kitchen, attacked the sandwiches, potato salad, and pie that Rita and Bertha had prepared anticipating the appetites of grown men after a long hard search.

The men had eaten their fill. One by one, they expressed their sorrow and left to go home. Murphy was the last to leave.

Ken assisted the women in cleaning the kitchen.

"Thanks for your help," he said to the women. "You and Bertha go on home now. I'll talk to you tomorrow. For now, I want to get some rest. Tomorrow will be a long day."

"Alright Ken, if you need us tonight you be sure and call, okay?"

"Okay. See you later."

He closed the door behind them and leaned against it for a few seconds then he noticed how loud the silence was and how the size of the lonely room suddenly seemed larger.

The search for Sasha continued throughout the next day. Sheriff Murphy stopped the search when the darkness overtook them once again, but promised Ken the investigation would continue...

Rosy Answers Letter #1

March 20, 2002

My Dear Friend Rene,

Our minds must have connected. I was thinking of you and now I hold your letter in my hand.

The wishes and dreams that plagued my days and nights for so many years are now a reality.

Mendy and I searched for years to get one clue as to where you were, but with no success. It seemed to us that you had vanished off the face of the earth. Now our hearts can be calm knowing you are still a part of our trio.

As fate would have it, I knew of Ken and Marsha. I haven't lived in Bartsville in such a long time and no longer have contacts there and I didn't hear about Ken's little girl disappearing.

My parents passed away, Mendy was married, so I had to make a change in my life and so I moved away. Mendy kept me informed for a while but we, too, lost contact. I will have to rely on you to tell me the rest of the story about Ken.

Now, I must tell you of Mendy's abduction, along with her little girl Misty. It was indeed a horrible ordeal for two such sweet innocent people. It was an ugly and heart-rending thing to happen to our loveable Mendy.

The police offered no hope for their return. The abductors made no ransom call or attempts to contact Trevor. We still do not know for sure if Misty will recover or if she will continue in the state of denial.

Mendy married Trevor Arnold. Their union seemed perfect, but on the very day Mendy was abducted, her so-called loving and devoted husband was having a torrid affair with another woman. He was not aware that his girls were missing until he returned home late that night.

Can you possibly visualize Trevor cheating on Mendy? I couldn't, but it did happen. He was the talk of the town. His father-in-law would have killed him had he been in town at the time. It was a sad day for everyone.

The woman Trevor had the one-night stand with was Sheila Martin. This Sheila lived briefly in Bartsville but I don't remember her at all.

The sheriff took Trevor's deposition and Sheila verified it. They cleared him of any suspicion. Sheriff Murphy found out that the abduction happened in Atlanta, so he had to turn the investigation over to them.

Trevor's sister, Elaina, knew the investigator, Nathan Girrod, who took the case.

You haven't told me anything about yourself. What have you been doing with your life all these years? What about marriage and family, do you have one? Please catch me up-to-date on your activities through the years.

Rene honey, it has been too many years without you. My body fails me rapidly but I can withstand the strain of writing now that you have suggested we write separate notes to relieve the pressure of writing all at once. I have been writing down the details of past events, worth remembering, so I, too, will send segments along with my letters.

It's good to be in touch once again. The memories are rushing back, good and bad.

Remember our sleepover and the murder of my beautiful Peppy, oh how I loved that cat! I will tell you about the fiend that did it.

However, I must stop writing for now. My notes will explain everything. Take care, my friend, and write very soon. I am anxious to hear the rest of Ken's story.

Love,

Rosy

1

Mendy

Trevor and Mendy were married and Misty was born. She was a beautiful little girl and bright as a penny. Mendy adored both Trevor and Misty.

She had seldom dated until Trevor came along. She had set her sights for that special someone to come along who would not allow her to lead him around by the nose, but would tolerate her strong will to be her own person.

She found her special man in Trevor Arnold. He was an important executive at the Saturn Publishing Company in Atlanta. She met him at a dinner-dance hosted by his country club. She sensed, in the moment her father introduced him, that he would become her husband.

He totally ignored her that first meeting but she could not take her eyes off him throughout the evening. From that day forward, he consumed her every thought. Through her father's connections, she made sure she received an invitation to all the functions Trevor might be attending. Her persistence paid off, he did ask her out and she accepted with enthusiasm. There were many dates following the first and they became 'an item.' A year later, they were married.

The wedding was the event of the season. The entire population of Bartsville and half of Atlanta were invited. They spent three weeks on their honeymoon in the Caribbean.

Mendy finished college and became a forensic pathologist. She sure had the stamina for that job. Her family had a fit, but this was something she wanted to do and she normally got what she wanted.

Her position consumed many hours. Trevor was also busy at his firm. Children were not on their list of priorities in the early stages of marriage and careers.

Eventually, they did have a little girl whom they called Misty, short for Margaret. Mendy agreed to set aside her job so she could stay at home and give her full attention to raising the little girl.

Mendy's father had given her fifty acres of his land as a wedding gift. Mendy was on the site every chance she could muster to witness the building of her dream house. The design of the house had a growing family in mind. Their terrace was pink, gray and blue mosaic tile situated outside the huge ballroom. She had placed the potted plants strategically around the terrace so a viewer could grasp the overwhelming view of the mirrored-surface lake of crystal-clear water just a stone's throw from her terrace. There was a natural spring situated on the property that fed clear water to form a large lake so there would be a grand view from the terrace.

Trevor sat on the terrace this particular morning, as he did every morning before leaving for work. He needed this time to get his thoughts in order for the day. He anxiously anticipated Mendy strolling out to join him, as was her custom each morning. His little Misty slept beyond his leaving for work so he and Mendy took advantage of this quiet time to share their moments together.

Mendy was recapping her schedule for the day and mentioned that she would take Misty to the Elite Dance Academy, in Atlanta, for enrollment. Trevor liked the idea, "That's a great idea. Nothing is too good for my princess."

As time neared for him to leave for work, he took Mendy in his arms and kissed her goodbye.

"I won't be home for dinner, honey, we have a late meeting and I'll grab something during break," Trevor said.

"Okay dear, Misty and I will eat before we get home."
Trevor grabbed his briefcase and left for his office.

Mendy dreaded seeing him drive away, she loved him so much. She continued to linger on the terrace to enjoy the beauty of two swans as they romantically glided through the water as if the lake belonged to them and them alone. Her thoughts were interrupted by the girlish giggle of Misty as she sneaked up behind her.

"Good morning princess, give me a hug, okay."
She giggled as she put her little arms around Mendy.

"Do you remember what we have to do today?" Mendy asked, as she gave Misty a squeeze.

"Oh yes," she giggled. "We have to see that funny lady at dance school."

"That's right! Now run up to your room, I'll be right there to help you pick out something pretty to wear." Misty skipped into the house and disappeared up the stairs.

Mendy gave a sigh of relief then suddenly shivers crept up her spine and startled her. She dismissed the thought and took one more look at the gorgeous scenery before her. She was reluctant to go in and wished she could just sit on the terrace all day, but, alas, that was not to be. She would take Misty out for breakfast, do her errands then be at the dance academy by 3 o'clock.

Mrs. Merchant, a prim, tall matron from the 1800s as Mendy had described her, stressed the fact that she would not tolerate tardiness. Her academy was so well known she could afford to be picky in choosing her clients. She was a famous dancer in her youth and she still commanded respect. In her studio, her word was law.

Mendy remembered her words, went into the house and up the stairs to check on Misty.

Misty was playing with her dolls as usual and still in her pajamas. Mendy pleaded with her to hurry so they could have a good breakfast, get her errands taken care of and arrive at Mrs. Merchant's in plenty of time.

Misty was excited about the dance classes so she put away her dolls and Mendy assisted her in dressing.

They arrived at the academy not a moment too soon. Mrs. Merchant was pacing impatiently in her office. The secretary showed the two into her office and she asked them to be seated.

Misty was interviewed first and then Mendy. After the interview was complete and Misty was accepted, the stern-looking Mrs. Merchant gave Mendy last-minute instructions to be certain Misty had the proper attire and shoes ready for the first lesson that was to begin the next week. They left the dance academy around 5:00 p.m. The interview had taken longer than expected.

They left the building and were out of ear-shot when Mendy exhaled a healthy "phew." Misty began to giggle. Mendy started to convulse with laughter. They had to sit down on a sidewalk bench until the hysteria had passed. When they had regained their composure, Mendy looked over at Misty and said, "I'm so proud of you honey. I was afraid you would burst out laughing right in the poor woman's face."

"Oh Mommy, I really wanted to."

"Well, I'm proud that you held it in. What do you think of Mrs. Merchant?"

"She's funny, but I like her." Misty replied.

She slid off the bench and took Mendy's hand.

"Let's eat over there Mommy," she said as she pointed. She pulled Mendy toward a quaint little restaurant called "PEPPY'S POP-EYED OWL."

She and an excited Misty went inside and the décor was indeed a child's haven. A variety of wildlife adorned the walls, corners and counter.

Mendy thought it odd that she had not heard of this place. She made a mental note to ask Trevor.

The waitress seated them in a booth that had a glass top. Underneath the glass was an aquarium with tropical fish of assorted colors.

As she watched the graceful fish gliding through the water around the perimeter of the tank, Misty became mesmerized. The waitress was becoming annoyed and asked her again, "what are you having to eat little lady?" Misty quickly ordered a burger and fries without looking up.

She was very slow at eating and Mendy had to keep urging her to finish. Although they were in no particular hurry, it would be dark soon and they should be getting home.

The girls finished eating and Mendy paid the check. They stepped outside and darkness was fast approaching. Mendy took Misty's hand in hers and they started toward the parking garage. They had walked a mere two blocks when Misty saw something shiny near the curb. She jerked away from Mendy and ran to pick it up.

"Look Mommy, it's a little angel," she said excitedly. She turned to show Mendy and her mouth dropped open as if to scream, but no sound escaped her. She was viewing a nightmare as she watched two men dragging her mother into the pitch black of an alley.

Before she could utter a sound, a huge hand clamped over her mouth. A very strong arm went around her body and they literally flew between two buildings. Mendy and Misty were gone.

2

The Affair

Trevor cancelled the meeting he had scheduled for the evening and accepted a more exciting offer.

He did not return home until late, and that was when he discovered that something was wrong; the grounds were dark. Mendy always had the outside lights on after dark. His family was not home. He entered the house, turned on the lights and checked the answering machine. The lights were not flashing so he knew Mendy had not called him.

Trevor telephoned Murphy only after he had called everyone he could think of. None of their friends had talked to Mendy that day. His heart was beating so fast, he thought it would jump out of his chest. He could not contact Mendy's parents at this time. They were away on vacation and would not be at their destination until later in the week. It would be a terrible shock for them to read about it in the papers.

It seemed an eternity before the sheriff arrived. Trevor was pacing up and down, trying to think where they might be. There was no message on the answering machine to indicate they might be late or staying over with a friend.

He had to let her parents know but dreaded to be the bearer of bad news. On the other hand, he knew he would have to tell Murphy about his afternoon in the country. How would he react to this bit of news? He felt lower than a rat's ass in a sewer. How could he have betrayed Mendy? He had been so faithful up to now and what if Mendy already knew about this afternoon? Did she take Misty and leave him altogether? The answers he sought, eventually, would become known.

Trevor saw lights appear in the driveway. He hurried to the door and stood on the stoop to wait until the sheriff came up to him. "Murphy, I'm so glad you're here. Come in."

The sheriff instructed his deputy to start canvassing the grounds and report anything out of the ordinary.

"I'm going out of my mind," said Trevor. "I can't locate Mendy or Misty," he said, with beads of perspiration soaking his forehead. The sheriff and Trevor sat down at the kitchen table.

"Calm down man and tell me, when was the last time you saw Mendy, and what you talked about? What plans did she have for the day? Did she mention anyone she might be visiting that you may have forgotten?"

"She mentioned taking Misty to a dance school in Atlanta. The Elite Dance Academy on Peachtree Street, I believe." Trevor said, as he put his head in his hands and leaned over. Murphy put his hand on Trevor's shoulder.

"Let me do some checking. We will talk some more later. You get some rest tonight. I will be out here around 10 o'clock tomorrow morning to officially take your statement. In the meantime, you may get a call from Mendy or from a kidnapper. In any case, you let me know immediately, okay?"

"I'm taking tomorrow off so I'll be here when you arrive. Thanks again Murphy."

The sheriff left and joined his deputy. They had found nothing strange around the grounds.

A million questions were cluttering Murphy's mind as he drove home and he did not sleep any that night. He finally gave up and headed for the kitchen. Living the bachelor's life, he reached for the cold pot of coffee, poured a mug full and put it in the microwave for a full minute and a half. He was accustomed to drinking day old coffee and this was no different.

He went into his living room and sat down. Grabbing his pad from the coffee table, he scribbled some notes, his "to do" list he called it. This list was invaluable to him so he would not forget important matters. His friend's family was in grave danger. This he knew from experience.

He had not had a single missing person case in his district since the little Mitchell girl had disappeared. However, his training told him either something had happened and Mendy took her daughter and fled the county, or someone knew there was a fortune here and it could be theirs.

He dreaded his next move. There was that question hanging in his mind. Where was Trevor the day of the disappearance? The husband is always the first suspect in a missing wife case.

He laid his head back on the couch and drifted off to sleep. His dreams were plagued with that one question, where was the husband? About 7:30 a.m., the trash men collecting the garbage jolted him awake.

Murphy took a shower, put on his uniform and headed for his office. He always stopped at the Diner to have breakfast as usual before going on duty. He phoned his office and checked in. He informed his deputy he was on the way out to Trevor Arnold's place to get his statement. Trevor had assured him that he would be home, so he was in no hurry.

On the way to Trevor's house, Murphy was struggling with the task of asking his friend to account for his whereabouts for the time of the disappearance. *The trouble I'm having with this investigation is that everyone is a friend*, he thought, rubbing his head.

As Murphy pulled into Trevor's drive, he saw Trevor sitting on the terrace. He parked his patrol car and got out. Then he heard Trevor yell.

"Come on up Murphy, I have some fresh coffee. Do you want a cup?"

"My God, yes. I can't refuse a fresh cup of java," he said, as he took off his cap and sat down at the table where Trevor was seated.

"You have to realize one thing buddy," he said as Trevor poured his coffee.

"I'm here on an official visit. I have to set aside our friendship during this interrogation. Do you understand?"

"Of course, I do. What's the problem?"

"Where were you all day yesterday, up to the time you discovered your wife and daughter were not at home?" Murphy wasted no time in beginning the interrogation.

Trevor hesitated a moment and said, "Murphy, you will find this hard to believe, but I was with a woman from about 12:30 yesterday until shortly before I called you last night."

Murphy was taking a swig of coffee about that time, and spewed it all over the table.

"What?"

"That's correct." Trevor said.

"Murphy, I have been in a vulnerable state for several months and Mendy's time is taken up by Misty. I love her beyond words, and I know I couldn't love another woman as completely. There are no doubts in my mind of her love and devotion to me, but my concern is for her obsession for Misty. She spends every minute fussing over her. It really preys heavy on my day-to-day existence. I have been trying to find a way to convince her that I am hurting for some of that attention she showers on Misty.

She's always too exhausted to respond to my advances. I have been working later and later lately. Coming home has not been exciting. I loved that little girl as much as Mendy, but something has to change so we can exercise our rights as husband and wife.

My work is suffering and I can't do it effectively when my every thought is consumed by the situation at home."

Murphy wanted to console his friend but thought otherwise. This was not the time to interrupt Trevor's flow of his activities of the day so he kept silent.

Trevor paused and took a drink of his coffee then continued with his story...

"I drove into the parking lot at Saturn this morning, turned off the ignition and sat there for a while. I was trying to clear my thoughts and focus on the day's agenda; suddenly there was a tap on the window. It startled me and I looked up. Two of the most beautiful eyes were peering in my window. Murphy, you should have been there.

"Excuse me sir, you have my parking spot." She said.

"What? I asked. She surprised me and I felt stupid. She repeated her statement. "You are in my parking spot."

"Oh," was all I could say as I looked around at the surroundings and did notice I was indeed in the wrong parking space.

"Forgive me," I said. "I was preoccupied I guess."

I started the car and moved three spaces down. I parked again, then, went over to the beautiful creature as she was getting out of her car. I introduced myself and said, "how about I atone for my sin by taking you to lunch today? It's the least I can do to make up for my preoccupation and your inconvenience."

"Very well, if you insist," she replied, "but it is totally unnecessary."

"By the way, I'm Sheila Martin. I have an office on the ninth floor." She said as they entered the elevator.

"I'm on the eleventh." I replied.

When the elevator arrived at her floor, she stepped out and just as the door was closing, she gave me a sexy wink and smiled. I knew this was the beginning of something I should control, but it felt so good. My pulse was racing and I felt warm all over.

I was thankful my workload was light yesterday. My thoughts were on her and the lunch date. God, I tried Murphy, but was unsuccessful. I tried to convince myself to call and cancel the date, but I couldn't. I was hooked into the idea.

When the noon hour approached, I left my desk, walked into my secretary's office and told her I was leaving for lunch. When I stepped onto the elevator I was so deep in thought, I didn't realize Sheila had gotten on the elevator until someone called her name and began a conversation. I turned toward the voices and there she stood only three bodies from mine. Her shoulder-length auburn hair encased her face, as would a silver frame for a treasured picture. For a second time, my pulse began to race. I could feel my heart pounding my shirtfront.

The elevator stopped on the ground floor. Only then did Sheila recognize the parking space thief she had encountered earlier. Our eyes met and she smiled.

"Ready to pay your debt," she asked with a smirk on her face.

"Of course I am. I'm a man of my word." I lifted an eyebrow and smiled.

We went into the restaurant, which is on the ground floor. Sheila asked the hostess to seat us by the window then she spoke first.

"I've felt so shut in all morning and that sunshine looks most delightful. I just may take the afternoon off and drive to the lake," she said as she gave me that look.

"That sounds interesting, want some company?" I asked.
She didn't answer my question. I felt as if she didn't hear me and I could not believe I had said it. The table was nestled in a cozy corner, which had a clear view of the plaza's park. I saw the people outside milling around. Some were having their brown-bag lunches on a bench under a shady tree near a fountain with its water smoothly flowing over colored stones and figurines of mermaids lounging lazily in the sun. The picturesque scene enhanced the pleasure of two people lost in a world of their own.

I broke the spell and said. "Were you serious about taking the afternoon off?"

"I'm thinking about it. Why do you ask?"

"Well, if you are, we won't have to rush through our lunch. I am in no hurry to get back. Things are sort of quiet today."

"Were you serious about keeping me company?" She asked.
"Yes, I was quite serious. I thought you hadn't heard my offer," I replied.

"Oh I heard it alright." She said. "I just had to think about it before I gave you my answer. I have a little summer place on a very secluded lake in Ackmon. We could sit quietly and enjoy the wildlife there. How does that sound to you?" She asked. She waited a few seconds as if anticipating my response.

I knew damn well I couldn't back out now. I fought like hell to control my thoughts that pushed my feelings and my body to the limits. Shit, I felt like a teenager trying to get his first piece of ass.

Murphy wanted to laugh but suppressed it. He was delighted to watch Trevor sweat, "Go on with your story man."

"I finally got up enough courage to take her hand in mine. It sounds crazy now, but being there was a different story. Then, I said, "it sounds like exactly what I need right now."

It was well past noon and the patrons in the dinning room were thinning out. I got up and pulled out Sheila's chair.

"Give me about 20 minutes to wrap up my desk. I will meet you in the parking garage. Will that give you enough time?"

"I believe so. We can go in my car, okay?" She stated the fact as if I had no say in the matter.

I met Sheila in the parking garage as agreed. We greeted each other and got into her car. She started the engine and while she was backing out, her dress inched up her leg above the knee. I did not miss an inch as it crept its way up her thigh. I reprimanded myself for even being in the damn car. My thoughts, of the possibilities for the afternoon, had me sweating again. Then the guilt trip started nagging at me.

We both rode in silence, as each was lost in our own private thought about where this trip would lead.

Sheila was the first to speak.

"It will be interesting to get your honest opinion about my little getaway. I designed it and supervised every nail and rivet put in it. I spend all my free time there. Eventually, I plan to make it my permanent residence."

"Well, I can only give you a layman's opinion. The publishing world hasn't prepared me to give an expert evaluation." I could tell my statement had impressed her.

She smiled as she spoke again.

"It has taken me two years to get it in a livable condition, but so far I'm pleased with the results. The view from every window is breathtaking. There are no neighbors for miles around. I planned it that way by purchasing 400 acres to make sure no one could move next door. I revel in my privacy." The manner in which she pointed that out made me a bit more comfortable with the situation.

The drive to her place from Atlanta took about an hour. The pleasant ride had relaxed us and casual conversation came easier.

She turned the car into a thicket of vines, natural foliage and bushes. The branches were swiping my window as she drove through the entrance to her property. The entrance was so obscure one would not have suspected that it was a driveway.

When she drove into a clearing, a most unique structure came into view. Its flagstone driveway was lined with the most beautiful Georgia pine trees. At the end of the row of pines stood a completely round structure perched high upon geometrically placed, perfectly round, columns. I figured each column could easily be 6 to 8 feet in diameter. It reminded me of a scene from a *Star Trek* movie. It appeared there was no entrance to the building.

She drove the car underneath the building and shut off its engine. She reached above her head and touched a panel located on a remote control. The car began to descend. I was speechless. We descended below the earth into what appeared to be a metal-lined closet, only big enough for the doors of the car to open comfortably.

Sheila could tell that I was amazed at what she was doing with the car. To reassure me that I was in no danger she made a comment.

"Believe it; this room is big enough for a large RV to park."

"Will I ever again see the light of day?" I laughed as I asked the question. We both started laughing and Sheila replied.

"I firmly insist upon security. I have had professionals try to break in, not here, of course, but when I completed the model. We went to several prisons and offered a substantial amount of money to anyone who could figure a way in. I left a model in place for one year. Alas, there was no penetration. Only I have the knowledge to enter."

"What if someone takes your remote?" I asked.

"It won't do them any good. There have been many tries and failures. The remote is programmed for my body chemistry and fingerprints. Should there be a genius come along to override that, then they must break the code. If only one digit of that series of codes is out of place, a self-destruct mechanism will activate. The digits are timed. Once the main entrance lock is penetrated, there is a chain reaction and the next lock, on the upper floor, will freeze. Once frozen, it is impossible to free the inside mechanism, therefore, no entry."

Her explanation was far above comprehension. However, I had to ask.

"If that happens, then how will you ever get in yourself?"

"Simple! There is another hidden entrance, equally as hard to figure out."

A panel slid open where no opening was evident. Sheila led the way into a beautifully decorated area with pink marble surrounding a swimming pool. There were several Grecian statues standing alongside the pool that made it appear as if each statue was a Siamese twin. The artificial lighting was fantastic.

I loosened my tie as I stopped to admire the surroundings. Sheila motioned for me to follow her into an elevator. Its round shape was spacious and could lift at least six people. She explained the elevator was one of the pillars holding up the building.

"My God, you designed this entire thing?" I asked in astonishment.

"Of course, right down to the last detail." She answered proudly. "You see now why I had to witness each rivet that was used? My security is important to me and I can't afford even one error to be made," she stated with pride.

"There is a backup generator that starts immediately if the power is interrupted."

"Do you have special people to maintain your equipment?" I asked.

"Yes, I search constantly for people in whom I can place my trust. I have several young men and women who are in training as we speak. Enough of this nonsense, let's have a drink. I will meet you on the terrace. Get comfortable. I'll only be a moment." She instructed. "I felt like a very special person to be invited to such a luxurious secret hideaway. I was still in awe as I removed my coat, tie and slipped out of my loafers.

She is correct, I thought. *The view is spectacular*.

I was lost in thought until I heard a movement behind me. When I turned, my God what a sight, Sheila was entering the terrace nude as the day she was born. She held two drinks and smiled as she handed one to me. My gaze devoured every detail of her lush body. I think I was in shock as I took the drink from her. I felt my face getting hot as well as every part of my body."

Murphy was getting a little uneasy himself as he listened to this fantastic story. He was fidgeting in his chair. He faulted himself, *for God's sake man, you are the sheriff, stop it. Get control of yourself*.

"Trevor, you don't have to go into such details. It's not necessary for my report," Murphy pleaded.

"Murphy I will tell you something, I have been around some in my time, but the vision I saw was far lovelier than anything I have had the pleasure to behold..."

She handed me the glass and I started to reach for her then she slowly backed away. I could still smell the aroma of her perfume teasing my nostrils. She chose a lounge chair that would allow me to view all of her assets and view I did. When she finally spoke, my mouth dropped open at her words.

"Take off your clothes, darling," she commanded. "The freedom is fantastic. You'll see."

I placed my glass on the table and began to disrobe. With each piece of clothing I removed, I could sense the feeling she described. It did indeed feel wonderful. This is something I had not experienced before. I have often wondered how the people at a nudist camp could walk around without clothes on. Now I knew first hand, and I could respect them from that day forward.

"I may never wear clothes again. This is great!" I said as I walked to the edge of the terrace and spread my arms toward the sky. I felt the sun beaming down over my nude body.

Sheila got up from her seat and strolled over to where I was standing. She put her arms around me from the back. I could feel her firm breasts gently pressed against my back. I slowly turned and took her in my arms. My passion was evident. She gently pushed me forward.

"Let's not rush a beautiful afternoon," she stated.

"With you looking so delicious, how do you expect me to be calm and less anxious to take advantage of such an invitation?"   "In due time darling, have a seat." I obeyed like a puppy and sat down. She picked up her drink and proposed a toast.

"Here's to whatever comes." She winked and gave me a seductive smile.

She noticed how ready I was to make love.

"I can tell you haven't dared to be adventurous. Have you? Let's take care of that so we can relax and enjoy the scenery. Shall we?"

"The scenery from my view point is breathtaking, but if you insist, we'll see what can be done to alleviate the problem."

I walked over to her and pulled her into my arms. Our eyes drew us closer and the lips parted slowly as they came together. She could feel that I needed her desperately. Her arousal was apparent by the short gasps of breath. She could stand it no longer. I knew her body was aching for mine.

She led the way to her spacious bedroom. There were no curtains on the windows and the room glowed from the sunlight streaming in. She eased herself upon the satin coverlet that made the bed so inviting and held out her arms to me. I was most anxious to join her. I had to struggle with my very being in order to keep myself under control. I just couldn't prematurely spoil this moment in my life."

Murphy got up, and turned facing the lake. He did not want Trevor to notice the story was affecting his professionalism.

Trevor continued his story...

"I had committed myself the moment I entered her car back in the garage. I vowed to take it to the limit of my talents as a lover.

Sheila was determined to take advantage of this situation to satisfy her needs. Needs that were aching to be fulfilled and she had the very man in her bed that could take care of her.

As I took her in my arms, she could feel my need for release as well as her own. She was ready to receive me with open willingness. I needed no invitation. I was ready and willing to be seduced into oblivion. Without much effort, I slowly lowered myself on her and the penetration was complete. She softly moaned and pulled me closer. Only seconds had passed then the climax hit the number eight on the Richter scale.

We relaxed and I kissed her with all the passion I had remaining in my body. We lay there and reveled in the aftermath of sheer ecstasy. As I lay beside her and being fully sated, we both dozed off.

Later, I awoke with a jerk. At first, I didn't realize where I was. My arm was still around Sheila; I looked down at the long red hair draped on my naked chest, I looked at my watch. It read 10:30 p.m. *My God,* I thought. *I have to get home. Mendy will be frantic.*

Sheila lifted her head as I removed my arm from beneath it.

"I have to be getting back." I told her.

"That goes for me too. I have a horrendous day tomorrow." She said as she slid out of bed.

The ride back into Atlanta was a silent one. We both were thinking over the event of the evening. I was sorry, in one way, that it happened, but on the other hand, I enjoyed the experience I had at that moment and it will stay with me for a long time to come, as guilt. I must admit I did have one hell of a fantastic day, one I will never forget.

Well Murphy, there you have the entire story from beginning to end."

Sheriff Murphy was still stunned and said nothing for a few seconds.

"Damn Trevor, that's some story. You know it will have to come out. Maybe not in as much detail but it will go in the record," he finally said.

"I understand." That was all Trevor had to say.

"I think I have the necessary information I need from you. I'll remind you again, if anything develops from this end, you call me."

"I sure will, and the same goes for you. I need answers."

Letter #2

15 April 2002
Dearest Rosy,

I read your letter and I am most distraught about Mendy and her daughter. I am so ashamed to have gone so long without letting you both know what I was up to.

Time passes so fast and other things take priority in our lives. It seems that someone has to die in order for family and friends to realize their priorities were incorrect. Do forgive me. I will attempt to make amends by revealing the reason for my misguided priority list.

Ken was doing fair but not good after they stopped searching for Sasha.

Word came to him that Marsha had tragically died. Grief overtook his existence; he barely made it through the funeral. Poor Dr. Howard tried to console him but his efforts fell by the wayside.

Ken went into seclusion; saw and spoke to no one. He dropped out, so to speak. The burdens on the man's shoulders were a heavy load to carry all at once.

Had it not been for Dr. Howard, Ken would have passed away and no clue to anyone that he was gone. However, the doc came to his rescue, again. To have a friend, as well, in your doctor is a blessing very few people have or appreciate.

I must close for now. Your love and friendship are two of my favorite treasures.

My enclosed notes will continue Ken's story. I look forward to your next letter.

Love,
Rene

FIVE

The Cruise

Ken Mitchell closed the door behind him and leaned against it for a few seconds, then noticed how loud the silence was and how the size of the lonely room suddenly seemed larger. Slowly, he forced himself toward the kitchen, set down in a single chair and lowered his head in his hands.

The next morning, a sunbeam had found its way through the kitchen curtains creating a perfect path to the table. Ken lifted his head and quickly closed his eyes. The bright light tortured his bloodshot eyes. Reality set in and he knew he had not gone to bed the night before. He felt terrible, his back hurt, his joints stiffened from holding one position so long. His nightmares had left rings under his bloodshot eyes. He made coffee, took a shower and was ready to continue the search with Sheriff Murphy.

The search for Sasha continued until nightfall. Sheriff Murphy stopped the search but promised Ken the investigation would continue.

Sasha's disappearance was still heavy on his mind and his defenses were weakening, yet another bit of tragic news came via Dr. Howard. Marsha had passed away. One evening the orderly had brought her dinner tray. While she was eating, he received an emergency call and had to leave neglecting to remember that her restraints were off. She went spastic, throwing things around the room and broke a flowerpot. She picked up a flower that had a metal tip on the end of the stem. While flaying her arms she struck an artery in the groin area as well as a vein in her arm causing massive bleeding. She was dead when the orderly returned.

His thoughts were running amuck; he could not think straight. How could he get past his wife's death and the disappearance of Sasha? In his state of mind, it was too much to comprehend. He barely made it through the funeral. Dr. Howard took him home and wanted to stay with him for a while, but Ken refused. He wanted to be alone to grieve in his own way.

Two weeks had passed and Dr. Howard decided to stop in to see how he was faring. He parked his car in Ken's driveway. As he opened his door to get out, he spotted Ken, walking as a zombie portrayed in a horror film, toward the house.

Dr. Howard was beside himself from disbelief that a person could punish his body so badly in such a short time. He approached Ken and gently took hold of his arm.

"Come with me my friend," he quietly said and led him into the house. Ken hardly acknowledged that the doctor was even present. There was no resistance on his part as the doctor led him into the bathroom and sternly insisted he take a shower then come to the kitchen. Dr. Howard found enough food in the cupboards to throw together a decent meal. During the meal, he insisted Ken come with him to his office for a thorough physical.

During the drive to Dr. Howard's office, he told Ken he knew of a couple that were seeking a position and he thought they were the answer to his recovery and that of the farm.

Ken felt better after the shower and solid food in his stomach and began to talk for himself. He explained that he had already done some serious thinking and decided to sell the farm and try to relieve himself of the memories the farm held for him, but he was willing to talk to the couple.

Doc did not waste any time. He phoned the Browns, Bud and Patsy, and told them to come out to the farm immediately for an interview and that his friend needed their help, now! The Browns were waiting at the farm when Dr. Howard and Ken arrived.

The introduction went well and Ken accepted their help. Dr. Howard gave the Browns instructions on how they could help Ken to recover his health.

The arrangement worked very well and Ken improved rapidly. The farm was in good shape and Ken was strong enough to help Bud do the work. During his recovery period and working with the Browns, Ken's affection grew deep for Bud and Patsy. He felt confident he could now leave his home, while he took an extended vacation to figure out what he wanted to do with the remaining years of his life.

His research of Germany had created some enthusiasm and the excitement of the idea drove him to choose sailing to Europe. The extra time would allow him to think and plan for his future.

After his extended leave, he resigned his position at Saturn Publishing. However, the door was left open for his return if he so desired. Before he left, he obtained a contact in Germany for possible employment.

He set sail on a Monday morning from the New York harbor. Dr. Howard, the Browns and twenty or more of friends saw him off. Dr. Howard gave Ken a clean bill of health and wished him well on his journey, but requested that he let him know how he was doing from time to time.

Ken was not even one day into his cruise when he met Bridget, a shapely, tall blonde beauty. Her friendly demeanor captured his attention and he so easily slipped into her circle of rich friends. She invited him to join them for dinner his first night at sea. He continued partying with Bridget and friends until the wee hours.

The next morning, Ken awoke with a terrible hangover and immediately started feeling guilty. *How could I have so much fun without Marsha,* he thought. This started preying on his mind. He thought he had overcome the hurt. He felt he had to talk to someone or his trip would prove to be useless. He dressed and went to find Bridget. He had forgotten that her cabin was next door to his. He reached the coffee bar and recognized a few of Bridget's friends.

Shortly, Bridget appeared fresh and beautiful. She asked him if he remembered meeting Phil. Phil was a psychiatrist and a friend of Bridget. Ken acknowledged his meeting the night before and realized how fortunate for him that Phil was a shrink. Phil started a conversation with Ken and they both found lounge chairs on the deck. Ken wanted to be well acquainted with Phil so he would feel comfortable discussing his problem, but now was much too soon. He could wait.

The friendship between Ken and Bridget really progressed. All was going well until Bridget's ex-boyfriend showed up on deck. He had boarded the ship in New York without her knowledge. She had had a brief romance with this Steve fellow, but, as far as she was concerned, the fling was over and forgotten. She told him he was too possessive and was making her life miserable and to get lost. It was over between them. However, he had other ideas.

When her ex realized Bridget was not to waste her time on him, and his anger reached its peak and needed an outlet, he started an argument with Ken. However, when Ken refused to feed the anger, Steve took a swing at him and missed. Ken retaliated with a direct hit right in the nose. Steve fell backwards and lost his balance. Over the rail, ass and elbows he went, right into the ocean. Everyone started yelling, "Man overboard!" When the captain got the word, poor Steve was bobbing up and down in the ocean screaming like a stuck pig. The security crew arrested Ken and took him to the brig to await the outcome of the investigation.

The sharks missed an excellent opportunity to dine on angry human flesh that day. The Gods were watching over Steve in that ocean. There was, at that time, another vessel in the water to rescue Steve.

The captain made a thorough investigation. He questioned the passengers who were present during the fracas, particularly one man, a friend of Bridget's, who had witnessed the entire event from beginning to the time Steve went overboard.

The captain was satisfied that Ken was defending himself, and, therefore, released him.

The captain informed him that Herr Von Hussen, a passenger, had given a full account of what actually happened. Ken apologized for the whole matter and left. Twelve hours in the brig was a lot to endure on a so-called pleasure cruise.

Ken was in no party mood when released from the Brig. He went back to his cabin, took a shower, had a stiff drink and went to bed. He did not even stir until the next morning. A knock on his cabin door startled him awake.

The ship's Steward had a cable from Bud Brown in the USA. Ken became concerned as he read that a vicious storm had hit the farm and the damage to the house and barn was extensive. Of all things, he did not need another tragedy added to the list of things that already had taken place. He wondered what terrible deed had he done to deserve such strife in his life.

He dressed and started toward the upper deck to get a much-needed cup of coffee when he ran into Bridget walking with a distinguished gentleman he had not met.

"Ken, are you okay?" Bridget asked.

"Yes." He extended his hand to Bridget's companion.

"Ken Mitchell."

"Eric Von Hussen. Glad to meet you." Eric replied.

"Eric's traveling with his daughter Angelica," Bridget announced.

"Sorry about your ordeal with Steve," Eric apologized.

"Thanks. I understand it was your statement that got me out of that mess." Ken had forgotten all about Steve, but acknowledged Eric's statement.

"I just told it like I saw it and it satisfied the captain."

"Thanks again. What happened with Steve? Did they find him?" They told him that Steve had been rescued and that he was safe and unharmed.

Ken mentioned that there was a problem back home and he must take care of it either on the phone or perhaps he would have to disembark and head back to the states. They talked for a while longer and Ken excused himself and headed for the captain's station. He wanted to handle this problem as quickly as possible.

He was thankful Steve was okay. He surely did not need yet another death on his conscience. Reliving the death of Marsha and the disappearance of Sasha was bad enough.

At this point, only Bridget knew about his wife and daughter. However, he fully intended to talk to Phil about his nightmares and his constantly looking at every little girl to see if she was Sasha.

Finally, the call Ken had placed to Bud in the USA came in. Expecting the worst he took the call immediately. Bud informed him the farm was a mess. One horse had perished when lightening struck the barn. The roof over the porch and living room had blown off and the rain soaked some furniture.

The sun came out the day after the storm and they had moved all the furniture outside to be sun-dried. Bud had patched the roof as best as he could but there was too much damage. He needed to get estimates to get it fixed.

Ken advised his friend to go through his desk and find the insurance policy. He would send him a "Power of Attorney" so he could get everything repaired with no problems. He also authorized Bud to upgrade the roof and buy new furniture. The soaked furniture was unsatisfactory for use. Bud agreed and the conversation ended.

Ken sent a cable to his attorney in the states and gave him the authority to initiate his Power of Attorney in order for Bud Brown to handle the repairs with the insurance company. Satisfied that all was in order, he breathed a sigh of relief, stopped into the nearest bar with the intention to get fully intoxicated.

He was well into his cups when Bridget and a few other passengers entered the bar. They were surprised to find the well-sodden Ken pouring his heart out to a patient bartender.

Bridget and Eric led Ken to a table, ordered a round of drinks, except for Ken. He got very strong coffee. He had mostly gotten everything off his chest while talking to the bartender and he was acting more cheerful at this point. He began to laugh with the others and he forgot his troubles for the time being.

When they started back to their rooms, Ken seemed to be okay and rational. He attempted to apologize for his actions but he was talking to himself. No one was listening. They all went to their cabins to freshen up for the evening activities.

They partied all night long. Ken was plagued with guilt about having so much fun without Marsha, until he finally got the opportunity to talk with Phil. They talked extensively for a few days and Ken began to feel much better. He admitted the passage of time had eased some of his pain, and the nightmares were occurring less frequently. He could not accept the death of Sasha and would not have a funeral service for her until he actually saw her body.

After his talks with the shrink, he was beginning to see the way things were. There was nothing he could do but accept what had happened and move on with his life.

That night, at the Captain's dinner, Bridget's group was seated at the same table in the dining room. Eric had not arrived. They suspected that Eric would be bringing his daughter, Angelica, to dine with them. Idle chitchat was flowing. All of a sudden, a hush came over the dining room; all heads turned toward the entrance. Ken's back was facing that direction so he had to shift his body in order to see what had captured everyone's attention.

Coming down the aisle were Eric, in a powder blue tuxedo, and Angelica. Her little gown of blue matched that of her father. She wore a tiny tiara on a head of silver-white hair. It sparkled as if silver flakes had been sprinkled there for the effect, as women often do for a New Year's Eve party.

They approached the table and Eric proudly introduced his daughter to those who had not yet met her. Ken could only stare at her perfect features and beauty.

Cold chills ran up his spine. Angelica was a perfect twin of his little girl, except for the hair. Sasha's hair was jet black as was Ken's.

Eric seated his daughter across the table from Ken and Bridget. Ken could not take his eyes off her. At one point, he looked over at Phil with a questioning look on his face. Phil knew what he was thinking and gave him a discrete shake of his head.

Ken thought for sure he had found his Sasha, but what about the hair? He took Bridget's hand underneath the table and gave it a squeeze. His message was clear.

Everyone had finished eating. They were highly impressed by Angelica's manners and poise. She was the main topic during the dinner hour. Eric rose and excused himself and Angelica.

"We must get my angel back to her quarters. It's getting late," Eric said, as he took his daughter's hand. She and Eric left.

Sensing that Ken was about to blow, Bridget asked him if he would like to accompany her out onto the deck for some fresh air and conversation. He gladly accepted. He needed to talk and talk urgently.

They walked to the railing and Bridget turned to Ken. They discussed the resemblance of Sasha and Angelica.

"What do you know about Eric? Where is his wife?" Ken asked.

"Stop it Ken! You will drive yourself crazy. Let it go. She's not Sasha and Eric is not married. He adopted Angelica. I don't know when or why, but you can see that hair doesn't lie. Have another session with Phil. However, for now, let's set it aside and enjoy the dance tonight, okay?"

Ken regained his composure and they entered the ballroom. The band was warming up for the evening. Eric had already returned and was sipping champagne. Ken ushered Bridget to the chair next to Eric.

He was still plagued with the thoughts of Angelica and turned to Eric. He complimented him on Angelica's display of grown-up intelligence. Eric swelled with pride. He began to tell them some facts about his little princess, but not the facts Ken really wanted to learn. He did not disclose his suspicions to Eric at this time. He just listened. Eric's conversation was that of a proud father's boasting of his daughter's accomplishments.

The music began and couples were strolling onto the dance floor. Ken asked Bridget to dance.

During the entire time Ken and Bridget were dancing, Eric's attention was on them. He recognized a sudden interest in her that he was not aware of before now. His thoughts were certainly not on the present conversation.

The dance ended and another began. Before Eric could say a word, another man was asking Bridget to dance. He felt his face getting hot and felt foolish for being so slow to act. He let it pass and entered a heated discussion with others at the table. The song had ended and Bridget returned to the table and heard the uninteresting conversation, so she excused herself and went to the powder room.

Eric did not get the chance to hold Bridget in his arms as he had visualized. This thought did not set well but he accepted the fact and dismissed it. He was preoccupied and the time had slipped away.

The band announced the last dance. Eric knew it was protocol for Ken to have the last dance with Bridget, so he reluctantly asked someone else to dance...

Rosy Answers Letter #2

May 20, 2002
Dear Rene,

Your letter has me so excited. My goodness, one never knows what is in their neighbor's closet, do they?

Ken was not as lily-white as we thought. It seems as if turmoil constantly plagues the poor man. He surely didn't need that scuffle with Bridget's boyfriend at this early stage of his recovery.

My anxiety is soaring while waiting to learn what happened next.

Honey, don't feel bad about Trevor. He made a horrible mistake.

Sheriff Murphy took Trevor's statement. His secretary and the woman, Sheila, verified it. How he could let a sexy woman lure him into an embarrassing situation is beyond my comprehension. He had been so sure of himself and his family. I can surely say; he really did screw up on that one.

The sheriff found out that the abduction had originated in Atlanta, so he had to turn the investigation over to the Atlanta Police Department.

Trevor's sister, Elaina, is an FBI agent. She has a good friend, Nathan Girrod, in the Atlanta Police Department, Detective Division. She recommended that he take over the investigation.

I have to stop for now, but my notes will clarify a few things. Take care, my dear friend, and write again soon.
Love,
Rosy

3

Nathan Girrod

After the initial shock of Trevor's story of his affair, Sheriff Murphy finished the deposition as quickly as possible and left.

He checked with Sheila Martin, determined Trevor had accurately stated the facts of the affair, and Murphy deleted him as a suspect.

Murphy's investigation revealed that the abduction could have occurred in Atlanta, out of his jurisdiction. He was contacted by Nathan Girrod of the Atlanta Police Department. Trevor's sister, Elaina, was an FBI agent and she had requested that Nathan take over the investigation. She knew Nathan Girrod and was confident he would find Mendy and Misty.

Nathan always had the desire to become a police officer. His father and grandfather were in the service. He grew up under very strict rules. Honesty and fair play were words spoken every day in his world. Since he was old enough to talk, the meaning of these words had been drilled into his head.

He was the youngest of four boys and learning to be tough was a matter of survival, but there was always honesty and fair play.

During Nathan's training at the Police Academy, he had questioned his instructor regarding the use of deception in many cases.

During his visits at home, he would have long conversations with his father, grandfather and his brothers, who were also police officers. He could not shake the feeling of honesty and fair play that was now being questioned in his mind. However, through these conversations with his family, he finally accepted their solution of getting around the deceptive part of police work without feeling guilty or harboring remorse when he had to apprehend a young teen for a heinous crime.

He would analyze fair play in each situation, exercising fairness to the victim on one hand and leave the fairness part up to the courts on the other. The difficult part was showing any compassion for a criminal, for in his gut he knew on first contact that the person, in many cases, was guilty as hell. However, it was not his job to judge. He had to work with facts that fit together to make a perfect picture, or case, as it were. Facts that any cop determined would hold up in the arrest and the eventual trial.

When a smart, crafty lawyer freed a guilty suspect on a technicality, his guts seemed to be torn out and casually scattered about the courtroom and kicked aside like a piece of garbage. The emptiness and feeling of betrayal hung heavy for days after a trial of this nature. Restraint on his emotions had to be exercised every moment of his life.

There was no end to the number of officers who had to swallow their pride and advance to the next case, and try to avoid making a little mistake that attorneys could twist and make the police look like irresponsible idiots.

Nathan wanted to make sure he covered all the bases in the present case of the two missing females. He owed it to Elaina. He could not feel sorry for the husband in this case. It was the timing of the affair that was unfortunate. He had promised Elaina he would do his very best to find Mendy and Misty.

Nathan had not met Trevor and Elaina had not told him much about their childhood, and what her relationship with Trevor meant, but he needed to know.

4

Trevor and Elaina

Being the oldest of three children, Trevor Arnold adored his sister Elaina. He and Elaina were inseparable as children. To them, their world was perfect. He did not consider her to be his little sister but his equal. In their youth, they did everything together. They had very few squabbles; no fussing over toys; sharing came natural. Little did they know their world would be shattered.

Trevor, at six years of age, and Elaina at five, sat very still as Mrs. Arnold smiled and took her husband's hand, both looking very pleased with themselves. With a coy look on her face, she made the announcement.

"Children! Soon there will be a new member of the family, a little sister for you to play with. How would you like that?" She waited for a response.

Trevor and Elaina stared at each other, not moving a muscle or even a blink of an eye. They did not say a word at first, just sat comprehending this new development in their lives. Finally, Elaina spoke.

"A little sister will live with us?"

"Of course darling, won't that be fun?"

"What's her name, Mommy?" Elaina asked

"Well, your father and I decided Deborah would be a nice name. Do you like it?"

Elaina shrugged her shoulders and looked at Trevor. He did not speak a word.

A few months later, Deborah came screaming into a world that had been fun and peaceful to Trevor and Elaina. Their lives as they knew it would change drastically. The attention they were accustomed to was now diverted to Deborah.

"Deborah, Deborah, Deborah" is what they heard when they tucked themselves into bed each night and upon awaking in the morning. A screaming Deborah is how the day began. It seemed to little Trevor and Elaina that this fun little bundle, as their mother called it, cried and bellowed the entire first year as a member of the Arnold family.

After that first year, Trevor and Elaina had had enough. Their disgust for Deborah grew into dislike and mistrust. The more they shunned the little brat; the more attention the parents showered on her.

At age two, Deborah had developed into a beautiful child, and due to her first year of difficulty, she was quite spoiled and ruled the roost.

Trevor endured her tactics throughout his teen years, and was relieved when he left his shattered world to enter college.

His relationship with Elaina was tested many times after Deborah came into the household. However, they became even closer as they only had each other to gain comfort. They relied on each other to keep their sanity in check.

While Deborah was running wild as a young teen, Trevor and Elaina prepared, worked hard and waited until they were old enough to escape. College was a welcomed outlet for both Trevor and his sister Elaina.

Elaina was so upset the day Trevor left for college. She could not visualize a year without him to comfort her. How would she cope alone against Deborah and her parents?

Tears were streaming down her cheeks as she put her arms around, the now tall and handsome, Trevor.

"Hang in there kid! Do what we planned and you will be okay," he whispered as he held her for the last time.

Elaina did endure her life for the next year until the time came for her to leave for college. No one was on hand to wish her a safe trip. Her parents were off attending an event involving Deborah. Again, and for the last time, Deborah had robbed Elaina of yet another important moment in her life. The moment all girls look forward to with anxiety. Receiving the blessings from mother and father was supposed to be very special to an eighteen-year-old.

Her only comfort was the phone call she received from Trevor. She would always have her brother and friend to take her troubles to, if she had any. Her tuition had been fully paid, thanks to her father's planning before Deborah came along. She picked up her suitcase and looked around the room. She knew for certain, it would be a long time before she saw it again.

During her senior year in high school, her grades permitted her to enroll in the work program. She attended class half days and worked half days. She saved every penny she earned as a part-time employee with the FBI. Her superior was so impressed with her interest and drive to succeed, he had assured her a job after her graduation from college and arranged for a part-time position with the FBI in her college town during the four years she would spend in school.

Her school was located miles and miles from Trevor. She was confident they would see each other as often as their schedules would permit. She had to complete her law training and law enforcement courses as soon as possible. Therefore, there would be little time for any extracurricular activities. She was prepared and had the drive to complete her tasks.

As for Deborah, Elaina no longer cared. She just prayed that her parents would not be crushed by Deborah's hard determination to wreck everything she touched. She barely had passing grades to finish high school. College was a definite no for that one. She relied on daddy's money to sustain her lifestyle and antics.

Elaina thanked God that her parents had provided for her and Trevor, in writing, and Deborah could not touch their legacy.

It was a long, hard road, but Elaina graduated with honors. Trevor and Mr. & Mrs. Arnold attended. For once, in the many years of her training, Elaina was pleased they were there to share in her receiving a hard-earned diploma.

They had not heard from Deborah and had no clue where she was. She had not been in contact with them in a long time. They seemed to be adjusting to her absence.

Trevor had earned some time off and he planned to spend some of it with Elaina before she had to report to work.

As for Trevor's graduation, Elaina was the only family member there for him. As often expected, it was Deborah again, this time with the law. Trevor had learned the hard way to accept what was to be.

After the graduation ceremony, Trevor and Elaina celebrated until the wee hours of the morning.

Elaina was quite pleased when Trevor met Mendy. She thought they were a perfect match.

Mendy and Elaina became good friends, although they could only talk on the phone. Elaina's job did not allow much time for visiting family or otherwise. Some cases required that she be out of the country for long periods.

Mendy was not eager to meet Deborah. From what she had learned from her husband and Elaina, she did not want to meet her, but she had prepared herself in the event they did meet, and a meeting at some point was inevitable...

Letter #3

6 June 2002

My Dear Rosy,

I was so thrilled to receive your letter and so shocked to learn of Mendy's abduction. I trust she survived and they found her and her daughter. This is terrible.

I did not know when she married nor had a child. You must tell me everything you know.

To answer your question, no, I cannot imagine anyone crossing Mendy. She is a sweet person, however, she can be nasty if need be. I hope Trevor's little trek was worth it. It really is amazing how little one knows about the weaknesses their partner harbors.

Trevor and his sister Elaina really did have it rough. Lucky for Mendy that Elaina knew Nathan Girrod and his reputation as an investigator.

Ken had it rough also, and Phil was afraid he was not getting through to him. Bridget agreed to stick with Ken awhile longer and help him to get established in Germany. Without someone to call 'friend,' Germany can be a very lonely place.

There were many surprises in store for the two and many new people that might become friends. Bridget was a mystery when the story began but more and more about her became known.

Honey, I will stop for now. Please read my enclosed notes as they will clarify many things. I look forward to your next letter.

Love,

Rene

SIX

Playtime Ending

The group met at the breakfast buffet the morning after the dance. Conversation flowed regarding the events of the last evening. Eric seemed to be in a particularly good mood. He announced that he would be spending most of the day with Angelica at the pool. Ken flinched at the very mention of her name. He simply had to stop this nonsense of imagining Angelica to be his Sasha. It was driving him mad. He decided to talk again with the psychiatrist.

After eating, Ken asked Phil if he had a few minutes to spare. They both found their way to a far corner of the upper deck. Ken proceeded to tell the shrink about his problem. Phil had, since previously talking with Ken, devised an alternate plan to help Ken if he came to him again. They talked for more than two hours about Ken's dilemma. Afterwards, Ken felt the conversation had left him better equipped mentally to cope with the situation.

They started back and when they passed the lounge, Ken suggested they have a quick drink. Ken really needed something to soothe his nerves. Phil ordered a Bloody Mary for each of them. The conversation regarding the subject at hand continued while they were in the lounge. Phil convinced Ken he was making more trouble for himself by refusing to admit his little girl was gone, perhaps forever. However, if, by some miracle, Sasha appeared at some point in his life, only then should he deal with it. For now, he had to let it go and get on with his life.

Ken invited Phil to join the group at the pool later. He accepted as he stood to leave the lounge.

It was still too early to go to the pool when Ken entered his cabin. He sat down on the bed and remembered he had to call the Browns in the USA. He wanted assurance that everything was okay. He had so much on his mind; he stretched out on the bed and fell fast asleep.

When he awoke, it was later than he expected. He freshened up and the call to the Browns totally slipped his mind. He put on his swim trunks and slipped into a robe. He did not knock on Bridget's door. He surmised she was at the pool with the others.

Ken spied his group at the pool and went over to take a seat. He settled himself comfortably beside Bridget. Eric was also sitting beside her. Ken explained his unexpected nap. It was evident he needed the rest, as he felt totally relaxed until he looked up and saw Angelica in the pool with a friend. His heart, again, started pounding. He looked over at Phil with a terrified expression on his face. The doctor gave him a reassuring nod and Ken understood, but would not let it go.

He asked Eric if Angelica was born in Germany. He immediately got on the defensive. "Why do you ask?" He replied. Ken commented on her perfect English. Eric gave him a strange look then said "Angelica had an excellent teacher. My mother took the responsibility of educating her in languages as well as all the graces a young lady needs to become a debutante."

"I am a confirmed bachelor but the good Lord decided to bring Angelica into my life." Eric ended the subject by saying "I will be happy to tell you the entire story another time."

Ken knew it was time to stop talking as Eric had changed the conversation to other topics.

Bridget received a challenge for a game of shuffleboard. She accepted and off they went. Eric had started a conversation with Phil that was of no interest to Ken, so he busied himself with a dip in the pool.

The cool water seemed to bring him out of his obsession with Angelica, for the moment at least. He did glance at her a few times while he was in the pool and she appeared to be so completely happy. This made him feel much better about the things that were bothering him.

Ken stayed in the pool until he felt he could contribute something intelligent to the conversation. He left the pool, picked up his towel and robe then sat down again beside Eric. He began by asking Eric about the publishing trends in Germany and expressed his desire to obtain employment in Berlin. Eric, being a writer, was well aware of the happenings in the publishing world. He offered to assist Ken when he arrived in Berlin. A phone call was all that was necessary.

The cruise was nearing its destination and everyone was enjoying the last few days that were remaining. Many parties and games ensued during that time. The food was fantastic, and the evening shows were enjoyable. All agreed that it was about time the fun ended and the work began.

Ken had had many sessions with Phil and his obsession was still with him, however, he had it under control. He, most of all, was ready to get down to business and see where his destiny would lead him...

SEVEN

The Apartment

Ken took stock of what he had accomplished, so far, on this cruise. The ship would be docking in a few days and it would be over and he had not fully decided what his plans were at present, but he was sure he wanted to stay in contact with the people he had met on this cruise, especially Eric and Phil.

There had been so much that had happened in the short time he was at sea. He started wondering how Bud made out at the farm and promised himself, again, to call when he settled in Berlin.

He thought about Sasha, and her disappearance. He could not be sure she was not alive. He pictured in his mind Sasha and Angelica side by side. *It is amazing. They are identical except for the hair,* he thought. The pain in his gut kept nagging him. *There was a connection somehow and he planned to find it.* He planned to stay as close as possible to Eric until he was satisfied the connection was only his hopes and dreams and nothing else.

Eric was a writer and Ken had a few years working in the publishing field. They had talked at length many times while on the cruise. Eric mentioned he would meet with his publisher in about three weeks to arrange a book-signing session for his new book. He promised a signed copy to Ken and Bridget when the publisher had released the book.

Ken tried several times to bring up the subject of Angelica. Eric had a smooth way of changing the subject. This action kept Ken's mind peaked to find out what their story really was. Eric was a very private person and it was difficult to pry any information out of him. In time, Ken felt sure Eric would tell him the story.

During the last few days of the cruise, Angelica had not appeared. This, also, made Ken wonder what Eric was not telling him. He decided to stop thinking about it for a while and start concentrating on where he would begin looking for a place to call home.

He had gotten some leads from his firm in Atlanta and planned to follow up on the suggestion as soon as he settled in Berlin.

He and Bridget did a lot of planning and decided to find lodgings near each other. Their relationship had grown much deeper than suspected.

The ship docked in France. Eric and Angelica were the last to disembark. The entire party of friends awaited their arrival in order to bid them farewell.

Ken asked Phil to keep in touch, not as a shrink, but a very good friend. Phil was staying in France and he told Ken it would be his wish to keep in contact. He also told him to call if he had further difficulties with his thoughts.

Ken had contacted Herr Gustaf; a representative for the publishing company he hoped would be his start in a new life. When the plane landed in Berlin, Germany, Herr Gustaf met Ken and Bridget at the airport.

Unknown to Ken, Herr Gustaf had previously arranged the living quarters for him and had tentatively set up an interview, with the Editor-In-Chief of a publishing firm in Berlin. When he learned this welcomed news, Ken began to relax and concentrate on the more important chores.

Bridget had quite an impressive resume. She had worked her way up the ladder in the fashion world. She was the CEO of "ELITE APPEARANCE" magazine in New York City. They were opening a branch in Berlin. She had yet a month before she had to report to work.

There were too many details to cover on such a short ride from the airport and Herr Gustaf told Ken to settle in and rest for a few days. He explained that the fatigue from the long journey would impair his judgment and he would need to adjust before making any important decisions.

"I will give you a call on Thursday to set up a meeting and go over all the details," Herr Gustaf said.

"Herr Gustaf, Bridget needs a temporary place to live. Is there ample space for two in my quarters?" Ken asked.

"Of course, the apartment is quite large if that is satisfactory with Ms. Barteau."

"Yes, I think that will work for now, and thank you. I have reservations at a hotel until I find suitable accommodations near my company," she replied.

Herr Gustaf took them to their new home, or rather, the residence they would use temporarily. The apartment building was in an elite section of Berlin. The streets, lined with very old beautiful trees, were clean and neat. This section of Berlin was somewhat spared during WWII.

Ken and Bridget were in awe as they entered the apartment. There were two bedrooms with separate baths. Bridget chose the master bedroom, of course, with a walk-in closet and dressing room. The four-poster bed was so regal. The red velvet canopy hung in perfect folds to the floor. Bridget felt the sensation that she had stepped into a fairy tale and she was the princess. As she reached out to touch its softness, a smile came to her lips. She was accustomed to luxury but she sure did not expect such grandeur here in Berlin.

Ken's bedroom was a bit more conservative, but elegantly decorated to perfection. The view took his breath away as he opened the drapes that led to a spacious balcony overlooking a magnificent park. He was lost in peaceful thoughts when he heard a rustle behind him. He turned and Bridget glided next to him. She looked out over the park that was before them. She looked up at Ken and their lips almost touched.

"Is this a dream, or will we suddenly awake and have imagined it all?" She asked softly. He looked into her beautiful eyes and replied, "I believe its real, honey."

Then, his lips met hers. Their embrace seemed to be some sort of seal upon their life together.

The apartment was quiet until late the next morning. The sun was peaking through the opening in the drapes. Bridget opened her eyes for only a second and then returned to the depth of unconsciousness.

Ken, on the other hand, had gotten up, showered and was on the balcony sipping a hot cup of coffee. Many things were occupying his thoughts. One item, particularly, the farm. He vowed to himself to call the Browns this very day without fail. He began to catch up on his paperwork while the house was quiet. He would think about eating when Bridget got up.

He started shuffling his papers on a writing table next to the window. He arranged his notes for his meeting with the publisher. There were a few bills to pay, etc.

The thought came to his mind that some vital information he needed was left in his desk at the farm and made a note to discuss it with Bud when he called him.

It was much too early to call Bud at this hour so Ken decided to make the call around 7:00 p.m.

Now that his papers were in order, his bills paid and the necessary papers in his briefcase, he decided to take a walk. He scribbled a note to Bridget in case she got up before he returned.

During Ken's walk in the park, he tried to place himself in the position of being there before the war when all was peaceful and one could wave to his neighbor without fear of the Gestapo. He imagined himself safe and that life was good and would continue that way forever. He was in a dreamlike state, and did not realize he was not alone. An older man had walked up beside him. He spoke and brought Ken back to reality.

Startled, Ken turned toward his intruder. The man apologized for the interruption of his solitude.

"Rudolf Von Seegan is the name, sir," he extended his hand toward Ken.

"Ken Mitchell. I was just enjoying the beauty of this place."

The old man started reminiscing about the past and started telling Ken about his neighborhood and his children.

"Our children were born here. There were three boys and a girl. This was before the war. Our home stands there." He pointed to Ken's building.

"It was passed along to my father then to me. It was one of the most elegant estates in the City of Berlin. It was taken from us when Hitler decided he wanted to live there. We were sick at the thought of leaving the only home we had ever known, so we made a deal with the Gestapo. My wife and I were allowed to stay in the house if we agreed to be the caretakers, but the Colonel didn't want our four children under foot. We protested, but there was no choice. Had we not agreed we would have been taken away, along with the children." The old gentlemen wiped a tear from his eye, and continued. "The children would not have been allowed to go with us anyway, so we made the decision to stay in our home. They took the children away. We never heard from them again."

"I'm so sorry, sir," Ken said.

"It was a long time ago," the old man said.

"After the war, we had very little money, but we had our home. We had to make it into flats and rent it out. There was no other way to survive. We had hidden my wife's jewelry in a safe place. We left out just enough for them to pilfer and not become unduly suspicious. All and all, the soldiers weren't too smart. We could out maneuver some of them.

"One was so stupid; he told us our little girl was taken to America by an English couple. We were relieved to know she survived. There were no leads about our boys. I trust God to have given my Bridget a good life in America," he said.

"What did you say? Your daughter's name was Bridget?" Ken asked in astonishment.

"Ah yes, and a little angel she was," he replied. "She had the most beautiful blond curls. Her mother was so proud of those curls she fussed with them constantly. She wanted to put Bridget on a shelf to admire as one would a delicate Dresden doll. I had to step in many times to get the child away from her. My little princess loved to play on this very spot where we stand."

"My friend and I arrived late last night. We are housed in your building. Our flat is number 4."

"Welcome my friend, such a coincidence." Herr Von Seegan said. "I should have recognized the name. Herr Gustaf recommended you highly. I do not normally rent without meeting my tenant first, but in this case, I made an exception. Number 4 is my favorite. My wife and I spent many memorable times there. You will enjoy it," he said.

"Herr Von Seegan, I would like for you to meet my companion. If you have no plans for this evening, would you like to join us?"

Rudolf was reluctant to accept the invitation without first Ken clearing it with his friend. Ken assured him it would be all right. He did accept and promised to come around five o'clock. They walked back to the building together. Ken's heart was beating so fast. He could hardly wait to get back to the apartment and tell Bridget of the old man and his tale of woe.

EIGHT

The Surprise

Ken was excited about meeting Herr Von Seegan. He thought, *this is no coincidence that the old man's daughter's name is also Bridget and she was originally from England.*

Ken said goodbye to Herr Von Seegan and went back to the apartment. He took the stairs two at a time. He reached his door, stopped, and ran his fingers through his hair in anticipation of how he would break this bit of suspicion to Bridget. She had expressed her love so many times of her beloved parents. In their conversations, sometimes, she would mention her childhood, but Ken let it pass with little or no concern, as he was preoccupied with his own troubles. She had told him of her adoption and he began to put the pieces together and was almost certain that her natural father lived downstairs.

He fumbled with the key to the door and almost dropped it. *Whoa,* he said to himself. *Get a grip man. You must find the right words to approach Bridget.* The voice in his head was so clear he let out a long sigh and aloud he murmured, "Wow!"

As he entered the apartment, he saw Bridget. She was standing in the hall as if waiting for him. He looked her square in the eye and the look on his face brought out the concern Bridget felt at that moment.

"Ken, what's wrong? You look as if you have seen a ghost." Ken silently stared at her.

"Ken?" She asked again. "What is it?"

"It may be nothing but we have to talk, now!" He said. "Is there any coffee?"

"Yes, of course. I made a fresh pot," she answered. "I will get a cup for you. Go to the balcony and I'll be back in a few minutes."

Ken settled himself at the table and thought, *oh God! What have I started?* He was trying to figure what his next words would be when Bridget came out with his coffee.

"Sit down, would you? I have something to tell you." Ken gave a long sigh.

Puzzled as she was, she seated herself across the table from Ken and waited until he spoke again.

"Honey," he finally said. "I went for a walk in the park." His voice cracked as he attempted to say his next line. "I met the landlord of this building. Herr Rudolf Von Seegan is his name. We had a long talk about the history of this place.

"At the beginning of World War II when Hitler took over, the Gestapo seized most of the homes in this section and this building was one of them. Herr Von Seegan, his wife and 4 children lived here. The Gestapo came to their home and demanded they give up the house for Hitler's headquarters. Being a fast thinker, Herr Von Seegan began negotiating with them. He told them they would need someone to care for the house and grounds. He and his family were willing to be caretakers for only a small portion of the house to live in. The Colonel agreed but refused to allow the children to stay.

"He said his youngest; a girl named Bridget was taken to America by an English couple."

Bridget continued to stare at Ken for a few more minutes. Then, in a weak voice, she uttered, "It does make a lot of sense, or could it just be wishful thinking."

"Well, we'll see. I hope you don't mind, but I invited him over here for a visit this evening." Ken replied.

"You invited him for today?"

"Yes, do you mind?" He asked. "We might as well see what he has to say. Jump in and get the feet wet, as the saying goes."

She stood and headed toward the kitchen to wash up the cups and saucers they had used.

A million thoughts raced through her mind. *I do remember some things,* she thought. *I can barely remember a little song, something special I remember at bedtime, but it could have been my mother.* She reprimanded herself and stopped trying to make it fit. If Herr Von Seegan were her natural father, they would know it. He could set her mind at ease.

As she reached into the cupboard to put away a cup, her hands were shaking so badly she dropped it on the tiled floor and it shattered into a million pieces.

Ken heard the crash and rushed into the kitchen. Bridget was leaning on the counter sobbing uncontrollably. He eased himself near to her and gently put his arms around her shoulders.

"Easy, honey," he whispered. "It's okay let it go."

She laid her head on his chest and cried so hard she could not speak. Ken held her close without a word until she regained her composure.

Finally, after what seemed an eternity, Bridget lifted her head and their eyes met. He fully understood and waited for her to speak first. She smiled and faintly said, "thanks." She brushed her lips against his cheek, turned and left the room.

Ken cleared up the broken cup and went back to the balcony. Bridget was standing there looking out into the park.

"Shall we go out and have a leisurely lunch? I think it will do me a world of good and give us time to discuss this," she turned to Ken and asked.

"Sure, honey. Are you ready now?"

"Yes. I'll get my purse."

Ken took Bridget to a quaint little café and the two sat quietly for a while.

"What if he is my father? How will it affect him?" she asked.

"Let's just wait and see how it goes, okay?"

"That's a great idea. I think I'm making more of this than I should," she replied.

They returned to the apartment after they had spent some time wandering the streets of Berlin. Bridget had picked up some coffee cake to serve that evening when Herr Von Seegan arrived.

The hour was getting near for their guest's appearance. Bridget was getting nervous about meeting Herr Von Seegan. She and Ken were sitting on the balcony talking and the doorbell rang. They looked at each other and Ken knew she wanted him to open the door. He made the first move and went to greet their expected guest.

Bridget walked slowly behind Ken and when he opened the door, Ken extended his hand in welcome. He introduced his companion as Bridget Barteau. She welcomed Herr Von Seegan and he presented her with a beautiful bouquet of flowers he had picked from his garden. As their eyes met, it seemed they knew at that moment, a bonding was taking place, a bonding only they could feel. Still holding her hand, he said, "My dear, it's a pleasure of a lifetime to meet you. You must tell me about yourself."

"Do come in. You are welcomed in our home," she said without taking her eyes from his.

The two men followed Bridget to the balcony. "Please have a seat. Do you take coffee?" She asked.

"Yes, with just sugar, if you please."

Ken started a conversation and it appeared Bridget and Herr Von Seegan were just going through the motions and heard not a word of what he was saying. Herr Von Seegan spoke, not realizing he had interrupted Ken's sentence.

"Bridget, my dear, tell me, who are your parents?" She was not at all hesitant to answer his question.

"Andre and Regina Barteau," she answered. "I was adopted at a very early age. They were the only parents I have known and loved. They were the best. As an only child, I fear I was a bit spoiled."

"Are your parents still living?" Herr Von Seegan asked further.

"Unfortunately, no," she said. "A horrible illness took my father and my mother followed shortly. The doctors could not say of what she died, other than a natural death. However, I suspected it was from a broken heart. They were so devoted to each other. She never accepted his death."

"I feel so sorry for your loss. I, too, lost everything that was dear to me." Herr Von Seegan replied, with a big lump crowding his throat.

Ken spoke up at this time and said "Herr Von Seegan, I've told Bridget part of your story. Do you prefer to tell her the rest of the story?"

"Yes, I would like to, if I may," he answered.

"Please, I would like to know," Bridget said sweetly...

Rosy Answers Letter #3

July 26, 2002

Dearest Rene,

It surely seems a long span between letters. I all but tackle my mailman each morning expecting your letter. The poor man practically runs past my house when he doesn't have a letter for me. He became aware of the importance of my getting your letters. He now plays games with me. He holds my letter at arms length so I can take the letter and not his hand.

I guess I am getting a little overanxious to learn more about Ken and Bridget.

Again, you are not telling me about you. Is it something horrible like a big wart on your nose and you are ashamed to tell me? Seriously, I care about you and want your reassurance that you are okay.

Trevor and Mendy's father kept after Sheriff Murphy every day until he told them he was not handling the case anymore. He had told them this before but they insisted that he inform them of anything this Nathan person found out.

It was difficult for them to reach Nathan. Lucky for him, he was too far away for them to be constantly under foot.

I am sure they were worried sick by not hearing any news but there was nothing the authorities could tell them that would give them any hope to believe the girls were alive.

My note is more detailed and written as I remember. Therefore, I will stop for now and look for the mailman.

I think he might be avoiding me by putting the mail in my box and scurrying away.

Do write to me soon. Your letters have my blood racing through my veins and that indicates that there is still life left in this old body.

Love,

Rosy

5

Jason and the Boys

Nathan would not give up. Maybe there would have been a glimmer of hope, if that ransom call had come, but too much time had elapsed and no contact.

His people had to keep digging. Someone somewhere had to have seen the girls. They did not vanish in thin air. He was staring into space trying to visualize the girls leaving the academy. They would be walking in the direction of the garage, anticipating their ride home.

Nathan grabbed his coat and asked one of the officers to accompany him. He wanted to walk from the dance academy to the garage where they had found Mendy's car. He had his man park in the garage so they could take the same route Mendy and Misty had supposedly taken. His keen eyes were combing every inch of the way for anything that might be a clue.

He came upon an alleyway between two buildings. He turned in and slowly walked the full length. There was a small parking area behind one building, and something caught Nathan's attention. He bent down and picked up a small object attached to a chain. In further examining the object, he saw it was a tiny gold angel with its wings spread and arms upward. A slight ripple crept up his spine. He didn't like the feeling at all. He made a mental note to ask Mr. Arnold if Misty owned such a trinket. He further scrutinized the area and behind the dumpster and, in plain sight, he saw a woman's purse. "Damn!" He said aloud. He picked up the purse with two fingers and laid it on a nearby box. With his pen, he tried to open its flap to examine the contents. He had left his office in such a hurry he neglected to grab a pair of latex gloves. He reached inside his pocket and took out his walkie-talkie. He reached one of the other team members who were combing the area. He told him to go to the car and call the CSI team. Nathan said he would do nothing further until they arrived. He was thankful no one had found the purse and made off with it. He slowly backed away from the area so the CSI team could go over what he considered the crime scene.

One of the other officers located Nathan and reported that he had found nothing unusual on his tour of the street. He was surprised when Nathan told him what he had found.

The CSI team arrived and taped off the alley between the buildings so no one could enter.

The General, his team called him, was the brains behind the team.

"What do you have here?" He asked as he walked up to Nathan.

Nathan pointed to the purse and the General opened the flap and peered inside. He took out an identification card bearing Mendy's photograph. Further search revealed her driver's license and her credit cards were in place and nothing seemed to be disturbed.

Nathan showed the General the little angel he had found. He took it and slipped it into a plastic bag.

"The identification in the purse says it belongs to one Mendy Sue Arnold," the General stated.

"Oh, God help them," Nathan said shaking his head.

This was the first lead they had gotten since the abduction. No way was he leaving until he had exhausted every effort to find something or someone that could give them some picture of what had taken place.

The CSI team had thoroughly covered every inch of the space in the lot behind the building and had given Nathan the "all clear" to continue.

"Would you give me a copy of your report as soon as possible?" Nathan asked.

"Yes, I will. It shouldn't be too long as we have too little to go on," the General said and walked away.

Nathan had noticed an exit at the other side and decided to walk around to the other alley beside this building and the next. He might find one of the very few homeless people that might have been searching for food or other items to enhance their life style and saw something, but they most always were reluctant to tell what they saw, if anything.

There were no tenant houses overlooking the alley so he ruled out an eyewitness from that angle. He and his partner walked slowly down the street. On the corner, there were three teen boys hanging out on the steps of a tobacco shop/poolroom. Nathan recognized the boys immediately.

Jason, a tall lanky 15-year-old Afro-American had a record for petty theft.

Wally was shorter than Jason, a year older and had a great physique. He was a physical-fitness freak and proud to flex his muscles at any given time. He, too, had gotten into trouble. He beat up his old man for abusing his mother. He beat him up real bad and while he was in the hospital, Wally told him, in no uncertain terms, that if he touched his mother again, he would rip his arm off and stick it up his ass. His father, of course, had him arrested.

While his father lay in the hospital, he got serious about his situation and his temper and he knew Wally was capable of carrying out his threat so when he returned home from the hospital he apologized to his wife and dropped the charges against Wally. Things at home changed drastically after the incident and Wally didn't mind going home more often.

The third teen was Rollo, a more severe case. He had been abused since he was a young child. His mother was a crack addict and he did not know who his father was. He only knew there were a lot of uncles and cousins spending the night in his mother's bedroom.

Rollo was sick a lot and very malnourished. His mother, uncles and cousins forced him out on the streets to steal and buy drugs for them. He hated them all but could not do anything about it until, by chance, he met up with Wally and Jason. He was only 11 years old when Wally and Jason took him under their wings.

He was forging for food in a dumpster behind a restaurant when Wally and Jason appeared. They felt a connection the moment they spoke to Rollo. He told them he was so hungry. Would they give him something to eat? The two boys bonded with him at that moment. They took him to Jason's house. His mother was putting together a meal for Rollo while Jason made him take a shower. He gave him some of his old outgrown clothes and made him put them on. From then on, his life became much easier and he ate regularly. His health improved and through the protection of Wally and Jason, he was becoming somewhat a normal unafraid kid.

Nathan had helped each one tremendously to cope with their individual situation. The boys didn't forget. They trusted Nathan and they knew what was happening on the streets so they helped Nathan by gathering information. Nathan knew all three were, basically, good boys. They just needed some outside person they could respect and rely on.

He wanted to talk to the boys alone. He sent the other officer down the street to see if he could locate anyone who might have seen something.

"What's happening, guys?" Nathan said as he walked up to Jason.

"What's up man?" Jason answered and gave him "the" handshake of the street.

"Got a little problem guys. You may be able to help me." "Maybe," Jason grinned. He wanted to act coy.

"Had a kidnapping Friday night about 6:30 p.m. or so, a lady and a little girl, both well dressed and pretty. We think it might have been in back at the end of that alleyway. He nodded in the direction from which he had come.

"Hey, it was Friday night we saw them three dudes cruising in a black van," Rollo said.

"An ugly piece of crap it was, too."

"Oh yeah!" Wally commented.

"One of the bastards gave me the finger. I got me one good look at him. He grinned when he flipped me the bird. His kisser was jammed with rotten teeth. The one driving had sort of a sourpuss look but a fair-looking dude. I wondered bout that, this guy didn't fit in with the other two."

Jason rubbed his chin and with a puzzled look, he told Nathan he noticed them coming out of the back alley about 7:15, but there were only two of them in the front seat, the guy with the rotten teeth and the good-looking dude.

Nathan felt a glimmer of hope. His next question was the kicker.

"Jason, would you be willing to give a description of the men to a police artist?"

"No way man," he snapped.

Nathan frowned when Jason at first refused to give a police artist a description of the three men he saw in the van.

Jason was nervous about going to the police station. Again, Nathan asked him to do this for him.

"Man, I need you to do this for me," Nathan stated.

"I don't know man," Jason said. "Maybe I can if it ain't at the station. I don't like that place none." Nathan knew what the boys had been through.

"What if I can get the artist to meet you someplace? Will that work for you?" He asked.

"Yeah, that's better. How about the park six blocks over on our turf."

"That's fine." Nathan agreed.

"How about 4:00 o'clock today?"

"Okay, we'll be there right by that Grant statue. You coming, too?" Jason asked.

"If nothing happens between now and then, I'll be there, but just in case, the artist's name is Janice. She's a short red head with a beautiful smile. Thanks guys, I won't forget this. You take care of Janice if I can't come."

"No problem man, just glad to do your job for you." Nathan grinned as he left to join his partner.

Nathan didn't mention the boys to his partner, but asked if he had any luck.

"One old guy said he was walking up this street with his daughter Friday night. They were going to the movies on Peachtree Street, said he didn't like to park in the garages, so he parked down this side street and they walked up."

"I asked him if he saw anything strange. He said no, at first, then he said he saw a black van parked in that alleyway over there." He pointed to the alley where Nathan had found the purse.

"He didn't know exactly what time it was, but the movie was to start at 7:30. Just as he looked into the alley the head lights came on and he and his daughter just kept walking."

"Did he say where he lived?" Nathan asked.

"Yeah, he said he lived ten blocks down this street and he works as a doorman at the Peachtree Plaza building. He was going back to work from his lunch break.

"He didn't see anyone in the van. It was too dark at that time. He did say he saw three young men on the steps of that tobacco shop."

"It fits," Nathan said. "I talked to the guys on the corner. I believe we got us a real lead. It's something to go on at least, instead of farting in the wind. Let's head back to the station."

Nathan entered the CSI Division and went directly to the General's office. He tapped twice on the window. The General looked up and motioned for Nathan to come in. He entered and closed the door behind him.

"Nate, my report of the crime scene is finished." Handing a folder to Nathan, the General started a synopsis of his findings.

"As you know, the purse was indeed that of Mrs. Arnold. However, we found nothing to indicate there was foul play. Everything we examined just indicated the lady lost her purse. There were two different prints on the angel you found. One was a match to those we obtained from the little girl's birth certificate Mr. Arnold gave us. But, the other has yet to be identified. It was a small print, indicating another child had held it. Perhaps Misty found it. Mr. Arnold said he had not seen it in his daughter's possession.

"How about a midget?" Nathan added.

"Can't be," the General replied. "They have a distinctive print. This one doesn't fit in that category. It belongs to another child, for certain. We are checking the school records, hoping to get a match. We have a partial tire print, which indicates the tire belongs on a utility vehicle. It could be a van, or a small delivery truck. There are foreign dirt particles, indicative of an area where there is new construction such as sawdust and masonry powder."

"We didn't see any repairs or new building of any nature around the area," Nathan added.

"We questioned the maintenance supervisors for the office buildings on both sides of the alley. They stated that there was no new construction occurring in their buildings," replied the General.

The General had completed his report and handed it to Nathan. He put his hands behind his head and leaned back in his chair awaiting a response from him. There was none.

Nathan stood and walked out.

He was pondering the information and thought, *we may be looking for plumbers or carpenters...*

6

Mendy/Misty

They disappeared between the buildings. The only thought that Misty had, at that moment, was how dark it seemed and she could not breathe. It seemed like forever to the little girl, before the hand let go and roughly threw her into a huge van and closed the door.

Misty was confused so badly she did not notice her mother lying across from her. Suddenly, someone put a piece of tape across her mouth, hands and legs and it seemed to her someone was playing a mean joke. She was thrown into the van with such force it had dazed her.

The van began to move, slowly at first then it sped up and moved very fast. With each bump, the floor of the van hurt her back. She started to cry, as the pain was getting more and more intense. Her eyes were so blurry, she could see very little. After a while, her eyes cleared up and she could see a little better but it was still dark in the van. Her mother was lying very still and the man in the back with them started opening Mendy's blouse and roughly squeezing her breast. Misty did not know what was happening. She had never seen anyone, not even her daddy, do this to her mother.

The man looked over at Misty and gave her a satanic grin as he unzipped his pants and made an obscene gesture toward her and said, "Don't you worry little darling, I'll get to you later." He let out a roar of laughter. This gesture made him more anxious. He pulled up Mendy's skirt and ripped her panties off. He untied her feet and mounted her between her legs. When he did this, he entered her roughly without hesitation and began pumping furiously. Misty could only watch. She had no clue what the man was doing to her mother, but she sensed that it was not right.

The man laying on Mendy began to grunt and groan. Misty witnessed each strange move the man made. Mendy lay motionless with her eyes closed. The other two men had no idea what was happening in the back of the van. There was no window to see in the back. Misty was so terrified she could not make a sound.

She knew by now she and her mother were in real trouble. She kept her eyes on the man who was lying on her mother. The man was oblivious to his surroundings. Having his fill, he rolled off Mendy. He was so exhausted he did not bother to zip his pants. Gasping for breath after his bout with Mendy, he lay back and closed his eyes. Shortly he was snoring.

Misty thought she heard a moan from her mother and saw a slight movement of her eyelids. She moaned again and opened her eyes. She could not comprehend what had happened. She looked over at Misty. She could not move. The sedation was strong, her eyes slowly closed and she was still once again.

Misty wet her pants and again started crying. The tears were burning her little cheeks but she lay helpless. She did not understand the thoughts that were running through her innocent little head, and that made her even more afraid. She wanted her mother to wake up. At this minute, she thought there was never a more lonely moment in her whole life. She wanted to go home to the safe haven of her own room...

Letter #4

26 August 2002
Dear Rosy,

I'm not quite sure my nerves will hold out before you tell me the rest of the story about Mendy, but I will try to keep calm.

My heavens! What an ordeal. Mendy must have been out of her mind with worry about Misty.

It is unfortunate for Mendy that this terrible thing happened to her and her daughter. My blood is boiling with thoughts of what they could do to Mendy and that little girl. My heart aches for them.

The boys really came through for Nate with that composite. It seems that he is honestly searching for the girls.

As I told you in my last letter, Ken & Bridget arrived in France. Bridget had said her farewell to Eric and the others.

Ken said he had a difficult time in France because he remembered very little French. He wished a million times he had taken French in school instead of Spanish. However, he was in luck. Bridget did know the language and could speak it fluently. She taught him enough to get by when he was out alone. He glowed with confidence that he could make a decent showing as he talked his way through France. Although he did get into a few minor confrontations by getting some vital words incorrect at the wrong time.

He and Bridget stayed only a short time in France then boarded a plane to Germany. He relaxed somewhat, knowing his German was 100% better than his French.

Enclosed is a more detailed description of their life in Germany.

It is beautiful here. I can enjoy the sunshine on this old body. My patio is perfect for viewing the many different flowers in my garden. I can relax and meditate.

A visit to my doctor today yielded no good news so I must hasten to finish the story.

Age has caught up with us, hasn't it Rosy? My notes will further explain the exciting events destined in the lives of Ken and Bridget.

Take care of yourself, my special friend. Unfortunately, I will not be able to carry out my plan to visit you. It's too late. However, we will continue to communicate until Gabriel blows the horn, right?

As for now, I will close this letter and await further news of Mendy.

Love,
Rene

NINE

The Truth

Herr Von Seegan insisted Bridget tell him as much as she could remember about her childhood before he finished his story.

Bridget began. "My parents told me they were living in Germany when the war broke out and things were in such turmoil. The Gestapo was selling a group of children just to get rid of them. Like slaves, each child was going to the highest bidder. My parents were passing by at the time and I caught their eye.

They put up a bid and the German soldier accepted it. They prepared adoption papers, in a fashion, which was legal, according to them, and my father and mother fled to America. Thank God, I don't remember any of it. The Gestapo told them I was an orphan and they couldn't take responsibility for any of the children."

"Tell me of your wife and children," Bridget asked.

"I've told you just about everything I remember. I never learned if any of the boys survived. There were Jeffery, Helmut, Bernhard and Bridget. I tried everything to get some word about them but, alas, nothing. So many years I ran ads, hired a detective, the police and every agency I could think of but no help came from any source. I kept a file of every attempt that I made. I shall let you see it sometime. But, for now, I truly believe, by the grace of God, you are my princess."

He finished his story then went to Bridget. As they embraced, Bridget whispered, "I just knew somehow there was a connection when Ken opened that door and I saw you standing there." The emotions evident convinced them that there was no doubt in either of their minds; fate had brought father and daughter together again.

She and her father were together almost every waking hour after that moment talking and comparing their experiences, further sealing their bond.

Bridget did not return to work as previously arranged. Her new-found father was more important. Besides, he would not hear of her going to work. He felt, and Bridget agreed, too many years had passed to be spending precious time on such a trivial thing as a job.

On the other hand, Ken did meet with the executives of the publishing firm and accepted the position offered.

There was so much happening since Ken and Bridget came to Germany, he totally forgot to make the call to the Browns at the farm back in the USA.

Ken did not know, at this early stage of his employment, that Eric Von Hussen was a top client of his firm. He was not in the department that took care of authors; he handled the publishing end of the business. Of course, Eric was writing under a pen name and Ken did not recognize the name associated with one of the projects he was working on. Through conversations with a fellow employee, he learned that Eric Von Hussen was the "aka" of the book.

Ken was so astonished at this turn of events; he felt he must read the book. He was so obsessed with it. Every second of free time, he spent reading it. He was certain that this book held some of the answers he sought about the disappearance of Sasha.

As he progressed into the story, the more he was driven. The plot was beginning to fill in the blanks in Ken's mind. It brought back the terrible memory of his little Sasha and how she was lost forever to him, or so he thought at the time. When he finally finished reading the last word, he wiped his eyes and thought to himself, *is it possible?* This question nagged at him all day, even into the night. He would not reveal his thoughts to Bridget. He did not want to spoil her newfound happiness. He set the matter aside for the present knowing he would eventually hear the real story from Eric himself.

Ken went about his task of getting Eric's book ready to release. Ken wanted to sit in on the conference with Eric.

The conference was set up a few days later. Ken stuck to his decision to keep the subject matter of the book to himself and get the facts before telling Bridget.

Only final changes remained in order for the book to be ready for the author's final approval.

Satisfied that he had covered all bases regarding the book's publication, Ken cleared his desk, looked around the office and, with confidence, he left for the day.

TEN

The Farm

Ken returned home about 4 o'clock that evening. Bridget was not at home. He did not expect she would be. She and her father were taking a grand tour of the museums in Berlin. Ken suspected she would be coming in shortly.

He prepared himself a cocktail and went out onto the balcony to relax. As he was clearing his thoughts of the day, he remembered he was to call the Browns at the farm. He felt terrible that he neglected to contact them in such a long time. However, he was not concerned about it. He knew the Browns were capable of keeping the place up far beyond normal standards. Even though it would be late there, he picked up the phone and dialed the number anyway. A few minutes passed without an answer. Ken was about to end the call when Mrs. Brown answered the phone.

After the normal chitchat was over, Ken got down to the reason he called.

"Patsy, may I speak with Bud?"

"Yes, Ken, just a minute." She called out to Bud. He got on the phone.

"Hello, Ken. How's it going?"

"Hi Bud. Everything is fine here. Listen Bud, I have to take you and Patsy into my confidence. I have some pretty shocking papers in my file. The contents are not to be revealed to anyone. I know I can I trust you two."

"Of course you can." Bud said. "We have already seen some confidential information. When you asked me to send you the other papers, we couldn't find them in your desk, so we went to your file cabinet to search for them. We didn't intentionally snoop into your private affairs. We opened that file but you have no worries here, Ken. What we saw is of no concern to us. You have our word. Absolutely nothing has been or will be revealed by us."

"I appreciate that Bud. You two are a blessing to me." Ken confidently replied.

"Here is what I need from you. I know now that I will not be returning to the farm. There are just too many bad memories there. I want you and Patsy to have the farm. That is, if you want to make it your permanent home." Bud was beginning to get choked up.

"Thank you, Ken. We feel this is where we belong and we were not certain just how long you would keep us on here. We have done our best to make the farm profitable. This year, we are beginning to think we're getting our heads above the water."

"Bud, I know what you have accomplished and I truthfully say at this moment, I want to sign over the farm to you and Patsy. I have no need for it and surely, I don't need the money. You two have earned the right to own it. I have no heirs and do not expect the circumstances to change at my age. I will contact my attorney there, Sam Jacobson, and have him prepare the necessary papers. After I have signed them, I will return them to Sam and it will be a done deal. Consider it yours now."

"Would you box up all my personal papers and ship them to the address Sam will give you? Please include personal pictures, cards and letters, which are in my desk. I think that's about all I will want. Any clothes of mine you can use for work or toss them. It's your decision," Ken instructed.

Bud was speechless. He could hardly utter another thank you. He did manage to say he would do as Ken requested and asked Ken to keep in touch. They were extremely fond of him and cared what happened in his life. Ken assured Bud he would indeed keep in touch as they, too, meant a lot to him.

He was ending his call as Bridget entered the apartment. She was the happiest Ken had ever seen her.

ELEVEN

The Invitation

Ken made all the arrangements to sign over the farm to the Browns, he let out a sigh of relief. *One problem solved*. He thought. Now to solve the mystery of Eric's book. The matter of Eric's story weighed heavily on his mind. Even though he read the book, he couldn't seem to figure out how much was fact and how much was fiction. He did know that he would get the real story at some point.

Ken and Bridget had a pleasant evening and Ken enjoyed hearing about her adventures with her father. He seemed to be such a delightful old gentleman. Ken never tired of hearing the stories told by someone who had lived in each tale he told.

Bridget talked so much she was exhausted by one thirty in the morning. She apologized for keeping Ken up so late. He didn't mind in the least. The enjoyment he was experiencing was most refreshing.

Ken entered his bedroom with a smile on his face. He took off his shoes and fell on the bed and the comfort of it took him immediately.

The next morning the sun, through a part in the drapes, cast its golden ray across Ken's face. He opened his eyes and realized he had slept in his clothes. He forced his frame off the bed, undressed and hit the shower.

By eight o'clock, he was fully dressed and ready to face the unknown events of the day. A familiar aroma eased its way up his nostrils, leading him to the kitchen. He poured a cup of coffee and sat down at the table. Bridget must have made the coffee.

Eric's book popped into his mind. He asked himself. *Why are these things happening now? Could I be imagining what I wish to be true or is it real? I fully intend to find out just how much is true and what is fiction.* His train of thought was broken as Bridget cheerfully entered the kitchen. Startled out of his stupor, Ken turned and said, "Good morning." Bridget settled in a chair across from him.

"Papa and I will take in the Festival today. Can't you come along with us?" she asked.

"No, I'm afraid not. Too much going on at the office today and I can't get away."

"Ken, he's so happy, I can't believe I love him so much," she said with a smile.

"You are blessed to have found him after all these years. Most people are not that lucky," he stated.

"I know, and I thank God every day," she replied.

Ken finished his coffee; put his suit coat on, and kissed Bridget goodbye.

"I want you to enjoy a great day with your father. I'm not sure what time I'll be finished today. I'll call if it's too late." He picked up his keys and left.

His thoughts were racing as he eased his car through the traffic on the Kudamm, a main thoroughfare in Berlin. He was confident all the details for the meeting with Eric were covered. He must be very careful and patient so his suspicions would not spook him.

The conference was for ten o'clock. Ken was ready with his end of the publishing and made sure each one attending the meeting had a copy of Eric's book, *The Mystified Angel.*

Ken was a little nervous now, so he picked up a coffee. As he entered the hall outside his office, he encountered none other than Herr

Eric Von Hussen walking toward him. A little surprised but pleased, he smiled and extended his hand to him.

"Eric! It has been awhile. How in the world are you? And Angelica, is she well?"

"We are both well, thank you," Eric replied.   "Congratulations on your book. I think you have a winner there," Ken said.

"Thanks, I believe I do. At least I hope so. There was a lot of hard work put into it. It's such a relief to have finally finished it to my satisfaction," Eric answered.

"I'm sure your labors will be well compensated for. Would you join me for a coffee?"

"Don't mind if I do. Is the conference on schedule?"

"Yes, I believe so. Let's go into the conference room. We'll have a few minutes to catch up since we last talked," Ken said.

"I hear you are doing an excellent job here. My book couldn't be in more capable hands."

"Well, it's for sure I didn't do it alone." They both laughed.

They seated themselves in their assigned seats at the conference table. Ken started another conversation by asking, "What have you been up to since the cruise ended?"

"As you can guess, I finished my book in between Angelica's activities.

"It is my first priority to escort her to ballet class plus her music sessions and school projects, which never seems to end. My mother has taught her languages since she was very young. Mother is, and has been, an excellent teacher since she was a young adult, as well as an excellent physician. Angelica is an astute pupil. She speaks French, English and German fluently. Now, she has almost accomplished the Russian language. Unbelievably, she loves everything she does. I couldn't have been more pleased in having a child with so much enthusiasm. She is our shining star and she knows it, too."

Ken felt so much pride in his heart as he commented to Eric. "You must be so proud. Angelica is such a beautiful young lady. She doesn't seem to be spoiled as people would suspect."

"No she is not," Eric replied. "She works hard for everything she gets. That is how she is being educated. She sure knows the value of money and she practices that knowledge every day."

"Are you still in touch with Bridget?" Eric asked.

"Oh yes, we share an apartment here in Berlin. By a sheer stroke of luck, Bridget found her biological father. He owns the building we live in. She has been spending every waking hour with him. They are getting to know each other in ways I cannot comprehend. I don't object and I give her as much support as possible. There is plenty of time for us."

"Do I detect a serious note between you two?" Eric asked.

"We do have deep feelings for each other. I plan to ask her to marry me as soon as her fascination for her father subsides a bit."

"That's great, Ken. I hope it works out for you. I noticed on the cruise that special something between you two." Ken asked Eric to keep this information quiet. He did not want to hasten things too fast. Eric agreed and gave him his word he would not reveal any information on the subject.

The executives of the firm were beginning to wander in so Eric and Ken stopped their chitchat.

The conference went well. Eric signed each copy of his book the executives held and, of course, requested they not let their friends or family read it until it was well into sales. They all knew this and pledged their secrecy as was normal in their business.

After the conference, Eric pulled Ken aside and told him it was his intent to invite him and Bridget to dine at his estate and stay the weekend, but other subjects started and the invitation slipped by for the moment. Ken accepted the invitation tentatively. He informed Eric he would call him later to confirm. That was satisfactory with Eric. He gave Ken his telephone number and directions to his home. They shook hands and Eric stepped over to converse with someone else.

Ken left the meeting and went back to his office very pleased at the turn of events. He left the office a little early. The Chief Editor said a job well done deserved some time off. Most of them planned to leave after lunch. The top executives were to meet Eric for lunch. Ken managed to leave a little after three o'clock. It being Friday, he stopped at a florist and bought a huge bouquet of roses for Bridget.

He was parking the car at the same time Bridget and her father were getting out of a taxi. They didn't see him. They went into the building and parted for the evening. Bridget was at the door when Ken came up the stairs.

"You are home early, why?" Ken asked.

"Papa wasn't feeling up to all the activity, so we cut it short. How about you? You are home early also. Was the conference a success?"

"It was a total success. Guess what?" He asked.

"I can't imagine what, tell me."

"The author I met today was none other than Eric Von Hussen. What do you think of that?" he mused.

"Oh my!" She said in surprise. "How is he? And why has he not contacted us?"

"He's been very busy. However, he did invite us for the weekend. What plans do you have with your father?"

"We have no plans at all. Papa will spend the weekend with an old friend. It's great timing, we are free. Did you tell Eric we would come?"

"I told him I would call to confirm after clearing it with you."

"I'd love to see him again. How soon will we be going?" she asked.

"Saturday morning, if you like, we can return Sunday afternoon. His estate is not far from here."

They entered the apartment, kicked off their shoes and Ken made a cocktail for each of them. They settled down on the balcony to relax.

The day was so warm with sunshine beaming on the balcony. It was so pleasant. Ken phoned Eric and he insisted they come right over to begin their fun-filled weekend.

They finished their drinks and as it was only about fifteen minutes to Eric's home, there was no need to rush. He told them dinner would be at six o'clock. They planned to pick up flowers for Eric's mother.

Rosy Answers Letter #4

September 30, 2002

Dear Rene,

      Your letter was retrieved safely and the mailman went on his way unharmed. He seems more relaxed lately as I, too, have a calm demeanor about getting your letters. The old saying goes "Don't kill the messenger," that means don't you go jumping on your mailman. Abuse to one deliverer of the mail is enough for both of us. Just kidding, my mailman is very tolerant of an old lady. I've known him for a long time and he understands my joking. In fact, I think he looks forward to it.

      Our lives are dull, aren't they, compared to the lives of our friends. Oh, how people and their circumstances change. Rest assured, my dear, when we have finished with these stories, we will tell each other about our years apart.

      It brought tears to my eyes when Ken gave his farm to the Browns. It seems he is leaving no bad memories to face in the future by having to return to the farm; however, it seems that he is adjusting well.

      He appears possessed in finding answers to his missing little girl. I don't blame him, I would do the same until I was satisfied that she is truly gone. He is wise to keep an eye on Eric. I, too, believe there is a connection and there is something Eric isn't telling at this point.

      I am so sorry you will not be coming to visit me. It would have been so much fun to talk about old times.

      Germany, nor France, was never on my list of vacation spots, but I can envision how lovely Germany would be and what I have read about the customs, it would be most entertaining to visit. Alas, it is not to be. I am not in good health at this writing and could not make the trip.

It is as you said; "until Gabriel blows the horn," we will continue to communicate via the post.

As for my story of Mendy, my notes cover the continuing story. Nathan is getting closer to locating the missing girls. That man is a smart investigator, don't you think?

Until the next letter, take care and enjoy your garden. The outside sunshine has its healing effect.

I trust my notes are explicit enough for you to get a clear picture of Mendy's situation. I so look forward to your letters so write soon.

Love,

Rosy

7

The Suspect

Jason did indeed agree to meet with the police artist. She was a cute little thing, but Jason and the boys stuck to their promise to Nathan to watch out for her. Jason's turf was a rough part of town and he pretty much controlled the action there. The girl had nothing to fear.

Nathan cautioned her to trust Jason. He had given him his word; his word had been good in the past. Nathan had no reason to doubt it would be good now.

Jason, Wally and Rollo were standing by the statue of Grant, as they promised, at precisely 4:00 p.m. They spotted a little red Mustang circling the block. Action like this always alerted gang members to be aware of who was cruising their turf and why.

Nathan had given Jason a description of the police artist and he was certain she was in the red mustang. They watched when she found a parking place, got out and started toward them.

Jason thought, *wow! That's one good-looking gal*. The other two made no comment, either. She walked up to them and asked, "Jason?"

"Yeah," he replied.

"I'm Janice, thank you for being here. Nathan has a lot of respect for you fellows," she said as she took out her pad of sketch paper. "It's a pretty simple thing to get a picture of a suspect. All you have to do is answer a few questions, okay?"

"Yeah," was his answer.

"Okay, let's begin. You mentioned there were three men in the van."

"Yeah."

"Let's take one at a time. Pick out one and tell me, was his face round, like a fat person, oval or square?"

Little by little, they gave Janice a good description of the suspects.

When she had finished her sketches, she asked. "Are these the men you saw?"

"You betcha," Wally said. "Lady, you are good. That's them all right. You even got them rotten teeth that dude had." The three boys hi-five'd each other and began to laugh.

Janice put away her pad and pencil. "Gentlemen, thank you so much. You may have given Nathan the very tool he needs to catch these men and save someone's life." She shook hands with each one and said goodbye. The handshake was unusual for the boys. They did not get thanks very often. They were grinning as they watched her walk back to her car and drive away. As she passed them, she smiled and waved. The boys were pleased as punch, and felt good about what they had done.

Janice returned to the station, gave Nathan the sketches and said, "Nate, those friends of yours are something else."

"You know Janice, if the guys took to you, you won't have to worry about anything if you have cause to go in that neighborhood again," Nate stated.

"Why?" She looked puzzled as she asked.

"Jason runs that neighborhood. When he spreads the word, no one will touch you, except in the act of defending you, of course. You are a pretty lucky girl," Nathan explained.

The sketches were just what Nathan was looking for. Now he had something to go on. He put out an APB on the three suspects. In the meantime, he had one of his staff search the files for a match to the sketches. It would be nice if he could get a name for each of the three men.

More time passed and Nathan was getting restless. What was the next step toward finding Mendy and Misty?

As he was leaving for lunch one day, the clerk, who was searching the records, yelled at him just before he went through the door.

"Hey Nate, we got a match for two of those guys you are looking for. Here you go." He handed Nate the sheet of paper. Nate went back into his office and forgot about lunch.

He read the names on the list. "Justen (Jeeter) McFarland - Robbery and Rape. Time served - Released July 1960. Ralph (Tater) McFarland - Rape and Robbery - Time served - Released July 1960. No record, so far, for the third man."

Nathan's hopes for finding Mendy and Misty were encouraging after he got the composite drawings of two of the three men suspected in the abduction. Two of the men, he knew, wouldn't be hard to track. Both men were practically illiterate and did not have a clue as how to cover their tracks. They had been arrested once and he was confident he would get them again.

He contacted their parole officers and he stated to Nate that the two were, in fact, contractors. They did odd jobs, nothing big or complicated.

They made just enough money to buy food, beer and a place to stay. That is all they needed or wanted.

Nate got the last known address for the two McFarland boys and obtained a warrant to search their apartment. The search yielded very little, but Nate did find a scrap of paper with the name "Bern" scribbled on it. Not much to go on, but Nathan put it in the evidence envelope anyway. The apartment looked as if the occupants would return. There were some clothes still in the closet and the refrigerator had a sparse amount of food remaining. He arranged for a round-the-clock surveillance. This went on for a week. They did not return. Nate made a deal with the landlord to notify his office the moment either of the two men showed up.

Nate himself canvassed the neighborhood, the bars, poolrooms and grocery stores. There were a couple of kids, who lived in the building, who said they knew the men. They were ugly and nasty and were always chasing them away from the steps. The last time they had seen them was early on the day of the abduction. Of course, the kids didn't know anything about Mendy and Misty being abducted but the time frame was correct. Nathan felt sure these guys were involved.

The bartender at one particular bar the men frequented told Nate he overheard one of the guys, called Jeeter, bragging about becoming rich soon and made the statement, "I may just buy this place and drink myself to death." The bartender said they all got a good laugh out of it. He also stated the two brothers hadn't been around lately.

Nate concluded these two guys were not smart enough to pull off an abduction of this magnitude. The third guy must be the mastermind behind it. He just had to get a lead on this third guy.

He took out the composite drawings again and stared at the good-looking man. He memorized every detail of the drawing. If he ever saw this man, he would recognize him immediately. He had asked Jason to keep an eye out and his ears to the ground and let him know if anything turned up.

8

Mendy and Misty

Mendy was fully awake now. The sedative had worn off but she kept her eyes closed until she had shaken off the effects of the drug. She didn't want a further dose. She was fighting with all her strength to figure out what had happened to her. She couldn't open her mouth. It was taped shut.

She listened and heard no movement and she knew her hands were bound together behind her. Slowly she opened her eyes and lifted her head; pain hit her hard, the scream she let out was muffled, her lips were drawn tightly together. She closed her eyes again and momentarily held her breath until the initial shock had passed. She had to be careful and think clearly. She risked another peek and Misty came into view. Panic almost seized her when she saw Misty tied up with silver tape over her mouth. Misty's eyes were staring directly at her, as if to say, "Mommy please help me."

Mendy was analyzing the situation. She saw one man lying next to her. He appeared to be asleep.

Mendy knew without a doubt that she had been raped and judging by the pain and soreness she felt, that bastard had raped her more than once.

She examined Misty with her eyes to see if she had been harmed in any way, but she saw no apparent evidence of an assault. For this, she was thankful. She could endure almost anything but she had to protect Misty at all cost. A million questions raced through her mind. At this point, she had no answers.

She lifted her head again and looked around the van. There were no seats. There were tools scattered haphazardly everywhere. An electric skill saw, a miter box and various other tools were placed together just a little away from Misty's head. There were a few small pieces of pipe rolling around in the van at various times. She got very annoyed with the noise they were making. She didn't know how many men there were but she remembered two. From the tools scattered about she determined they were probably contractors or handymen.

Mendy thought it very important that she memorize everything in detail. The information would come in handy when they got away and she assumed strongly that they would escape. In her mind, these fiends would pay heavily for this dastardly deed.

A groan came from the man next to her. Mendy looked in his direction. She drew her feet underneath her and slid her way up the side of the van into a sitting position. As the man turned toward her, she immediately caught sight of his enormous erection. This sight didn't frighten her; it made her insane with fury. She knew her daughter had been watching this sight and probably witnessed her rape. She couldn't think of anything else but ripping this man's heart out and shoving it down his throat.

"Well, hi there sweet thang," he said with a crooked smile. "I feel like a little more loving right about now, before I take a leak."

Mendy could say nothing but the fire in her eyes told him to watch out.

"I had enough of you sweet thang. What I want now is to bust that little cherry over thar."

As he moved toward Misty, he licked his lips and let out a sardonic laugh. Mendy knew just what to do. She waited until he had Misty's dress up and started to pull down her panties. She drew her feet from beneath her, raised her knees up under her chin and forcing her feet and legs outward kicking him in the back with all the strength she could muster. She was surprised at the force with which her kick hit home.

The filthy man was caught off guard and went sprawling over Misty's head. His head hit the blade of the saw just at the correct angle. He made no sound as he relaxed in a face down position, his foot lying on Misty's shoulder.

The terror showing in Misty's eyes tore at Mendy's heart, her very soul hardened with hate for what her daughter was going through. She motioned to Misty to scoot over to her. Misty understood and began to wriggle her way toward Mendy. When she got close enough, Mendy touched her cheek with her own, giving her some reassurance that the man would not frighten her again. Misty was no longer crying at this point. Apparently, she was in a state of shock or in denial.

Mendy realized she was thirsty. She looked at Misty and wondered if she had had to relieve herself, then she noticed that her little dress was wet and soiled. This fed the fury she had built against these men.

The van had stopped briefly twice. She assumed the men had relieved themselves. That pleasure was not offered to the girls. They both were soaked from the results of them being denied the use of a toilet.

Mendy had no idea where they were or how far they had traveled. She just knew that her legs, back and bottom ached from bumping around on the floor. She hurt for Misty too. The poor little thing must be bruised and hurting from head to toe.

Misty had lain her head in her mother's lap and Mendy believed she was finally asleep, which both had had very little of.

Mendy was thinking clearly now. She would play it cool and cause no trouble, hoping their captors wouldn't think she had anything to do with their friend's death. She knew he was dead because he never moved after the fall. She had tucked her feet under her again so they wouldn't notice that they were free.

The van was slowing down and Mendy could hear the tires rolling over stones and gravel. Wherever they were taking them, they had arrived, she guessed.

The van stopped. The door was jerked open and the fresh air hit Mendy in the face. A man poked his head in and yelled. "Jeeter, get up, we're here."

For a brief moment, Mendy was grateful to see that ugly face peering in at her. He turned and stretched his arms out wide as if trying to get the kinks out of his body caused by the long trip. Mendy did not see anyone else. She did hear another voice so there had to be three men.

The man got back in the van and pulled at Misty, dragging her out and she fell on the ground. Then he grabbed for Mendy.

"Get out of there lady, we're home." He grinned as he roughly assisted her out. The stupid bastard didn't even notice her feet were loose. He took the tape off her mouth and she breathed a sigh of relief. Her mouth felt like it was filled with cotton. Then he turned to Misty, jerked off the tape. Misty let out a scream when the tape peeled the skin from her lips and face. Her tender little lips began to bleed. Mendy had to grit her teeth to keep from killing the hateful son of a bitch right then. He showed no feeling for Misty when he took the tape from her feet and hands. She said nothing further as a single tear eased down her cheek. Like the illiterate oaf he was, he also untied Mendy's hands. She rushed to her daughter and held her very tight until she calmed down. The blood was still fresh on her little cheeks and lips.

"Don't even think about running," the man said to Mendy. The jerk gave a big belly laugh and added, "thar ain't no place to run out here, but you can try. Them bears would love to have you for a playmate." He laughed again and started back toward the van.

"Jeeter, you lazy bum," he yelled. "Get your ass out here." He got in the van and saw Jeeter lying motionless on the floor.

"Jeeter," he yelled again. He stepped over to him and nearly fell as his foot hit a piece of pipe. He let out a string of profanity. He caught his balance and looked down at Jeeter. His mouth dropped open. He couldn't say a word for a few seconds. The pool of blood surrounding his brother's head told him, he was no longer among the living.

The man got out of the van and yelled at Mendy.

"What happened to Jeeter in there"?

"How do you expect me to know? You had me doped up. I thought the bum was sleeping when I woke up," She said.

He suddenly drew back his hand and slapped Mendy across the face. She was stunned by his sudden action. He turned to Misty and grabbed her by the shoulders.

"You little brat! Tell me what happened to Jeeter. Misty just stared at him and said nothing. He raised his hand to give her a slap. Mendy grabbed his arm, he spun around, let go of her and in a second his lights went out.

Mendy dropped the bloody rock she held in her hand and muttered, "stupid bastard." She took Misty by the hand and started running into the woods. They had to get away before the third man returned and found his accomplices dead. They walked and ran, stumbling often. Mendy was looking back to see if they were being followed. She saw no one as they approached a river.

"Oh no," she said with a terrifying look on her face.

She was about to explore the depth of the river when a male voice startled her.

"Taking an evening stroll are we?" he said very calmly.   She jerked her head around and saw a good looking, well-dressed young man leisurely leaning against a huge bolder near the river.

Quick thinking Mendy replied in a sarcastic voice, "we need to bathe. Do you mind? What do you want with us anyway?" She asked as she looked directly into his cold emotionless eyes.

"There is a bathroom in the cabin. Did you bother to check it out?" he calmly asked.

"Check it out," she screamed. "How in hell could we check it out? Your beautiful friends kept us a little busy." She was still holding Misty very close to her.

"I do apologize for your discomfort Madam," he coldly replied.

"What do you want with us?" Mendy asked.

He unfolded his arms and slowly walked up to Mendy. His eyes of steel were looking into hers as he spoke.

"In due time madam, for now you must get cleaned up. There's food and clothing for you both in the cabin." He motioned for them to walk ahead of him. When they reached the cabin, he saw Ralph lying on the ground. Blood was still oozing from his nose and ears.

The handsome stranger showed no emotion as he looked down at the dead man.

"Well, well, you have been pretty busy now haven't you?" he stated cockily.

"I had to hit the bastard," she said.

"He started to hit my daughter. As long as I am alive, no one will harm my daughter. Do you understand?"

"Fully Madam," he answered with a twisted grin.

Mendy and Misty went into the cabin and the man disappeared before she could even blink an eye.

Mendy thought to herself, *there must be a way out of here. He disappeared to fast. He must think I'm a complete idiot and didn't notice when he left?* She couldn't think about that for now, she had to take care of Misty.

They entered the cabin and to her surprise, the cabin was clean and there was food, in bags, on the table. She didn't bother to wash up. She tore into the bags and found milk, cheese, meat, lettuce and tomatoes and a loaf of bread. She made a quick sandwich for Misty and herself.

She finished eating and Mendy looked down at her blouse and skirt; *what a disgusting mess,* she thought. Misty was still eating. She got up to explore the cabin. There was a living area with a big fireplace completely filling one wall. She opened a door and to her amazement, a beautifully decorated bedroom with a huge king-sized bed. There were clothes on the bed neatly laid out. Off to her right, she discovered a bathroom with tub, shower, sink and toilet. The towels were neatly folded and hung on the towel rack with precision. She could not believe such luxury out here in the woods. She went back to the bed and examined the clothing. She found them to be their exact size. *What in the world in going on here?* Her thoughts made her uneasy.

Misty was satisfied, at the moment. Her little stomach was full and she just wanted to lie down and go to sleep. Mendy convinced her she would feel much better if she had a bath and clean dry clothes. She drew a tub full of warm water, removed Misty's clothes and helped her in the tub. Misty almost fell asleep. They finished bathing and put on the clothes that were on the bed. Misty was exhausted and lay down on the bed and went fast asleep. Mendy lay down with her and even though she tried to stay awake, she fell asleep.

Mendy began to feel eerie and she opened her eyes. The good-looking young man was watching her sleep.

"Who are you?" Instinctively she felt for Misty. "Where is my daughter?" She started to get up. The young man stopped her.

"Good evening Mrs. Arnold," the young man said very politely.

"Why are we here? How do you know me? What do you want with us?" Mendy kept asking the questions and she wanted the answers.

"In due time, Madam, in due time, be patient awhile longer and your questions will be answered," he replied in a very cold controlled voice.

"Where is my daughter?" Mendy asked again.

Mendy brushed past the man and started looking for Misty. She didn't care about him, he could go to hell. She was really getting scared. She couldn't find her Misty anywhere. She called and called, but no answer from Misty. It was getting dark outside and she could only imagine Misty out there somewhere alone and afraid.

"Oh my God!" She said aloud. She was getting furious. He didn't seem to care what happened to Misty. She sat down on the little porch and cried her heart out.

"Oh Misty my baby, where are you?"

Letter #5

1 November 2002

Dearest Rosy,

Forgive me for not writing sooner. I trust you have not killed your mailman or I wouldn't get a response to my letters. I spent a three-week period in the hospital. I'm a little weak but functional. It was a mild heart attack, not severe enough to get concerned. The rest in the hospital was what I needed. Actually, it was the pampering I enjoyed the most.

There was so much spare time, my notes grew and grew. I have almost revealed the entire story. If all goes well, it will be finished soon.

Are you feeling better now that the weather is getting cooler?

Your last letter and notes were very upsetting. Had I known what was happening to Mendy, I would have come to her aid immediately not that my being there would help Nathan find her any sooner, but at least I would have been with you and near enough to get any news of the investigation.

Mendy is smart and she would find a way to outsmart anyone.

As for Eric, he did not realize his attraction to Bridget nor did she. Ken was uppermost on her mind and did not detect the signs.

My granddaughter is taking me on an excursion this afternoon so I will stop for now and get this letter in the post.

I have explained the invitation extended by Eric to Ken and Bridget in my notes.

I am anxious to receive your next letter.

Love,
Rene

TWELVE

The Party

The invitation to Eric's home for the weekend had Bridget excited.

Both she and Ken were well off financially but such magnificence they witnessed upon arrival at Eric's estate was fascinating.

The valet took their car and an attendant took their bags and escorted them inside. Eric and his mother met them with open arms. Angelica was nearby and looked in their direction. She excused herself from her friends and hurried to the foyer where Ken and Bridget were standing. The Von Hussen family seemed to be delighted that they could be there for the entire weekend.

As Angelica put her arms around Ken, a fire was ignited throughout his entire body.

"It's such a pleasure to see you again young lady," he said as he released her.

"It is indeed my pleasure sir," she responded sweetly.

At that moment, she turned and embraced Bridget. Bridget thought her heart would burst if she held on any longer. She pushed Angelica out at arms length.

"My goodness Angie, you have grown like a weed." Bridget could hardly finish her statement; she was so moved by Angelica's gesture.

"Welcome to our home," Angelica replied gleefully. She excused herself and returned to her friends.

Eric introduced his mother as Frau Erma Von Hussen. As was the German custom, Ken took her hand in his; placed a gentle kiss on it, then presented her with a bouquet of flowers.

She was quite pleased, said an appreciative thank you and then welcomed them into her home. She invited them to follow her into the drawing room so they could get acquainted with the other guests.

"Eric has talked of you many times. Angelica was quite taken with you on her maiden voyage from the Americas," She said as they all seated themselves.

"Her poise and beauty are outstanding for one so young," Ken said with pride.

"She is quite an angel to us. Eric dotes on that child more than he should I fear," Frau Von Hussen said. "I wish for you a grand time this weekend and again, welcome to our home." She immediately excused herself to welcome the other arriving guests.

Eric summoned a valet to show Ken and Bridget to their quarters to freshen up before dinner. They followed the valet up the heavily carpeted stairs to a suite in which they could fit their own apartment. They were amazed that they had two adjoining rooms with separate baths. Ken told Bridget he would knock when he was ready to go down for dinner.

Bridget had chosen the appropriate gown to wear for the evening. Ken wore his black tuxedo. He was dressed to his satisfaction and he tapped on Bridget's door. She opened the door and her beauty made him speechless. He put his arms around her and she responded by moving into his arms snugly. He slowly brought his lips close to hers waiting for her to follow suit. She did so and the passionate kiss lasted until she pulled away. She took his arm in a saucy manner and the look on her face told him she was thrilled to have such a handsome man accompany her to dinner.

As the pair descended the stairs, every eye in the room focused on them. They could hear the approval by the many comments that were made. Eric made no comment; just stared at Bridget gliding down the stairs in the most beautiful gown he had ever seen on a woman. Its blue/green iridescent color shimmered as the light from the stair's chandelier bounced off her curves. One bare shoulder stood out like an enticing piece of candy a child would be tempted to steal. Eric's mouth turned bone dry. He could only pretend she didn't make him so warm all over. He could feel the heat upon his face as he suspected it was turning red.

Frau Von Hussen broke the spell he was in by touching him on the arm.

"Eric, would you lead us into the dining room?" She asked.

He was so embarrassed he would not face her. He knew she could read him like a book.

"Of course Mother, may I escort you?" he asked.

"Yes, my son that would be very nice."

Each couple followed Eric and his mother. Ken and Bridget were directly behind them. As everyone sat down, Eric was beside Bridget.

"You are lovely this evening my dear, we are so pleased you could join us," Eric whispered as he leaned close to her.

"Thank you Eric. I appreciate the opportunity to see you again. We have a lot to talk about."

"I'm sure we do and we shall," Eric's thoughts were very devious at that moment.

Everyone seemed to be enjoying the delicious meal and the camaraderie that went along with it. Angelica and her girlfriend were in a world of their own. Girl talk was flowing. Bridget noticed how pretty both girls were. Each had a distinctive personality. They were fashionably laughing with each other. Occasionally they would say something to the adult seated next to them. Bridget was awed at how Angelica could converse with adults and hold their attention for so long.

After dessert, the girls excused themselves and disappeared, probably to Angelica's suite to continue the fascination of teen talk and music.

Eric watched and waited until all his guests had finished the elegant feast. He stood and an announced that the entertainment would begin immediately in the ballroom. He invited those who would like to smoke to join him on the terrace. Frau Von Hussen, at the same moment, invited the women to accompany her to their seats to await the return of the men.

Attendants were everywhere tending the needs and comfort of each guest. The orchestra had been playing all through dinner. Their selections were soft and low. It was just loud enough to fill the atmosphere with pleasant easy listening.

Eric and the other men were returning and the look on the women's faces revealed they were pleased to have them back.

The Maestro announced the first arrangement of the evening would be a waltz. He urged everyone to choose a partner to begin the evening's festivities.

"Would you mind if I asked Bridget for this dance?" Eric asked Ken.

"Not at all," he replied.

Eric did indeed ask Bridget to dance this waltz. He led her to the dance floor; she fit perfectly in his arms. They began to dance. It looked as if they had been dancing together for years. Ken noticed how well they moved as one. A little tinge of jealously probed his mind for only a few seconds. What man would not envy the excellence of two people so well suited for each other, especially if one of them was the woman he loved? A more handsome couple did not exist on that floor. All eyes were on them. The dance ended and the applause and whistles from everyone were most complimentary. Bridget was a little embarrassed at the attention but quickly accepted the limelight for the moment. She thought the roar of the guests would never stop.

Eric mingled with his guests. He danced with each lady friend, but with no such fanfare as when he danced with Bridget.

The dancing, laughing and chatter continued well into the morning hours. Finally, an announcement was made that the orchestra would play the final number for the evening.

Eric thanked everyone for coming and said there would be a picnic by the lake the next day. He extended an invitation to everyone to attend.

Eric started back to the table. Ken suspected he would ask Bridget for the last dance. To his surprise, Eric asked his mother to join him for the finale. Ken was relieved. He took Bridget's hand and asked her for the final dance. She accepted graciously.

THIRTEEN

The Picnic

The party at Eric's went very well. All the guests had left and those who were staying the night were in their rooms. The house was quiet except for the clean-up crew. Satisfied that everything was shipshape, the staff went to their own quarters for the night. The morning staff was rested and willing to begin work at 5 a.m., which was not far off.

Eric's mother, Frau Von Hussen, was always the first to rise and the first cup of tea was hers to enjoy alone. She enjoyed the solitude of the early morning. Her very existence depended upon organization. She ruled the staff with an iron hand. They all loved and respected her, not one would dare to upset her, not through fear but respect. Her firm, but fair treatment was her forte. They knew, without a doubt, she would do anything to help any one of them if need be. Most of the staff in the Von Hussen household had been there for many years. Some of them traveled with the family. The realization that the family cared for them deeply in no way deterred them from performing their duties with professionalism. After all, to serve the family was their number one priority along with devotion and respect.

In one particular incident, several months before the party, Erma had to hire a replacement for one of the long-time maids who suddenly passed away. The replacement made the mistake of arguing with another maid. Frau Von Hussen, per chance, was passing the room they were in and overheard the nasty conversation. She listened for a few minutes to make a positive identification of the person making the fuss. Satisfied, she had the facts correct, she entered the room, called the person by name and invited her to accompany her to the library.

"Stacy," Frau Von Hussen said. "Please have a seat. Your services are no longer needed. I'll give you the wages you have earned up to this time." Stacy was shocked that she was being fired. Erma said nothing more. She reached into the desk drawer and brought out a letter. She handed it to Stacy and asked her to read it.

The letter was one she presented to all employees at the time of the interview. It explained her rules for employment, should the rules be broken, employment would be terminated immediately.

She waited until the girl had finished reading the letter and looked up.

"Do you understand why you must go?"

Stacy attempted to defend herself and Erma told her she had overheard the entire conversation. She informed her that she would have no discord among her staff and she was aware of this when she was hired. She also told Stacy that it was very important that she trust her staff and ensure a pleasant working environment for each. The trust Erma felt for Stacy had been broken and a second chance was out of the question.

Erma summoned the Security Chief. She told him to escort Stacy to her quarters to gather what belongings were hers and put her in a taxi. As far as Erma was concerned, the matter was over. It always made her very sad to dismiss an employee. She was thankful she did not have to do it often.

The guests were coming alive by now as the hour was approaching 11 a.m. They entered the breakfast area by twos and by the noon hour, everyone had finished eating. There was idle conversation and laughter, and some took their coffee or tea out to the terrace to absorb the delightful sunshine that was a blessing in November.

The bartender at the outside bar was ready to serve, should anyone care for a cocktail. Some of the women asked for a Bloody Mary. They thought this first toddy of the day would help to bring them back to their senses, so they could forget how badly they felt upon rising this morning. The men, of course, were huddled together talking sports or politics, which was of no interest to the ladies.

Eric, Ken and Bridget were slowly strolling in the garden. Their path took them to a lovely, secluded gazebo. The conversation had been Eric's book. He volunteered to begin his tale of what prompted the writing of his most recent book. The three seated themselves. Eric and Ken, both, pulled out a cigar, but first asked Bridget if this would offend her. She said no and for them to enjoy one if they liked.

Ken had not told Bridget anything about the story he had read at work. He felt that Eric would eventually tell them both when he was ready to do so. It appeared he was ready and willing to divulge his story now that the book was on the market. The day was gorgeous and the garden was so peaceful, the time seemed right to Eric. He let out a sigh and began his story...

"I needed an appropriate place to continue my writing. Therefore, Jacco, he is my brother, you will meet him today, he had leased a place far back in the swamps of Georgia. He had found it through a real estate agent in Atlanta. It was a real place of seclusion adequate for a writer.

The estate was surrounded by a swamp. The lighting was excellent during the day, but as evening set in, it became pitch black. I didn't mind because I only wrote during the day. My evenings I reserved for my family and private life. The only entrance to the property was by boat.

A wealthy recluse owned the property until he passed away. He had no heirs that could be located and after a time, the state of Georgia took possession and sold it at auction to the highest bidder. The buyer of the property put it on the rental market. The price was right and Jacco rented the property for a year.

We completed our plans for the move and left Germany in the capable hands of our staff.

We brought a small staff and their spouses to assist us during our stay in the US."

Eric told the story of Jacco, his friend, financial advisor and body-guard. They had known each other since their youth.

Young Jacco's parents were killed and Eric could not stand the thought of leaving him in the hands of the social system. He convinced his parents to obtain a guardianship of Jacco, which eventually led to his adoption. The two boys became brothers. It was just after the guardianship was legal that the Von Hussen family left Germany to travel to the United States. Jacco became Eric's companion. He had no other relatives that wanted to take in an active teen, so with no objections to his leaving, the Von Hussens gladly took him along.

As Jacco grew into a young adult, Eric suspected he had ideas of leaving to pursue a career of his own. Before Jacco could express his decision to break away, Eric approached him with a proposition. If he stayed with them, he was to become a financial advisor and bodyguard to Eric and, of course, a salary was inevitable as he became of age.

They discussed the matter thoroughly and Jacco agreed, with the stipulation that, if for any reason he wanted to change this arrangement, he was free to leave with no hard feelings. It was mutually agreed and never discussed again. Jacco was still with Eric at the time of this writing. They were so close sometimes they appeared to be on the same brain waves. All through their association, there were disagreements but never once did a fight occur between them. The two handled any dispute in a manner satisfactory to both.

"After we arrived and were settled in our new location, Jacco and I decided we needed to explore the surroundings. We took the boat out of the swamp and down the river. The scenery was so soothing and we relaxed and enjoyed each other's company. Being away from business was making us laugh, which we hadn't done in quite awhile, Jacco was joking and pointing out different wildlife along the way. He spotted a little clearing on the river quite a distance from the swamp. We decided to dock the boat and take a walk to stretch our legs.

We were talking and laughing as brothers do when we happened upon a pair of otters snuggled up to a muddy clump of something. As we drew near, the otters got very defensive of the muddy mass. We were cautious as we slowly approached the clump to see what it was. The otters hissed and screamed at us, but realizing they were at a disadvantage, slid into the river leaving behind the unprotected clump.

Jacco carefully examined the muddy mass and yelled, "Oh my God! It's a child, a little girl, I think..."

Rosy Answers Letter #5

December 2, 2002

Dear Rene,

    Your letter fills my mind with so many questions. Mr. Von See-gan and his wife were so strong and brave to survive that terrible ordeal without their children. I honestly cannot say I could have survived during that era knowing those people could take my children away. I understand, what other sane choice could they have made under the circumstances at hand. At least they could hope their children would be safe. Surely, they would not kill the children, or would they?

    As for my mailman yes, it has become a game now. He enjoys taunting me.

    I agree with you the cooler weather is nice but the cold weather to come is not in the best interest for bony swollen fingers.

    Mendy and Misty were going through hell with the thought that they were on their own and not one person could help them through it. Mendy knew eventually someone would find them, but would they find them in time? She did not even know what she was up against or who was involved in their abduction but she would go along with the flow for the present time. She had no choice in the matter.

    Misty was her greatest concern. The man with her would tell her nothing to relieve her anxiety.

    Dear, I must stop for now. My notes are enclosed and precise to the best of my ability.

    Keep me informed as to your health. I care for you very much and need your friendship.

Love,

Rosy

9

The Investigation Continues

Nathan was a little perplexed. He did not know where to go for more clues after talking with the landlord about the McFarland brothers. He hoped they would return and he would go from there. In the meantime, he had Jason on the lookout.

He started looking through some recent bulletins received from other districts. He came across one from the Ackmon Police Department. It read: (TWO FISHERMEN FOUND TWO UNIDENTIFIED MALE BODIES IN LAKE ACKMON. IF YOU CAN IDENTIFY THESE BODIES, PLEASE CONTACT THE ACKMON POLICE DEPARTMENT.) There were pictures of the two bodies.

A light went off in Nate's brain. He grabbed his coat from his chair and put the pictures in his pocket. He wanted to take the pictures to the McFarlands' landlord to see, if by chance, these were the men he was after. He skipped lunch and went directly to the McFarlands' building.

He parked his car in a NO PARKING zone in front of the building. If he got a ticket, he didn't care he was on police business. After looking through the entire building, he finally found the seedy-looking landlord coming down the stairs from, God only knows where. He immediately got on the defensive.   "I ain't seen either of them since you were here last," he said.

"I have a couple of pictures here I want you to look at." He handed the pictures to the man.

"Geez, they are dead?"

"Are these the MacFarland brothers?" Nate asked.

"That's them alright," he said and handed the pictures back to Nate.

"Are you positive?"

"Sure am," he said.

"Is the rent paid up on their apartment?" Nate asked.   "Yeah, until the end of the week," he answered.

"Do not, under any circumstances, enter that apartment until you hear from me, okay?"

"OK," he said.

Nate hurried to his car, radioed his office and told his Captain he was going to Ackmon to check out the bodies.

His mind was racing with more questions than he had answers. He looked up in his rearview mirror and saw the flashing lights of a patrol car. "Damn," he said aloud. He was driving faster than usual but didn't realize it. He pulled over to the curb, stopped his car and waited until the officer approached his car. He showed the officer his identification and explained his mission.

"Next time, put your 'reds' on if it's that important," the officer cautioned him.

"Thanks officer, I'll remember next time," Nate responded and continued on his mission.

Nate talked with the Duty Officer at the Ackmon Police Department. He told him that he could identify the bodies and knew where they had lived. Their apartment was secure as far as Nate could tell. He arranged, with the Captain, for him to work with the Ackmon Police in locating the point of entry where the men entered the lake. He explained to the Captain that he suspected these men to be connected to his case, the disappearance of Mendy and Misty.

He returned to his office and updated his report. As soon as the pathologist had determined the cause of death, he would proceed with his investigation. The results of the autopsies would not be available for another week. He called the McFarlands' landlord and instructed him to let no one in the apartment. He would send a team out to examine every inch of it. He wanted to get a lead on the third man. Nate decided to go home and relax for a while.

In answer to Nate's prayers, the phone rang. It was Jason. "Hey man, what's up?" Nathan asked on picking up the phone.

"Hey, Nate, I think I saw your man," Jason said.

"Which one?" he asked.

"That good looking dude, he was with an older dude and a blonde chick. It looked like the chick was with the old dude." "Where did you see them?" Nate asked.

"The guys and me was at that Jaguar place on Piedmont Avenue. We like to go down there and look around. They drove in and I recognized that younger one right away. We waited around to see if they wanted to buy something. They came out with the salesman and he took them to a silver Jaguar. The chick was acting like a kid, and I heard her say, 'I like this one

Jeffery. I love it. Can I have it?' Then the old dude said, 'Of course, Angel,' then he turned to the salesman and told him to have it ready for delivery tomorrow."

"They went back into the building. We tried to get inside to find out who they were but the security guy stopped us. He said if we ain't buying to get off the property so we left. That's all we know man."

"Jason, I owe you one man." Nathan hung up.

He looked at his notes again. He remembered the little piece of paper he found in the McFarlands' apartment with the name "Bern" scribbled on it. Is Bern the guy with the older fellow and the girl? He smiled as he made a note to go see the salesman at the Jaguar dealer. It was getting late so he would go tomorrow just after breakfast.

Nate was to meet the Ackmon police at the McFarlands' apartment in forty-five minutes. He had just enough time to grab a cup of coffee. He had a chat with his captain and left the building.

He decided, when he got into his car, he would get closer to the apartment then have his coffee. That way, he would not have to hurry. He remembered seeing a small coffee shop just down the street from the apartment building.

He parked his car in front of the coffee shop and went inside. There were some seedy looking guys at the counter. He sat down and said hello to the man next to him. He looked as if maybe he had just gotten off work.

"How's the coffee here?" Nate asked.

"The best around," the man said.

"Great! That's good news. Man, do I need a good cup of java. Good coffee is hard to come by," Nate stated. The girl behind the counter slithered up in front of him.

"What can I do for you?" she said in a sexy voice.

"This gentleman said your coffee is good. I'll take a cup with a donut, if you have any."

"Our donuts are fresh every day... coffee and donut coming up." She went down to the end of the counter. She returned with the coffee and a big fat donut. Nate took one sip of the coffee and thanked God he came early. He really wanted to savor this coffee and donut.

He struck up a casual conversation with the man next to him. Eventually he was talking to the counter girl and the man.

"You see those McFarland boys lately?" Nate casually asked,

"No, ain't seen 'em in awhile. They used to come in every day for breakfast. Why do you ask?"

"I hear they are pretty good at fixing things. Did they ever do any work for you?" Nate asked.

"One time we had a leak in the ladies room. We asked them to fix it. They did one hell of job. We haven't had any trouble since," the girl responded to the question.

"That's good enough for me. Do you know where I can get in touch with them?"

"Nope, they aren't ones for handing out cards," The girl added.

"Anybody know where they live?" Nate asked.

"Don't know that either and I'm not interested enough to find out," she replied.

"Oh well," Nate sighed. "I'll catch up with them later. For now I gotta go. It was nice talking with you folks. I'll be back for some more of that coffee. You take care now." Nate waved his hand and walked out the door.

He got into his car and drove to the apartment. The Ackmon police were waiting for him. They exchanged greetings and Nate walked ahead of them into the building to find the landlord.

They knocked on his door. The television was blasting so they suspected he was home. In a few minutes, he opened the door and peered out. It seemed to Nate the man had been asleep in his chair.

"What now?" the man asked.

"I told you I would be back. Didn't I?" Nate said in a sarcastic manner.

"You let anybody in that apartment?" Nate added.

"No," the man said rubbing his eyes.

"Well, we want to go in. My previous warrant still stands."

"Who are they?" he asked pointing to the two officers.

One officer flashed his badge and said, "Officer Blackwell, Ackmon Police Department. This is Officer DoLittle." He pointed to the other officer. "We also have a warrant. Would you please take us to the McFarland apartment and open it? What is your name, sir?"

"Beau Jenkins," He answered. "I don't own this building. I just look after it." He began to look a little scared.

Nate spoke up. "You indicated to me that you were the landlord. Now, you say you are not. What's the deal? Do you own this building or not?"

"Well, no. I'm just the super. Minoa Realty Company owns it," he said.

Nate made a note on his pad and walked down the hall behind the two officers.

Beau opened the apartment door and stepped back allowing the officers and Nate to enter. Nate had already looked through pretty much everything. He went to the closet and started looking through pockets of the jackets and pants that were haphazardly hanging there. He did find a pay stub, in the jacket, from the Harvard Plumbing Co., in Ackmon. He called out to the officers.

"Hey! I found something here. Do you know of a company called Harvard Plumbing Company in your town?"

"Sure I do. Ackmon is a small town. It's right on Main Street," DoLittle said. Nate handed the stub to the officer. They searched the apartment from stem to stern. The pay stub was the only thing found in the apartment. The officers fingerprinted the entire area. They took, as evidence, the remaining clothes and one pair of well-worn shoes.

As they were leaving the apartment, the Ackmon police officer told Beau that he could rent out the apartment. They had completed their search...

10

Mendy

Mendy had her cry. The handsome young man just stood there quietly and waited until she had finished. She stood and he politely handed her his handkerchief. It was so white it emitted a blue hue. She was quite impressed. She took the handkerchief from him and, as she wiped the remaining tears from her eyes, she vowed to herself, *I let my guard down and it really hurts, just as it did when I was a child. I promise I will not, ever again in my lifetime, let anyone or anything cause me so much pain.*

Mendy lifted her chin and her cold blue eyes burned into his.

"Okay, whatever your name is, let's get on with it. Where do we go from here? Or, do you plan to bore me to death?" She spat out her statement.

"This way Madam," he said as he extended his arm in a sweeping motion toward the woods. She started walking toward the woods in the direction she and Misty had gone earlier.

They had walked only a short distance and the young man asked her to stop. She turned to look at him and she thought he had gone bonkers on her. It appeared to her he was hugging a tree. In a second or two, a portion of the tree, no larger than a dollhouse door, opened up and he told her to step in.

"So, this is how you disappear so fast!" she said. She bent her head and stepped through the little opening in the tree. He followed her. She was amazed. There was an elevator in the tree large enough for two people. She was very uncomfortable with the closeness to each other. She could feel his warm breath on her face, but neither spoke.

It started moving downward. She judged it had traveled about two stories below the earth. It stopped and the side opened into a tunnel. He motioned for her to get out. There was an open-sided vehicle, resembling a golf cart, waiting for them.

He assisted her into the passenger's side and he took the driver's seat. The vehicle moved silently through the tunnel. Mendy could not determine how far they had gone but she thought it had to have been less than a quarter-mile. The walls of the tunnel were made of glossy tile of some sort. She could not remember seeing such tile anywhere. It was like traveling through a fantasyland. The temperature was pleasant and there were, of all things, paintings on the wall. The effects the lighting presented were fantastic. She was so mesmerized by her surroundings she had lost track of the time.

The vehicle came to a stop and she was jolted back to the present situation.

"What is this place? Those paintings back there are priceless," she stated.

Her companion said nothing, but inserted a key into a mechanism she thought resembled an ignition key.

"Okay, I'll play your silent game if that's what you want," she said.

A door opened and again, another elevator. She stepped in and he followed her. The door closed and up they went. In a few seconds the motion stopped. The door opened slowly and the first thing she saw was a well-groomed man holding onto Misty's hand. She was so relieved to see Misty that the man was oblivious to her.

Misty was wearing another outfit different from the one they had donned after their bath in the cabin. Her hair was in curls with a ribbon, which matched her pink and white dress. The patent leather shoes she wore had a highly polished shine.

Mendy had memorized every detail of her daughter's appearance in a blink of an eye.

"Misty! Honey, are you alright?" Mendy said and bent down to embrace her daughter.

"Mommy, I was so afraid I wouldn't see you again. I got lost in the woods and Bernie found me and brought me here." Rage tore through Mendy at that moment. She stood, looked the young man in the eye and snapped at him.

"You didn't even have the decency to let me know she was safe." Still the man was silent.

"Won't you say hello to an old school chum, Mendy?" The question startled her at first. She looked up to see where it came from. She starred at the man next to Misty, unable to speak for a moment.

"Jeffery! Is that you?" she asked.

"Jeffery Warren at your service Madam," he said rather sarcastically.

"This is my brother Bernard," he said, gesturing to the man who'd accompanied Mendy.

"It's very interesting to meet you Mrs. Arnold," Bernie said most politely. "Please, won't you join us for a cocktail in the lounge?" he offered.

"Jeffery, what on earth does this mean? We have been through hell these past few days."

"Well my dear, if you will pardon my limp," he emphasized "limp" strongly. "We will get on with the next phase of the agenda," he answered her with contempt.

He led the way into a room that resembled an exclusive hotel lounge. The hand-polished black leather covering the sides of the bar depicted its elegance. The carpet covering the floor had to be three inches thick. Mendy's feet sank out of sight when she stepped into the room.

A pretty young lady entered the lounge and announced she would take Misty to the playroom.

"Wait a minute," Mendy said. "What is this playroom? Is it some kind of torture chamber? She stays here with me," she demanded.

"My dear Mendy, your daughter will be just fine. The adults have to talk. She will join us for dinner."

"Okay then," Mendy agreed and added, "just how long do you plan to keep us here?"

"You and your daughter will be my guests for awhile, my dear," he stated.

Bernie handed Mendy a glass of white wine and a scotch and water to Jeffery. He took nothing for himself. He stayed behind the bar in case they needed or wanted another drink.

"It appears as though you have done well for yourself by the looks of this place."

"I have indeed, thanks to you. You destroyed any chance I had for a career in sports. Therefore, learning everything I could was my only salvation, working with my brain instead of the brawn, so to speak." He paused to await a response.

"How long did it take you to get smart instead of so cocky?" she asked.

"It didn't take very long, just a short year or two to learn how to walk again.

"Well, how do I fit in with this whole thing?" Mendy asked.

"You can't be serious, asking such a question. How do you fit in indeed? It will take some time for me to explain, or show you, how you fit in." Venom was spewing from his mouth...

Letter #6

20 January 2003

Dear Rosy,

It is amusing that you and your mailman are engaged in such a simple, but amusing game of 'Do you have a letter today or not.'

It is probably refreshing for him to know there is someone on his route to whom he can have a little fun without repercussions and break the boredom of delivering mail at the same time.

Honey, we must hasten our stories. Some days I do not feel like getting up. This old body is failing rapidly and I have so much more you have to know.

It seems that Mendy and Misty are safe for the time being. This Jeffery was a school chum of Mendy? How interesting, I do remember something about him. That appears quite suspicious.

The boys are a real help to Nathan. Of course, they would know what is happening on the street more than the authorities would.

Regarding my story, Eric and Jacco were enjoying their outing but it was suddenly interrupted. They both were perplexed at what they found when they docked their boat and began to walk along the river. It was imperative that they get back to their place as quickly as possible. It was a life or death situation.

Dear, I have written it all down in my notes. I cannot write anymore today, so I will close this letter. I look forward to receiving your next letter.

Love,

Rene

FOURTEEN

Eric's Story Continues...

"Jacco and I found something the otters appeared to be protecting. We thought, perhaps it was their baby.

I bent down over the muddy clump and looked more closely and sure enough, it was a child. I felt her forehead and she was burning up with fever."

The statement Eric had just made brought back some intense moments Ken had put on the back burner. Now he was living it all over again. He looked at Bridget and she had a strange look on her face. They continued to listen and did not say a word as Eric continued his story.

"We have to get this child back to the cabin as fast as possible." I said to Jacco. I knew my mother would know how to handle the situation. I took the little girl in my arms, mud and all.

"Give me your sweatshirt to wrap her in," I asked Jacco. He did so and also wet his handkerchief in the river and then said to me, "We must keep the fever from getting worse."

That was quick thinking on his part. I was too worried to think about that.

We ran as fast as our legs would take us back to the boat. Jacco helped me get into the boat, and then untied it. He slowly eased the boat out into the middle of the river. Satisfied that he was clear of any debris, he opened up the throttle and we were literally flying through the water.

The cabin was still some miles up the river, not to mention the stretch of swamp through which we could only creep. At last, we spotted the swamp's edge. Jacco cut his speed and we slowly entered the swamp. There were gators, snakes and all kinds of things to consider. The dock came into view, and I gave a sigh of relief, although I was still concerned for the child. Jacco eased the boat up to the dock, tied it off and ran ahead to make a place ready and tell my mother what had taken place.

When Jacco told mother what had happened, she went right to work. Out came her medical bag and she gave instructions to her maid to turn down her bed. She was cleaning her hands as I came through the door. I laid the child on the bed, stepped back and watched my mother take charge.

"We have to get this child into a tub of ice water, now!" she ordered.

Jacco had anticipated her order and was already preparing the tub in the bathroom. The ice he found in the house was not sufficient. He set out to locate more. He remembered the storage shed we had discovered with a small icehouse, out back.

Mother said it was time to put the child in the tub. What ice we had we packed around her body as close as possible. The mud on her clothes was the result of the otter's protective instincts. They sensed the child was in trouble and unconscious, and packed cool mud around her body. That's the only explanation. Their ingenuity probably saved her life. That act is something we will never figure out.

Her fever was excessively high. Therefore, it had to be monitored and quickly reduced. There was no way we could determine just how long she was subjected to the elements with only a nightgown as protection.

Jacco returned with a block of ice. He had found a pick and started chipping the ice into small pieces. We covered her body up to the neck. Mother knew just how long to keep the child in the ice water.

At the appropriate time, she asked me to take her out of the tub and put her back on the bed. She dismissed us and said she could do the rest, in other words, get the hell out of here and let me do my job. The maid removed her dirty clothes and she bathed her with tepid water. They now could see what a beautiful child we had rescued from the muck.

The child's white hair had us baffled. Mother told me later that she knew of only a few instances where a person's hair had turned white from a traumatic experience. However, had this child's hair turned white through the effects of the high fever? Or, was it natural. Only time will tell.

Mother borrowed one of my T-shirts to use as a gown. She called us in after she had finished dressing the little girl. We entered and she recognized the concerned look on our faces. Before I could speak, she asked me to take the child to my room temporarily until we could make other arrangements.

As I lifted the little girl, something happened within me. I felt this child belongs to me. I believe it was God's Will that Jacco and I came upon that exact spot at that precise moment. I felt this strange bonding with the child; I wanted to keep her in my arms forever. She was so precious, and so helpless, I wanted to protect her with my life just as the otters attempted to do. As gently as possible, I placed her in my bed, pulled the covers over her and kissed her forehead. "Sleep peacefully little one," I whispered faintly.

"Only an angel could possess hair such as that," mother said as she gazed upon the child.

"We shall call her Angelica, for now, until her parents can be located," she said.

I listened intently and repeated the name, "Angelica."

"It's perfect Mother, it fits her," I said.

My eyes were beginning to burn and a big lump came up in my throat. I knew it was time I left the room to join Jacco, who, only moments ago, had walked out.

We sat down on the porch and began discussing how to go about finding her parents. The first thing we would do is go back to that same spot where we found her and backtrack to see if we could find where she came from, then go from there.

"Her family must be frantic," Jacco stated.

"Yes, they most assuredly are. However, we cannot do anything tonight. We don't know the area. We can start out at first light tomorrow."

"Good idea," Jacco agreed.

We continued to make plans. First, we would contact the local authorities. Surely, someone had reported her missing.

We all agreed to take shifts to keep a constant eye on Angelica. Mother could not predict how long, if ever, the child would regain consciousness. If, and when she awoke, then she could tell us who she is. Mother gave her an antibiotic to curb the pneumonia. This was repeated every four hours without exception.

I volunteered to take the first shift. Jacco would take over in four hours. I wanted mother to take the last shift so she could get a good night's sleep. The hard part would be the following day. Mother would have to watch Angelica while Jacco and I went looking for her family.

I was alone with Angelica. The others had retired.

I pulled a chair close to the bed, took a book from a shelf and began reading to her. This child had captured my very soul. I spent the entire night reading to her. I made certain she got the antibiotic every four hours without fail.

My mother was furious that I didn't awake her for her appointed shift with Angelica. When mother came into the room I still sat by the bed with the book opened.

First, she asked how the child was. After I gave her a status report, she reprimanded me for not waking her. She told me she would take over from here.

"I will get Jacco up and we will begin the search for Angelica's parents immediately after breakfast," I stated.

Before leaving, I bent over her and kissed her on the forehead. I was confident she was in capable hands.

Jacco was already dressed and mad as hell because I didn't call him to take his shift. I explained the situation and my feelings. He accepted my explanation and cooled down.

The cook had our breakfast ready and while eating we discussed where we would start in order to locate Angelica's parents. When we had finished eating, we set out to find someone who could help us.

We had no clue as to where we were going. We had driven for about forty-five minutes and approached a fork in the road. There was a sign with two arrows; one was to Bartsville 2 Miles and the other was Meritville 1 Mile. We took the turn to Meritville. It was closer."

Ken started to perspire. How close he came to finding Sasha. *If only he had taken the other road*, he thought. Still, he said nothing. Eric was not aware that Ken or Bridget was uncomfortable with his story, therefore, he continued.

"We entered the town and saw only two buildings; one was a two-story, which badly needed to be repaired. The bottom floor was a small grocery store. Jacco parked the car and we went inside. I asked the proprietor if the town had a sheriff. He pointed to the ceiling indicating the police station was up the stairs.

Jacco asked me if the ill-repaired stairs would hold the two of us. They did and we safely reached the top step and looked straight ahead. There was no door just an open space. Behind an old wooden desk sat a rather large man. He had his feet on the desk and appeared to be sound asleep. I surmised that the man had to be the local authority. We approached the desk and made our presents known by knocking on the desk. The man opened his eyes and sleepily looked at us. Finally, he took his feet down.

"Welcome folks, what can I do for you?" he asked most annoyed that we had interrupted his nap.

We introduced ourselves then Jacco asked if he was the sheriff. The man said he was a deputy. He mentioned the fact that the town was too small to warrant paying a sheriff, so, he was it. I asked if anyone had reported missing a child. The deputy thought for a moment.

"Nobody told me nothing about missing a kid. Some folks here about wish some of their kids would go missing," he said with a big belly laugh. The statement was not funny to either Jacco or me.

"Have you got a picture of the kid?" He asked.

"No, we only found the child late yesterday. She's very sick and has not regained consciousness. She is about five or six years old with blonde hair. My mother is caring for her at the present time."

"Don't know what to tell you mister. Ain't heard nothing. Check back with me later. Maybe I'll get a message from one of the other counties. I know most folks around here and none is missing kids. Ain't no place a kid could get lost around here anyway. All the folks what lives around here knows their property like the back of the hand. So, no kid gets lost."

I was disgusted with this person I was trying to work with. In desperation, I asked the deputy how to get to Atlanta. He knew Atlanta was a big city and they would have a newspaper. He gave me his idea of the route to Atlanta. He said he did not know how far it was exactly because he had never been there.

"Where you fellas staying?" the deputy asked.

"We are temporarily staying at the Jensen Plantation," I answered. The deputy's eyes widened.

"That old Jensen place?" he asked. "Something's creepy about that place. Nobody around here will dare go out there. Once old man Tilton went up there. He ain't been heard from since. That was ten years ago. Folks said the gators probably ate him. You folks best keep your eyes opened or we won't hear from you again." He laughed again, longer this time.

We had had enough of this poor soul so we thanked him and went out the same way we came in, down the shaky steps. Once downstairs, we purchased a soft drink and went to the car.

The trip to Atlanta was very stressful by attempting to follow the deputy's directions.

Jacco said he should have been more inquisitive about the surroundings and the location of the cabin before signing a lease. Who could anticipate the present situation happening? As we drove past the city limits sign of Atlanta, Jacco spotted a roadside telephone booth. I suggested that we pull over and try to find a number for the local newspaper in the telephone book.

He found the number and initiated a call. He asked to speak with the editor. He briefly told the man what we wanted to do. That was, to send out a special edition announcing the finding of Angelica.

The editor introduced himself as Garrison Beam and asked Jacco if they could meet with us somewhere. He explained that we were not familiar with the city and told Garrison where we were at that moment. He knew exactly where we were and directed us to a restaurant near to them. He would meet us there for lunch.

Jacco had no problem finding the place. We went inside and took a seat at the bar to await Garrison's arrival.

It was early but we ordered a drink anyway and started to relax. Twenty minutes later, the editor of the *Atlanta Daily Journal*, arrived and joined us at the bar. We introduced ourselves and Garrison summoned the hostess, she escorted us to a table. After we gave our orders to the waitress I began to tell my story to Garrison. I explained what had happened and our meeting with the deputy in the small berg called Meritville. I explained my desire to find the little girl's parents as soon as possible.

Garrison stated he could put an article on the front page of the evening paper that would get plenty of attention.

"Give me a description and any details you have that will be helpful and we'll see what turns up. We can also alert the Atlanta Police Department, Missing Persons Division. I have a friend who is the Captain of that division. I'll call him and we can go right over now, if you have the time," Garrison said.

I was thankful we had found someone to assist us with our plight. We agreed to go with Garrison and speak with the Captain.

After a more extensive discussion and the meal had ended, we all left the restaurant. We had left our car in the restaurant's parking lot and rode with Garrison to the police station. We entered his car and sat down. He phoned his office and gave instructions for the article to run in the evening paper and the exact words to use in the article to get a positive reaction.

We met with the Chief, Garrison's friend was not available at the time. I gave a detailed description of Angelica. The Chief asked for a photo of the little girl. Of course, we did not have one. I explained that the child was very sick and unconscious when we left home to come here.

"When she regains consciousness, maybe she can tell us who she is and where she lives," I explained.

The Chief said there was not much hope of finding out much. Those small towns are so tight-knit. However, he would go down every avenue possible to get information.

I told the Chief we would keep him informed when the child woke up. I explained to him that my mother was an excellent doctor and she would do everything possible to heal the child of pneumonia. After that, it was up to the child to do the rest.

I also explained that my mother brought only the basic medical supplies with her on this trip. I asked him to recommend a pharmacy that would supply us with the necessary medication she would need to treat the child. He gave me the name and address. He volunteered to call the pharmacy to alert them that we would pick up the supplies mother would need at this time. I explained that my mother could provide a prescription for what she needed.

On the way back to our vehicle, I asked Garrison what the odds were of locating Angelica's parents. Garrison said chances were slim because the main papers did not go to the smaller towns that were out of circulation range.

"When you come back for your supplies, give me a call. I'll have an update on the progress we have made."

We started back to the cabin. We had spent more daylight hours than we should have and we figured it would be dark before we could get home. Jacco and I agreed to spend the night at a hotel and start out fresh the next morning.

Garrison recommended a reputable hotel. It was not difficult to locate. We checked in and requested adjoining rooms. Before going to our rooms, we went to the bar, then we began to relax and knowing we didn't have to take the trip home that night, we had more than a few drinks before going to our rooms. We were tired and felt dirty so we ordered room service. We thoroughly discussed the situation while eating.

In my heart, I knew Angelica would remain in my household. I vowed to raise her and love her as my own. However, if I had to give her up when, or if, her parents came forward, I would sadly do so. I would do everything within my power to find her parents.

Not having slept the night before, I was so exhausted I told Jacco I had to get some sleep. Jacco said good night and went into his own room. He had barely closed his door when I removed my clothes, and as soon as my head hit the pillow, I was out like a light.

We both had a good night's sleep. We slept in and did not get up until around nine o'clock the next morning. After we showered and ate breakfast, we started back to the cabin.

It didn't take as long to get back home as it did finding our destination in Atlanta. We parked the car and boarded the boat. We were in a better frame of mind than the day before. The ride to the cabin was quite pleasant and relaxing. We tied the boat to the dock and hurried inside to inquire about Angelica.

Mother was taking a break when we entered. She looked up from her teacup and smiled a welcome.

"How's Angelica?" I asked with anticipation.

"Her fever is down but she's still out," Mother answered.

I went to Angelica's bedside, picked up her little hand, and kissed it. I began talking to her as if she was just resting.

Days seem to be dragging. Finally, one evening as I was reading to her, a movement caught my eye. I looked over at the bed. Angelica's eyes were open staring up at the ceiling. My heart began to race. It was a few seconds before I could speak. I got up, leaned over her, and said softly, "Hi Angel, it's about time you woke up." I had tears of joy forming in my eyes as I gently took her hand in mine. She slowly turned her head toward the soft voice and smiled.

I didn't want to alarm her by calling out to the others so, I called in a very low voice.

"Mother, please come in here."

At first, I thought she didn't hear me. Then she walked up to the bed, looked down at the child, "Welcome home little one. I'll bet you are hungry for some real food? Nana will get you some broth," she stated. Frau Von Hussen removed the needle from her arm and went to prepare something for Angelica to eat.

I continued talking to her as I lifted her head and propped her up on two pillows. At this point she had not spoken, just smiled only once. Her eyes were shifting to different locations in the room as if she was thinking, "this is a strange place I've not seen it before." She did not appear to be frightened at all. I was pleased at that.

Mother brought in the broth and put the spoon to Angelica's lips. They parted and she took it and seemed to like it. My mother didn't want her to eat too much at this time as she was nourished intravenously since we found her. She took as much of the broth as she was offered. We praised her highly for her effort in taking nourishment as instructed.

As mother was preparing to take away the bowl, Angelica spoke for the first time.

"Thank you, Nana," she whispered.

Mother was so taken by surprise that she almost dropped the bowl.

"You are welcome little one." With that statement, she left the room.

I explained to Angelica that she had been on a long journey and I was happy she had come home.

"I love you Papa." This came from out of nowhere and I was very surprised.

"I love you too Princess," I put my head down on the bed and sobbed like a little kid.

"It's okay Papa, I'm here now." She put her little hand on my head as she said it.

Jacco never entered the room. He was just outside the door. His huge frame was shaking from head to toe. He did not want the others to see his emotions gone awry."

As Eric had explained to Ken and Bridget, the authorities had one lead. A small little girl did go missing in another county, but her description did not match. That little girl had long black hair. The sheriff there said they had to assume the child fell into the river. The body was not recovered.

Eric explained that they had advertised for about eight months. Every day they expected someone would come forward. No one ever did. Angelica had total amnesia and could not tell them anything to help find her parents. Of course, they did not tell her the circumstances by which she was there. They had asked her pertinent questions, in a subtle way, but the answers gave no clues.

Eric had not worked on his book for some time, but they all were sick of the inconvenience. They were ready and willing to leave the cabin and go back to Germany.

Angelica's situation was discussed, down to the last detail. Both Eric and Frau Von Hussen agreed that an adoption was the only solution to their dilemma. Eric filed the necessary papers and the hearing for the final adoption was only weeks away.

Eric and Jacco went back to Atlanta to see the Chief for a final update. They had been in contact with each other throughout the long process of seeking Angelica's family. On this last trip, Eric informed the Chief of the adoption and asked him to be a character witness at the hearing. The Chief agreed willingly. Garrison Beam was more than willing to testify on Eric's behalf.

The Chief testified in court. He told the judge his staff had exhausted every lead to find the parents. He also told the judge he had run a check on Eric, his mother and Jacco. Not one had any derogatory information on file anywhere. He had checked with Interpol. Their records were clean and ample funds were available to see to the child's needs and education. The adoption was final.

They avoided telling Angelica of the adoption until many years later when Eric felt she could fully understand the situation surrounding her adoption.

She did fully recover physically but did not remember anything prior to her waking up in the family of the Von Hussens.

The reading and talking to her by Eric, during her unconsciousness, led her to believe he was her father. She progressed into her youth as a well-adjusted happy child.

Eric informed them that finding Angelica inspired him to put the whole story in book form.

Both Ken and Bridget, in their mind, put the two stories together, but made no comment. Bridget only said it was a beautiful story and she was pleased that he was the one who found her. There were still unanswered questions that would plague them for a long time to come, but they were satisfied that Angelica was in such a grand family.

As they were leaving the gazebo, Eric's mother approached them. She reprimanded him for monopolizing Ken and Bridget for so long. She mentioned that they just might want to converse with some of the other guests.

"Not at all, Frau Von Hussen," Ken said.

"Eric has just completed his story of finding Angelica. We were so mesmerized by his storytelling, the time just flew by." "We are quite fortunate that she came to us but most unfortunate for her parents, whoever they are. I am sure there are hearts, somewhere, that are still aching. Maybe someday it will come to light," she said.

With her last statement, they all went back to the patio to mingle with the others.

The picnic was quite a success. It lasted until the early evening hours.

Bridget and Ken discussed Eric's story on the way home. This weekend would remain vivid in their memory for some time to come.

Rosy Answers Letter #6

February 27, 2003

My dear Rene,

It is a good thing that I have my notes up-to-date. My hands get more useless everyday now that it is so cold and damp. I, too, have progressed with my story and it is almost finished.

I could not go out to get your last letter and my good friend, the mailman, brought your letter directly to my door. We do not play games anymore and I do miss it very much.

Rene, I have missed you over the years and only you and Mendy can understand how happy it makes me to receive your letters.

I think Ken and Bridget are very strong people to sit there and listen to Eric's story without saying something that would ease their minds as to whether Angelica was indeed Sasha. However, the hair leaves some unanswered questions.

As for my story, Elaina, Trevor's sister, could not take part in the investigation but being friends with Nathan, she was abreast of anything Nathan found and she passed it along to Trevor.

Mendy was adamant about why she and Misty were abducted and she intended to find out.

It has been a long winter and I have not been out of the house in weeks. My husband is taking me to the theater this afternoon, if I feel up to it. Even if I don't feel up to it, I will go anyway.

So, my friend, I will close this letter and concentrate on the date with my husband.

My notes will continue revealing the progress of Nathan's investigation of the disappearance of Mendy and her daughter, Misty. Write soon. Receiving your letters keep my enthusiasm at its highest.

Love,

Rosy

11

Elaina

The business with the McFarlands' apartment was over and Nathan accepted the fact that he would not get any further leads from the dead McFarlands, unless of course the forensic pathologist discovered how and when the two died, which he would.

Nathan slept late the morning after meeting with the Ackmon police. Actually, it was his day off, but he was compelled to visit the Jaguar dealership. He promised himself he would try to forget the case, on his day off, after his trip to see the salesman. He had showered, dressed and wanted to get started. He picked up the keys to his car and started for the door.

"Damn!" He said aloud. The phone was ringing. He did not want to answer it but being a dedicated police officer; he could not leave with it ringing. He picked up the receiver and gruffly said, "Hello."

"Nathan?" A female voice asked.

"Lanie? Is that you girl?"

"Yes. What's happening with the investigation?" she asked.

"Honey, when can we get together? I really need to talk to you," Nathan said.

"It so happens, dear heart, I'm in town today. What's your schedule?"

"As luck would have it, love, I'm off today." He mocked her in a sassy smug voice. "Where are you?" He asked.

"I've just arrived. I'm at the airport."

"Stay there. I'll pick you up."

"No, no, I have to rent a car. There are several matters I must handle while here. Where can we meet?"

"How about the restaurant at the Peachtree Plaza Office building?" He asked.

"Great! That's where I have an appointment today. It will take me about thirty minutes to get there depending upon the traffic. I'll meet you in the restaurant there, okay?"   "That sounds good to me. I need some breakfast anyway."   "Okay, see you then."

"Bye love." He replaced the receiver with a smile on his face. *Boy! She's just what I need right now. What luck,* he thought.

He would not have time to see the salesman at the Jaguar place before meeting Elaina, so he decided to go directly to the Plaza. It would be a real treat to sit down and read the newspaper through for a change. He was feeling superb as he exited his apartment.

Nate drove his car into the parking space next to the exact spot they had found Mendy's car. He felt chills creep up his spine and his thinking started all over again.

He walked the few blocks from the garage to the Plaza as he did when he was looking for clues in the case. He instinctively looked around as if he was searching for something else connected to Mendy's disappearance.

He approached the doorman at the Peachtree Plaza entrance and with a smile; he said "Good morning, sir." He opened the door for him. This made Nate feel special. He straightened his posture and proudly went inside and purchased a newspaper.

He was content just to be alone to read his paper. He did not turn on his pager. If anyone needed him, they could leave a message. That is the way he wanted it today. He had not had any time for himself since this case had started. He was savoring his coffee when he heard a voice say, "Good morning Mr. Arnold!"

Nate jerked his head around and saw Mendy's husband approaching in his direction. He rose and spoke to him.

"Mr. Arnold, it's good to see you, would you join me?"

"Yes I will Nathan. I haven't heard from you in a while. Are you making any progress in finding my wife and daughter?" he asked. He sat down and gave the waitress his order. Nate didn't want to discuss the case today but it looked as if he had no choice, so he said to Trevor.

"I don't have a lot to report as yet. However, there are some rather good leads, but nothing very solid. Nathan changed the subject.

"I'm meeting Elaina here. Did you know she was in town?"

"Yes, she called this morning. She will be staying at my home while she's here." Trevor answered.

"I know you two have a lot to talk about so when she gets here I'll go back to my office."

"Thanks, Mr. Arnold, we do have a lot to talk about."

The two men were discussing Elaina when she entered the restaurant and shown to the table.

"My two favorite men in one place, how could a girl ask for more?" She said gleefully.

The men stood and Trevor took Elaina in his arms and whispered.

"It's been too long kid. Where have you been keeping yourself?"

"Busy," she said. Then, she turned to Nate and put her arms around him.

"Hi Nathan." She said.

"Hello, doll," was his response. "Have a seat. We were just this minute discussing how beautiful you are."

"Flattery will get you anything you want," She laughed. "Whoa! You are in the presence of your big brother here." Trevor joked with her.

"How are you holding up Trev?" She asked.

"I'm hanging in there kid. Not much else I can do, is there?"

"Let's talk tonight. For now, I have matters to discuss with Nate. Do you mind?"

"Not at all, I have to get back to work. I do have to make a living you know." He excused himself, shook hands with Nate and walked away.

12

Revenge

Things were heating up and Mendy was on the verge of finding out the reason why she and Misty were here.

"You, my dear Mendy, are the very reason you are here today," Jeffery said to her in a hateful voice.

"Me!" Her voice was getting a bit louder.

"Yes, you, Madam Arnold. I have waited and prepared for this day for many years, and I will fully enjoy your responses to my making your life as miserable as you have made mine."

"Jeffery for God sakes, tell me what this is all about." Mendy seriously did not make heads or tails of what he was saying.

"You honestly don't care enough to remember, do you?" He stated.

"Remember what? Stop beating around the bush and get to the point." She demanded an answer.

"If you don't know, you will just have to wait until I'm ready," he growled at her. "I have a special surprise for you. Our dinner will prove to be most interesting. Until then, Bernie will show you to your room. Before we have dinner, you may want to freshen up. We dress formal for the dinner hour. You will find adequate attire in your room." He said nothing else.

"This way Mrs. Arnold," Bernie said as he came from behind the bar. He escorted her up an elegant spiral staircase to a door.

"You will find everything you need for your comfort Madam. I will send Nanette to assist you," he said. She entered the bedroom and he closed the door.

Mendy was mesmerized at the sight of the bedroom. Its size and décor was astounding. There must have been thousands spent in decorating it as well as the rooms she had seen so far.

Misty popped into her mind. *Where had they taken her?* It appeared they did not plan to harm her. For now, Mendy was not worried. She was certain that Jeffery Warren was insane. She remembered his cold, fire-shooting eyes, as they looked her up and down. He scrutinized every inch of her body.

Okay, she thought. She would play his game to the fullest to see what she could find out and devise a plan of escape. She was sure he did not plan to let her and Misty just walk out of here. They definitely had been kidnapped, for what reason she had not figured out yet. She knew she could be as ruthless as he is. However, he had the advantage at the moment. She would bide her time.

The door opened and an attractive young woman entered.

"I'm Nanette, Madam. Your bath is ready. I will style your hair when you have finished. Your gown and shoes are there," she pointed to the bed.

"Hello, Nanette. Do you know where my daughter is?" she asked.

"Yes Madam. She is in the nursery suite. She is quite content and happy. There is no limit of toys to choose from." "Are there young children in the home?" Mendy asked.

"Oh no Madam. The room is especially for your daughter. This suite is yours. The closet is fully stocked with the latest fashions in your size," she added.

Mendy really did get worried at Nanette's statement. Why and how did Jeffery know their exact sizes and where they would be for him to abduct her and Misty? She had to play along until she could find some answers.

She disrobed and let her body down slowly in the tub of welcoming water. Its scented oil and bubbles was delightful even if her circumstances were not. In spite of her dismay of the situation, she lavished in the tub. When she had had enough, she got out and Nanette wrapped her in a soft body length towel. She handed her a robe of bright green silk and slippers to match. Mendy could not believe he had omitted nothing to enhance her comfort. Why? Was this the act of fattening a pig before the kill, She wondered.

Okay, she thought, *let's enjoy it while it lasts.*

She sat down at a huge dressing table and Nanette combed her hair and put it up into a French Twist. She had not worn her hair this way in years. Nanette handed Mendy the gown Jeffery had selected for her to wear to dinner. One shoulder was missing from the silver gown with diamonds encircling the waist. Mendy had some pretty gowns at home but nothing compared to this. *Were these real diamonds,* she wondered. They sure looked like it.

Nanette had put the final touch to Mendy's outfit when there was a soft tap on the door. Nanette opened the door and stepped back. Jeffery stood in the doorway.

"Mendy, you have never been lovelier than you are at this moment. Are you ready to dine?" He asked.

"If I have no other choice, let's do it," she snapped.

"It's not in character for you to act so defiant, my dear. You were always so sure of yourself. Was it because of your loyal followers?" he asked.

"You haven't seen defiant as yet Mr. Warren." He had no response and put out his arm for her to take. He escorted her down the carpeted hallway to the stairs.

They started descending the staircase. Bernie was waiting at the bottom step looking so debonair. When they reached him, he put out his arm and Jeffery transferred her hand to his brother's.

"May I escort you, Mrs. Arnold?" he asked.

"I really can't say it will be nice, but get on with it." It was not like her to be so rude. Under the circumstances, what could she do? She was not here at her own free will.

Misty was at the table when Mendy entered the dining room. When Misty saw Mendy, she ran to her.

"Mommy," she cried.

"Hi sweetheart, is everything okay?" They hugged each other and did not let go for a few seconds.

Jeffery had not arrived. Mendy and Misty sat down next to each other and waited. In a few minutes, Jeffery arrived with a beautiful blonde female on his arm.

"Mrs. Arnold, may I introduce my companion? Miss Deborah Arnold, please say hello to Mrs. Trevor Arnold."

Mendy was surprised for a moment.

"It's about time you surfaced Debbie," she stated.

"How have you been dear sister-in-law?" Deborah said sweetly.

"So! You are part of his conspiracy, are you?"

"I don't meddle into Jeffery's business dear," she replied. "I'm especially glad to meet my niece. She is a delightful child. You are raising her to be most polite. I can't stand a bratty child."

"It seems you, most of all, would understand a bratty child," Mendy added.

"Don't be hateful Mendy, I didn't bring you here."

"Now, now, ladies, we won't allow cat fights at the dinner table," Jeffery admonished the two.

Deborah started light conversation.

"How's my dear brother Trevor? We haven't seen each other over the past few years. However, I do stay informed. Speaking of being informed, there was a nice lengthy article in the papers lately regarding your husband. He was knee deep into an affair on the very day you dropped out of sight. Remind me to show it to you." Mendy did not know what to say, so she said nothing.

13

Nathan's Day Off

Trevor went back to work and left Nathan and Elaina to catch up.

"Nate, how's the case going? I have been doing some checking on the sly. There is very little information in the records that I could find about Sheila. She did live in Bartsville only a short time. Her father was an agricultural consultant. The family was there only while he completed his analysis for nine farms. They had a problem with the soil for a season and no one could figure out why, so they hired Sheila Martin's father to find out what was wrong with the soil. It took him about a year to find out. Then they moved back to Atlanta. Sheila was in the ninth grade at that time. Mendy had already entered high school and left the Bartsville Grammar School."

"Sheila became an architect and I understand very successful. She has an apartment in Atlanta. Records say she built a home in Ackmon." Elaina explained.

"Yeah, I found that out when I talked to the sheriff in Bartsville. She has a good reputation, personally and professionally, and as you can verify, Trevor has an impeccable reputation. I believe what he said that this was the first time to slip."

"I know I believe him, too. He is an upstanding person and honest as the day is long. I am not saying that just because he is my brother. He would have eventually told Mendy about it. What she will do with the information when she hears it remains to be seen. If she is alive and has access to a paper, she surely knows about it by now," Elaina stated.

"I could almost be convinced the town of Ackmon plays a big part in the disappearance of Mendy and her daughter," Nate said.

"Can you get me a recent topographical survey of the town and the surrounding area through your connections?" He asked. Elaina thought for a minute.

"I think I can handle that for you. It may take a week or so, if you want one as recent as today. Is that recent enough for you?"

"Damn, you are good. That would be great. Anything you can do, without getting in hot water, will certainly be appreciated," He said it as if he was humbling himself.

"It will be my pleasure. After all it is my family that's at stake."

They ate in silence except for minor conversation. Then Nate asked her, "Don't you have any free time today?"

"I'm afraid not dear. My schedule is so tight, I have to finish my business here and run. Trevor is expecting me for dinner tonight and I have two appointments to finish before then. I have to get back to Washington tomorrow then I'm off to only God knows where." Nate understood. She spoke again as she stood and took her purse off the table.

"I'll have the survey delivered personally to you at the station or wherever you are. Take care of yourself, my friend, I will call you from time to time to get an update on the case. In the meantime, my eyes and ears are opened." Nate gave her a big hug and she disappeared in the elevator.

It was his day off and he vowed to enjoy the balance of the day.

Letter #7

3 March 2003

Dear Rosy,

Do forgive me for not writing since January. I was very ill and my daughter stayed with me in the hospital until I was able to come home.

As you can readily understand, I am not in the best of health and my time is limited. I will try to finish my story soon and please, you do the same.

I am so worried about you. Does your doctor say why you are growing weaker by the day? Is it old age or has something terrible taken hold of your body as it is with me?

As for your story, Nathan is coming along nicely with the investigation. It is wonderful that Elaina and Nathan are such good friends and their jobs are so much related. I can see how much they have in common. It seems strange that she could not work with Nathan. I guess the FBI has their silly rules.

I do remember why Jeffery is so upset with Mendy. As I remember, she had nothing to do with the razor blade that damaged Jeffery's toes. I guess in his rage he did not fully investigate and find the real person responsible.

I remember Jeffery and his brother Bernie. As I recall, they were quite popular as jocks. However, he has met his match in Mendy.

Time does bring changes in people, doesn't it? I can hardly visualize so much turmoil and heartaches emerging from people who were so happy in that peaceful little town of Bartsville.

I will get on with my story. Things were getting interesting as Herr Von Seegan was exchanging stories with Bridget. She was being very cautious about what he was saying to her.

Honey, my health is deteriorating, as is yours, and I do understand we are in the same boat. Time is of the essence so we will have to hasten our stories to a conclusion.

Until next time, this letter must end.

My notes are enclosed.

Love,

Rene

FIFTEEN

The Proposal

Ken and Bridget returned home after a splendid weekend at Eric's estate. Ken recalled some incidents that took place at Eric's and it really opened his eyes. He wanted to waste no more time in proposing to Bridget. First, he must talk it over with Herr Von Seegen. After all, he did consider Bridget to be his true daughter. In Germany, it is protocol to consult with the father of the intended bride.

Bridget and Ken talked for hours about the weekend. Eric's story and the picnic were the main subjects. They both agreed not to pursue their suspicions regarding Angelica. She seemed to be happy and for them to open a can of worms at this late date would be catastrophic. If she wanted to check into her past later in her life, they would leave the matter up to her. However, if asked, they would have to tell her of the disappearance of Sasha.

On Monday, following the great weekend, Ken went to his office. He called Bridget's father, and extended an invitation for lunch. Herr Von Seegen was delighted.

There was man talk for a while then Ken asked Rudolf if he objected to his asking Bridget to be his wife. There was no objection there. Rudolf was ecstatic with the idea. Ken mentioned that his plan was to ask her that evening. As expected, he said yes.

The day seemed endless. Ken phoned Bridget, and then he phoned the Reinhardt Inn, an exclusive restaurant in Berlin and booked reservations for three. He had eaten there before and the decor was breathtakingly beautiful, the perfect place for a proposal.

Ken went to the jeweler's and there in the case, perched on a green velvet pedestal, was the ring he wanted to present to Bridget that night.

It was later than usual when Ken arrived home. Bridget was dressed in one of her gorgeous gowns. The vision of her took his breath away as she sat on the chaise with a cocktail in her hand. Her father had already arrived. Ken apologized for being so late, and then he excused himself to get dressed.

The suit he chose, he thought, would make him look extra special. He wanted everything to be just right in order to make her night the one she would remember always.

Suddenly Marsha popped into his mind. He wondered how she would feel about the engagement to Bridget. He had loved her so completely. However, he had laid her to rest and he was certain she would approve.

Satisfied with himself, he made sure he had the ring in his pocket. He stopped to make a drink, make a quick phone call, and then he joined the others.

They had finished their drinks and Ken asked if they were ready to leave. As they exited the building, a chauffer opened the door for their entrance into a sleek silver limo. Bridget was awestruck. This was something she was not expecting.

Their table was ready when they arrived at the restaurant. The champagne was cooling and the candlelight was perfect. The waiter poured the champagne and left the table. Ken raised his glass to Bridget.

"Here's to the most beautiful woman I have had the ultimate pleasure to know. Will you consent to be my wife?"

Bridget was so surprised; her mouth fell open as she looked at her father. He smiled and nodded indicating he knew and approved.

"My goodness Ken, you should have given me some hint," she said.

"Well, do you accept?" he asked.

"I do accept with pleasure." The toast and the proposal were finished. They stood and embraced. The entire dining room of patrons was staring in their direction. Before he took Bridget into his arms, he turned directing his attention to their audience and proudly announced, "This beautiful creature has just consented to become my wife." Everyone gave hoots and hollers, and started clapping. Ken put his arms around Bridget and said, "I love you." Their lips met and the proposal was official.

The evening was an enormous success. Rudolf had excused himself after dinner and instructed the chauffer to take him home.

Ken and Bridget danced the night away. Their eyes were only for each other. They acted as if no others were present. They danced the last dance of the evening and vowed to be together forever. The evening left them both pleasantly exhausted from the activities.

The next morning things were back to normal. Ken went off to work. Bridget slept in. She awoke feeling very content. She slipped out of bed, donned her silk robe and strolled into the kitchen. There was coffee left by Ken. She took her cup to the balcony and just stood there, taking in the beauty of her special garden, as her father called it. There were a million thoughts going through her mind. She had to plan an engagement party, set the date for the wedding, etc. She could get a guest list and maybe with Frau Von Hussen's help she could accomplish the task.

She phoned Eric's house. Erma was out at the time so she told Eric of her dilemma. He assured her there was no problem. The engagement party and the wedding would take place at his estate. He said his mother and Angelica would be delighted.

"The matter is settled," he stated. He invited them to his home to discuss their wishes. She accepted the invitation knowing Ken would be in total agreement.

Eric conversed with his mother regarding what he had promised Bridget.

"I'm sincerely happy for them. But it should be your wedding we are planning," she stated.

"I know mother, for now I'm okay with the bachelor's life," he sadly replied.

The engagement party was in one month. Everyone carried out the tasks allotted by Erma. It would go well if each did their assigned jobs.

Ken and Bridget were getting a little testy with each other. There were so many details to work out so the party and the wedding could take place without complications. After many days of hard work and tears, the arrangements for the party were complete.

Bridget had made an appointment to order her wedding gown. She and Ken decided it would not be a full gown with a train. Her age had to come into play. With Erma handling the wedding preparations, it would be tastefully done. She could think about all of that after the engagement party.

The party was the usual gala affair hosted by the Von Hussens. Their friends were never bored with a party made up by Erma Von Hussen. She was at the top of the elite list of people who gave the best parties.

It appeared as if Ken and Bridget were forever nursing hangovers. They felt like crap the morning after. They did not discuss the party until later in the morning when both were feeling better.

Ken expressed his satisfaction of how smooth the evening went. He was certainly grateful for Eric and his mother for helping them put on such a prestigious affair.

There were too many gifts to take home in a car. Therefore, Eric offered his storage space until after the wedding. His thoughtfulness solved yet another of the many problems they would encounter during the next few weeks.

Bridget was dividing her time between planning the wedding and her father. He demanded a lot of her attention. He felt he needed to make up for the time missed before he found her.

Angelica and Erma accompanied Bridget wherever she wanted to go shopping for her big day.

Ken and Rudolf were busy also. They were discussing the purchase of a home for him and Bridget. Rudolf informed Ken that finding a home was not necessary. He had already given his tenants notice to move. He expressed his desire to remodel the house to Bridget's specifications and present it to her as a wedding gift. He had been working with the city's government to purchase that portion of the park that was once the estate grounds, at least, most of it.

Rudolf asked Ken what he thought about the idea. He agreed to the plan with one stipulation. Rudolf would have his own apartment on the entire third floor with his own private entrance. He wiped a tear from his eye, blew his nose and agreed wholeheartedly.

The time it would take to remodel would be vast. His intention was to start the project the next week. He requested that Ken not mention this to Bridget. He wanted it to be a total surprise. They planned to stall the buying of another place for as long as they could.

As predicted, the work on the house began on schedule. Bridget was so inquisitive; Rudolf had to learn fast how to shade the truth a bit. He explained that he wanted to do this for a long time but was not motivated until he found his princess. He showed Bridget the original plans he had found and solicited any changes she felt would make the house comfortable. His plan was to make the house as close to the original as possible. He pleaded with her to modernize it to a woman's satisfaction. He asked her to visualize herself living there. He was too old fashioned and if it were ever to be sold, it would be up-to-date and quite enticing for some young couple. She agreed and was so excited that he included her in his plans. She was anxious to tell Ken what was in the works.

The plans Rudolf had the architect prepare had arrived and he and Bridget were studying them. There were only minute changes she wanted to make. The garden was not even in Bridget's mind and her father was relieved that she did not bring it up.

For the next few weeks, Bridget put the wedding on hold. She was much too involved with the remodeling. Ken was not concerned about delaying the wedding. He felt she had already committed herself to him in all ways. He totally trusted her.

Several more weeks passed and the house was almost finished. There were some inconveniences, but the concern was minute. They were forever moving from one room to another until at last Bridget and Ken ended up on the second floor as planned. Herr Von Seegen was on the third floor. The ground floor consisted of the kitchen, a sizeable ballroom and the dining room. Off the ballroom lay a vast terrace overlooking the beautiful park. All work except the final touches was complete.

Bridget was awakened one morning by loud pounding in the back yard. She thought the City was doing more work in the park. This had happened before. She paid little attention to it. A few days later, she was on her new terrace relaxing. Big trucks began pulling into the park. They were unloading brick. She did not understand what they were planning to do. She phoned her father. He told her he would check it out with the Parks Department and let her know. She busied herself with other things, mainly the wedding.

When Ken returned that evening, she reported the happenings of the day. He had no comment regarding the park work. He just said Rudolf would find out and we would know soon enough.

Bridget watched with wonder as a wall went up at the edge of the park. She asked her father many times about the wall. He always had some delay action ready to keep her in suspense.

The wall and the clean up of the debris had taken a long time. The plants and shrubs were replanted.

Rudolf told Ken he was ready to divulge their scheme to Bridget.

"I don't believe I have any more deceitful lies left in me," Ken stated.

"I'm sure we will be forgiven, once the story is out," Rudolf giggled.

Bridget planned dinner in the new dining room. She had already invited her father to dine with them that evening. He wanted to take this opportunity to present the gift. He came down to dinner at the appointed time. Bridget greeted him and of course, he had flowers for her table.

Since the completion of the remodeling, the place was much too big to keep up, so a housekeeper and a cook were hired to help Bridget take care of it. So far, they both were working out well.

After an excellent dinner, the three went to the terrace and seated themselves comfortably. Rudolf handed Bridget an envelope. She took it in her hand.

"What's this, Papa?" she asked. He said nothing until she opened it.

"Look out there Princess. It's your garden once again," he mused.

"You have in your hand the deed to this estate."

"Papa, what have you done?"

"It is my legacy to you, honey. I am an old man. I will not be around much longer and I want you to have it, raise my grandchildren here, and perhaps my great grandchildren as well."

Bridget was holding the deed reading her name embossed on the paper. Moisture was forming in her eyes.

"I don't know what to say. It is so wonderful. Are you sure this is what you want, Papa?" She dried her tears and went over to her father. He got up and put his arms around her.

"Thank you, Papa. You know you have a home here with us and don't you doubt it," she stated.

Ken was wiping his eyes as she turned to him with outstretched arms signaling him to come to her. She suspected Ken had a hand in the deceit. She expressed her gratitude for his silence and patience through the many months of remodeling. The stress of that phase of her life was over. Now, she must set a date and get on with the wedding plans...

Rosy Answers Letter #7

May 1, 2003

My Dear Rene,

I finally acquired enough energy to answer your last letter. I have added a few words to my notes as I felt like it. I am sending more to the story this time and probably within the next few days, I will finish my story. Things are not looking good for me lately, the doctor says it is the big "C" and there is less time than I expected, but I think I can finish the story in plenty of time.

Please hasten the adventures of Ken and Bridget. It appears things are going well for them.

As for Mendy, she received a bit of shocking news that she did not know what to do with or to believe. Her meeting Deborah was not what she needed at that moment. Jeffery was overly polite and Mendy wondered when the next shoe would drop. She did not trust him one bit.

As for the progress in finding her and Misty, Nathan planned to go to the Jaguar dealer and check out the information given him by Jason.

Mendy was getting tired of the game Jeffery was playing and wanted him to put the cards on the table and tell her what he planned to do with her and Misty.

The pieces to the puzzle were falling into place and she did not like it.

My mailman (Greg) has been so gracious since I have been housebound. It is a sad thing that our little game is over and no more anticipation. However, I did tell him about your story and he comes by every chance he gets to learn more about Ken and Bridget. I hope you don't mind. He is alone and a very good friend to my husband and me. They both listen intently and look forward to your letters almost as much as I do. I must stop and close this letter. I look forward to your next letter. My notes are enclosed.

Love,

Rosy

14

The Newspaper Article

Mendy could not stop thinking about what Deborah had told her about Trevor. She certainly did want to see that article. It was hard for her to comprehend Trevor being unfaithful to her. This changed everything. She looked over at Misty to see if, by chance, she understood the conversation. There was no indication. Misty was busy eating and she seemed to be contented.

Jeffery spoke to Mendy.

"Is your food satisfactory, Mrs. Arnold?"

"Quite delicious, thank you. My compliments to the chef, please." She said it in such a way he got the message.

"So, you are a Forensic Pathologist. That profession suits your cold demeanor, Mendy. How did you decide on such a profession?"

"I did it to piss off my parents. That's how," she snapped at him.

"And you succeeded I take it."

"Of course. Don't I usually get what I want?" Mendy felt terrible about talking like this in the presence of Misty, but at that point it did not matter much.

Her heart had been ripped out and she was running on pure vinegar. Before this mess was over, Misty would grow up at a rapid pace. Mendy knew if they escaped this madman, things would really get nasty and Misty had to learn to cope with it. She would try to get a chance to talk to Misty and warn her of the danger they faced.

Misty had witnessed a horrendous act in the van and her mother smashing that man's face with a rock and killing him. She had yet to mention either act. Mendy thought maybe her precious daughter had closed these incidents out of her mind. She seemed to be enjoying all the attention Jeffery and Deborah were giving her. It was too soon to know what plans they had for Misty.

"So, Deborah, what have you been doing all these years?" Mendy asked.

"Nothing you would be interested in, dear sister-in-law," she snapped.

"Oh, we were interested alright. Trevor spent a lot of time trying to find you when your parents passed away. Anyway, why are you so bitter toward Trevor and Elaina?" Mendy asked.   "Bitter? I'm not bitter. I just don't care. As far as I am concerned, they both can rot in hell. I consider myself an only child."

"From what I was told, you should consider yourself lucky they didn't decapitate you the moment you were born," Mendy responded.

Deborah was getting hot under the collar. She took a dinner roll and threw it, as hard as she could, in Mendy's direction. Her aim was not good. It landed on the floor over Mendy's head. Jeffery grabbed her wrist in his strong hand and twisted her arm.

"You may leave the table Deborah. Take your temper and your manners to your room," he ordered sternly.

"Jeffery!" She screamed. "How dare you take her side against me?" He said nothing and slapped her across the face. Bernie said nothing but clinched his teeth. The ripples in his jaw were evident to Mendy. Misty was watching this episode with wide-opened eyes.

"Get out! I'll talk to you later." Jeffery spat. She ran out of the dining room in tears.

"This is an interesting little act Jeffery. What do you do for an encore?" Mendy slyly asked.

"Don't push me Mendy. I'm in no mood for it."

"I do believe the dinner hour is over," Mendy stated. "May I have your permission, sir, to see that Misty is safely in bed?" He did not answer her. He turned to Bernie and instructed him to accompany the ladies to Misty's quarters.

"I will expect you to return when she is tucked into her bed. I will be waiting in the lounge." He stood and exited in the direction Deborah had taken. Mendy took Misty by the hand to leave.

Mendy was quite concerned that Misty had placed her trust in Jeffery, Bernie and Deborah. She would be eight years of age in a few days and she was so vulnerable. The thoughts going through Mendy's head, regarding her daughter, were overtaking her attention and she did not hear Jeffery when he told Bernie to wait for Mendy and escort her back to the lounge.

Bernie had summoned Nanette and led the way to the room they called the Nursery Suite. As they stopped at the door next to Mendy's Nanette took Misty into the nursery and before Mendy entered the room, she looked at Bernie, "Another little detail you neglected to tell me," she said.

"Your comfort is most important to us, Madam." Bernie spoke in an even well calculated voice. "There is a connecting door to your suite. Feel free to use it if need be. I will wait for you to finish your motherly duties and accompany you to the lounge. If I were you, I wouldn't take too long. Jeffery's patience leaves a lot to be desired." By his tone, Mendy knew what he meant.

"I'll be outside, Madam," he said as he closed her door. She heard a click indicating that the door was locked and secure.

Nanette prepared Misty for bed then left the room. Mendy tucked her in. Before saying goodnight, she took Misty's hand.

"Honey, pay close attention to me, this is very important." She spread her arms as if encircling the room, "all of this is only a pretend. You and I were taken away from our home and away from daddy and Jeffery won't let us go back. How do you feel about what's been happening?" she asked.

"Mommy, I don't want to talk about it. I just want to go to sleep."

"Oh Misty baby, can't you understand what I am saying?"

"Yes, Mommy," she said and closed her eyes.

Oh my God! She's in shock or something worse, Mendy thought. *I guess it is best for now, she is in her own little world.* She covered Misty, and went into her own bedroom.

She freshened up and looked around trying to memorize every crack and seam in the walls hunting for something that might be a clue to a way out of this place. There was a knock on the door and she knew it was her cue to come out.

She opened the door with no trouble. This was a mystery to her. *I know that door was locked, why is it unlocked now? What am I overlooking,* she thought. She had decided to pay close attention to everything that Bernie did in regard to keeping her and Misty in the rooms.

15

The Jaguar Dealer

Nathan did indeed enjoy his day off. After he left Elaina, reluctantly he went home. He really wanted to go the Jaguar dealer, but he said no. He had not had a day off in so long he could hardly remember. Therefore, he decided to loaf the balance of the day, even take a nap. *What luxury, to take a nap,* he thought.

When he entered his apartment, he picked up his mail. The superintendent always slipped it under the door. He had been doing this for as long as Nathan had lived there. He did not have to worry about somebody taking it. One never knows what will happen in his line of work.

He fell asleep while watching some dumb television show. It was dark when he came alive again. He decided to go out and find some interesting conversation at a local hang out. He could use a couple of beers. He was off duty and he might get stoned out of his mind.

He met up with a couple of fellow officers who were also off duty. They kicked around some funny stories and seemed to have had a good time.

How he got home was another mystery. When he opened his eyes in his own bed, it was safe to assume he had not killed anyone on the way home. He missed those sessions he used to have with his dad. Many times, like now, since his dad passed away, Nathan had wished for some good advice. His brothers were scattered throughout the country and they only got together once a year, if they were lucky enough to have time off together. He had been on his own for some time.

He dressed and went to his favorite diner for breakfast. When he had finished, he called his captain and told him he was going to the Jaguar dealer to question the salesman and that he needed a warrant just in case they would not give him the information he wanted. Privacy and all that crap would be their excuse and Nathan did not have the time to play their games. He stopped by the courthouse and picked up the warrant. He would not use it unless it was absolutely necessary.

He drove into the lot and parked his car, went inside and asked for the manager. The girl at the counter paged a Mr. Nolan. In a few minutes, an older man came in the front door and walked up to the counter where Nathan stood. The girl told him Nathan would like to see him.

"I'm Frank Nolan, the manager here, what can I help you with?"

"Nathan Girrod, could we go somewhere private? I have something confidential to discuss with you."

"Of course, come this way." He led Nathan to his office behind the show room. They both sat down. Nathan spoke.

"I am with the Atlanta Police Department." He showed his badge and identification. "I'm investigating the disappearance of a lady and her daughter. I have it on good authority that one of our suspects may have purchased a silver Jaguar from you last week. I would like to know who it was and where they live." Nathan told him which salesman had handled the deal.

"Mr. Girrod, I can't give out that information," he said.

"Mr. Nolan, Judge Henry Wilson says you can." He reached into his inside pocket and handed the warrant to Mr. Nolan. Then, he continued.

"We can do this the easy way or we can get a crew in here to examine everything in those file cabinets over there." He pointed to a wall lined with file cabinets.

"There's no need for that Mr. Girrod. I'll get my salesman in here and see if we can sort this thing out." He left and came back shortly with a man he introduced as Phillip Blake.

"What day was it that the silver Jag was supposed to have been sold?" Phillip asked Nathan.

"I suspect you sell hundreds and hundreds of silver Jags a day or week. Is this so?" Nathan asked.

"Well no," he answered. "But, we could narrow it down if you could tell me about what day it was."

"Let's start with Thursday, okay?" The salesman took out his note pad and flipped a few pages.

"I sold one on Thursday to..." he hesitated and looked at Mr. Nolan.

"It's okay Phil. We have to tell him."

"His name is Jeffery Warren. We delivered the silver Jag to his home in Ackmon. He paid cash for it and gave me a handsome tip."

"What's the address?" Nathan asked him.

"It's 4709 Plowhitch Road. It's outside the town of Ackmon and a hard place to find. It's a small cabin a ways back in the woods. I'll draw you a diagram." He gave Nathan the diagram and asked permission to get back to his customer.

"My little visit today never happened. Is that correct Mr. Nolan?"

"I understand Mr. Girrod." Nathan walked proudly out the door and went to his car.

"Now we are getting somewhere," he smiled as he opened his car door and got in. He had to hightail it back to the station and formulate a plan to go to the address he was given. First, he had to make sure of his plan. If Mendy and Misty were there, he did not want to put them in jeopardy. It had to be done correctly or not at all.

He went to his office and turned on his computer. He urgently needed to get any information on this Jeffery Warren he could use. It was necessary to find out who was dealing the cards before he sat down at the table.

He searched the files and found nothing on Jeffery Warren. He had no record. He contacted Interpol to see if the man had done any foul deeds out of the country. Interpol had no criminal records on Jeffery; however, they did have a record of a Jeffery Von Seegan and Bernhard Von Seegan entering the United States in 1945. They were stowaways on a troop ship from Europe.

The two boys were taken to an orphanage and fortunately were adopted by the same family, the Warrens. At one point in their lives, the boys resided in Bartsville, as did Mendy and Trevor.

Nathan's interest was peaked at such a coincidence.

16

The Confrontation

Bernie was standing outside the door waiting to accompany Mendy back down to the lounge where Jeffery was waiting. Mendy was reluctant to leave Misty. Mendy had a major concern that Misty continued to deny anything about the abduction and what had taken place. For now, she could do nothing as her hands were tied. Here she was, dressed to the hilt, her precious daughter was ill and there was a maniac demanding her presence.

They entered the dim lit lounge. Jeffery was sitting at a round table in a plush heavily padded chair.

"Won't you join me, my dear Mendy?" He said most politely.

"Do I have a choice, Your Majesty?"

"I think not," he snapped.

"Let's get down to brass tacks, Jeffery. What do you want of me? My daughter is ill. She witnessed my rape and she doesn't even know what rape is. Those animals that took us, it seems, paid a heavy price for their deeds. At the very least, you don't have to pay them, now do you? It is evident that you should be grateful they no longer are here to dirty up your fine carpet," Mendy said viciously.

"They were beginning to annoy me. I do thank you for handling that matter for me," he said with a crooked grin. "What happen to their bodies?" she asked.

"That's of no concern to you, my dear. Let us just say there is no longer rubbish cluttering my yard."

"So, tell me. That little tree trick with the elevator, and the tunnel, how did you accomplish that?" she asked.

"Through my sheer genius my dear thanks to you. I really should be appreciative of your little act of having the tendons in my toes cut. That forced me to turn to other endeavors in life. I am, I believe, considered one of the best architects in the world, if not the best." He answered her question.

"And I believe your act of killing an innocent cat deserves the utmost punishment. Don't you?"

"I must admit it was a childish prank directed in the wrong direction at the time. But a lifetime of punishment is a bit much, isn't it?"

"So... my daughter and I should suffer for it? Right?" she asked. "Where does it stop? You killed and you received your just reward. It should be over. Have you wasted all this time plotting how to get even? You have not grown up, Jeffery. You are still living in a vengeful state, still feeling sorry for yourself. Well, get over it! It looks like you have done okay for yourself. Why spoil it? You know very well the authorities will eventually catch you and then what? Your efforts will have been wasted on nothing." She finished her speech while he listened intently.

"Have you spoken to your cohort as of late?" he asked calmly.

"Who?" she asked.

"Why, Miss Roselee, of course," he answered.

"Who are you kidding? If you know so much about me, my habits, plus my dress size and food preference, surely you know the where, what, how and when about Rosy. She should be of no concern to you. She was not involved in anything you would be interested in," she said.

"Oh, but I am interested in everything she does, but first you, my dear. You were always in the lead of everything going on. And you shall be the lead topic here," he stated.

"Why don't we just spell it out just what's on your mind? The suspense weighs heavy on my mind," she snapped.

"In due time, my dear, let's not rush it. Anything worth doing is worth doing correctly. Make no mistake, Mendy, you will wish you had never encountered the likes of me."

"I already have. You have showed me nothing to change my mind about that. You are still too dumb to realize you have everything. Our kidnapping has ruined it all in a flash. When they catch you, you are smart enough to know they have you for rape or causing a rape, kidnapping and entrapment. Is it worth it, Jeffery?" she asked.

"At this point, Mendy, I haven't committed rape, not yet," he said. "It's late. Bernie, show Mrs. Arnold to her room. I have things to do. Sleep well Mendy. Tomorrow holds some exciting adventures for you." He left the lounge and disappeared.

Bernie went with her and closed the door. She hurried to Misty's room to check on her before going to bed. She was sleeping snugly and Mendy kissed her cheek and went to her own room.

17

The Plan

As far as the investigation goes, there was not much Nathan could do except get his plan in order then wait for Elaina's friend to send the topographical map. He closeted himself with his captain for hours on end. He was certain that Jeffery Warren was connected and he would leave no stone unturned to prove it and find Mendy and Misty. Alive or dead, he would find them. He preferred alive, if possible.

He thought it might be beneficial to talk with Sheila Martin again. He called her office and arranged to meet her for lunch at her office building on the next day. He had talked to Trevor a few times but got nothing more he could use in his investigation.

Trevor had eventually told Mendy's parents and they went ballistic. They immediately hired investigators to find their daughter and granddaughter. They were not talking to Trevor now that they knew he was messing around with Sheila. He could not convince them that it was a one-time-only thing.

The PI's they hired were getting in Nate's way. They were around every corner. He knew, for certain, that they would mess up his plan to raid the Warren place. Nathan had cautioned the entire police force, clerks and all, to give out no information no matter who tried to coerce them. The captain also issued orders. He stressed that the punishment would be severe if any information got out regarding the investigation.

Nathan had a little talk with Jason and the boys about the PI that was plaguing him. Jason promised him that he would put the word out to lead the PI, called Morgan, in a different direction by getting one of their white co-conspirators to let a false tip leak somewhere, so the PI would grab the information and attempt to be the first hero to find Mendy and Misty.

Jason and the boys would come through. Nathan told his captain not to worry. If the other PI became a pain in the ass, he would again sic Jason and the boys on him. The captain got quite a laugh from it.

As Nathan promised, he met Sheila for lunch. While waiting for her to appear, he treated himself with coffee and reading the paper. It seemed he never got the opportunity to finish a cup of coffee or read a paper.

She walked over to his table and sat down. Nathan folded his paper and said hello.

"What else can I tell you, Mr. Girrod?" She asked.

"Please, call me Nate. I like a more relaxed atmosphere to talk, don't you?"

"If you prefer, Nate," she answered.

"How long did you say you have been living in Ackmon?" he asked.

"I don't live in Ackmon...Nate. I only have a house there. I go there occasionally to get away from the rat race. As you know, I have an apartment in Atlanta."

"When you go to your little getaway, do you see anyone? A neighbor, a hunter, anyone?" he asked.

"Not usually. My house is very secluded, as I have told you. All the surrounding land belongs to me and it is posted. So far, I haven't seen anyone defy the signs."

"Do you know who your nearest neighbor is?"

"No, I don't have the time to visit anyone nor do I want to. It's not my intent to become one of the coffee klatch crowd. If you know what I mean."

"Do you still see Mr. Arnold?" he asked.

"No. That was a spur of the moment thing. How are you coming along in locating his wife and daughter?" she asked.

"We're making progress. That's about all I can say at this point. Would you give me a call if you should happen to run into a neighbor?" He handed Sheila his card.

"Don't get your hopes up Nate. I see no one when I go up there. However, if I do, you will be the first to know, okay?"

They both walked out of the dining room. She went to the elevator and Nathan went outside.

He went back to the station and shortly thereafter, there was a special delivery man directed to his office. He tipped the man and opened the package.

"Great!" he said aloud, "It's here." He discarded the envelope and opened the map. At first glance, it meant nothing to him. However, upon close examination, that is after he found a focal point, it seemed a little clearer. He spent a few minutes studying the map and dropping his pen on the map, he yelled, "Gotcha." He said it so loud that several people passing his door looked in with a puzzled look on their face.

Nathan picked up the map and went into the captain's office. They huddled over the map for a while.

"Let's do it," the captain said to Nathan.

18

The Garden

Mendy did not sleep much that night. Her thoughts filled her mind with disturbing questions. She had to be smarter than Jeffery, although she thought he had planned this abduction for a long time and had covered all bases to prevent an escape. Even the most efficient criminals make mistakes. Small things, she thought, may have eluded his sick mind.

She thought about Trevor. *How could he be unfaithful to me? He had not even given me a hint that he was unhappy with our lives. Maybe, I was too engrossed with Misty's activities to detect any clue.*

She and Misty were together constantly, and when Trevor did come home, she continued her catering to Misty until her bedtime. It became evident now that she had put some realistic reasoning behind it.

Trevor seemed to accept things as they were. What happened? She lay in bed with too many questions cropping up. She had to stop thinking about Trevor for now. She must figure out how to get out of this place. Misty would not be of any help as she was sick. Would she put up a fuss about leaving? They treated her as if she was a princess. What child would want to leave such a fairy tale existence?

Mendy started thinking of an escape. *Let me start at the beginning. The cabin, the grounds, the tree elevator and the river could play an important part in her escape. What happened to the van? It was still in the yard when Bernie took her away from the cabin. But it had Jeeter's blood all over the floor. They could not leave it in plain sight after they took the dead bodies away. That is another thing. Will they tell the authorities about my killing the two men? They might hold that over my head. How could I prove it was to protect Misty and not just a random, vicious act? After all, we were kidnapped. I cannot worry about that now... I will just keep my eyes and ears opened and wait. Jeffery will let me know soon enough what is in store for us.*

Mendy fell asleep from sheer mental exhaustion. A soft rap on the door alerted her that someone was entering the room. She sat up and Nanette entered.

"Good morning, Mrs. Arnold. Mr. Warren is expecting you for breakfast."

Mendy wondered why Nanette didn't open the drapes. That act was usually part of a maid's responsibility in the morning. She did not mention this to Nanette, but filed it in her memory to be used later when she was alone. That is, if she were ever allowed to be alone again. She was living from day to day in wonder.

"Is my daughter up yet?" she asked Nanette.

"Yes she is, Madam. She has had her breakfast and she is in the garden with Mr. Warren. He is showing her the fish pond," she answered. "Mr. Warren will have his breakfast in your company."

Nanette laid out the clothes Mendy was to wear on this day and went into the bathroom to make a bath for her.

She expertly assisted Mendy in dressing to perfection. Her hair and makeup was perfect. She took a last look in the full-length mirror before departing. Nanette commented on her beauty and perfection.

Nanette opened the door. Mendy noticed again what happened with the door when they went though it. When it closed, she said quickly, "Oh, I forgot something. Nanette will you open the door for me?" She reached for the doorknob and Mendy watched very intently. There was something very strange about the way she put her hand on the knob. With no key, she opened the door easily, as if it was unlocked. Mendy went back into the room and pretended some act, and then she came out again. This time, Mendy opened the door from the inside with no difficulty.

She was still trying to figure out the lock when her thoughts were interrupted by a male voice.

"Good morning, Mrs. Arnold, this way please." It was Bernie. His impeccable appearance impressed her highly. She was versed in the need for formality but this crew was carrying it to the extreme. She responded to his greeting.

"Good morning, Bernie. And what surprises are in store for us today?" He said nothing but led her into the formal dining room and seated her on the side of the table next to the head seat.

Shortly, Jeffery entered holding Misty's hand. She was smiling.

"Misty, honey," Mendy cried. Misty made no effort to run to her as she did the first time, she saw her, when the elevator opened.

"Good morning, mother," was her response. "I have had a delightful morning with Jeffery. Now, I must go to my room and see if my dolls have been good while I was away." She let go of Jeffery's hand. "Please excuse me," she said politely. Mendy was shocked as she watched her daughter ascend the stairs.

"What have you done to my daughter, Jeffery? She is certainly not acting like a seven-year-old," she stated.

"My dear Mendy, a little kindness and suggestions goes a long way with children. Is this not true?" he answered her with a satanic smile.

"You have done something to her. Brainwashing I would suspect. She was rather too polite and too formal for this time of day. What have you told her?"

"I think that's between me and the Princess. It is of no concern to you, my dear."

Mendy had not yet been outside the house and she wondered if he would allow her to do so.

"Well, Jeffery, what exciting plan is in store for me today?" she asked rather civilly. "I can't imagine this life of luxury will continue for very long. When will you begin your revenge on me?"

"Oh, dear heart, my revenge started some time ago. Have you not noticed? Today, I will show you around the grounds and point out how magnificent my estate is. In the event you deem it necessary to depart our company, you will see, first hand, that it's not so simple. If you leave here, it will be at my discretion, not yours, right?"

"Know this Jeffery, impossible is not a word used in my vocabulary."

They finished eating and Jeffery started for the door to the terrace. He held out his hand.

"Will you accompany me to the garden, Mrs. Arnold?" She did not take his hand but stood and walked in his direction.

She walked ahead of him and stopped on the terrace to look around. The garden appeared to be sunny and pleasantly warm, it was mid-morning and bright so Mendy determined there was artificial lighting, it had to be in these underground surroundings. She observed birds flying around and a pleasant breeze touched her face ever so slightly.

Jeffery took her by the arm and created a sensation she could not understand but it was pleasant. He led her down a few steps to what appeared to be the lawn. It spanned the length of a half football field. Beyond that was a wall of shrubs. They looked real but were different in some strange way.

"I see you have the proper attire for a hike today," Jeffery mentioned.

"I imagine you knew, well ahead of me, what my attire would be for today. Your choice of outfits is most satisfactory and in the latest fashion, I might add."

"You wear them well, my dear," he said politely.

"I would like to know, just why you are being so nice to me. It is unheard of that a kidnapper would treat their victims so royally."

"My dear Mendy, haven't you heard of killing someone with kindness?" he asked.

"Your precious child is a delight to behold. I do not have any children but I have decided that your daughter would be very happy in this household. It appears that she feels the same."

"So, that's it. You intend to take my daughter, win her over with luxury and then what? What will you do with me? Do you expect me to stand by and let it happen, just like that?

"I would hope, in some small way, you could become content living here also. Haven't you realized that you are perfectly safe in my home?" he said.

"Yes Jeffery, I have not been afraid once since I came here and I have often wondered why," she said softly.

Mendy knew he had her over a barrel for now, and she would not cause any trouble, just bide her time until she could figure out a good means of escape. She was confident he would not hurt Misty. Through her experience, Mendy felt that, now, the attention was the perfect therapy for Misty. She was in denial and pampering would keep her stable for a while. When the time came, she knew she could get help for Misty.

Mendy was still trying to figure out how this place of Jeffery's came into being. She knew for sure it was underground. Except for the missing sun, anyone would think this is the real thing.

"May I ask what happened to Deborah?"

"You may ask, but don't concern yourself with Deborah she gets over her tantrums easily. I do apologize for our behavior last evening. I am quite certain her display of emotions will not happen again."

"Does she really dislike her brother and sister so much?"
"I cannot, and will not, speak for Deborah. She has expressed her feelings adequately, I believe."

They were approaching the shrubbery as if to walk over them. Mendy was taking in everything she possibly could. Actually, she was enjoying her surroundings and delighted in Jeffery's company. Her feelings for him were changing. He had treated her and Misty with grandeur, except for the hateful way he acted at first. Then he had acted as if he wanted to rip her heart out.

Suddenly she gasped; a little rabbit came across the path and startled her. On instinct, she quickly stepped backwards and turned into Jeffery's arms. Their lips were inches apart. Jeffery made an intelligent decision within seconds and released her.

"I see you are delighted with my friends. There are more, come I'll show you," he commented.

His knees were a little shaky as he led the way through an opening between the shrubs. This disturbed him as he had not experienced such a sensation with anyone.

A beautiful garden lay beyond the row of shrubs, not visible from the yard.

A magnificent pair of black swans nestled side by side in a crystal clear pond. There were four baby swans swimming nearby. A variety of wildlife scurried away as Jeffery and Mendy stepped into the garden.

After shaking off the initial wonder of it all, Mendy spoke to Jeffery.

"You have a paradise here Jeffery. Why do you need me here to spoil the tranquility of it all?"

"I must admit, my dear that you and Misty have added to the tranquility. I have loathed you for too many years. Since you have been my guest, my feelings toward you have changed. You seem to be a very pleasant person to have in my presence, not the arrogant bitch I have hated all these years. You were correct, I should be grateful that my hate led me to achieve my success, leading to my wealth. My designs are world renowned, you know. My reputation is impeccable." His eyes softened as he looked at her.

"Your reputation may be impeccable, now. What will it be like when they execute you for kidnapping? That is still the penalty for the crime, is it not?" she asked.

They had started back toward the house. Mendy spied Bernie rushing toward them. When he approached, he leaned in and whispered something to Jeffery. He turned to Mendy.

"Do excuse me, my dear. I have urgent business that needs my attention." He and Bernie left her standing in the yard. She continued to walk toward the house. A void fell over her as she watched him walk away and out of sight. *I cannot let my guard down now; I do not completely trust him.* She thought. She felt this was a good time to find Misty and see what she had heard.

Mendy went into the house and met Nanette in a hallway.

"I would like to see my daughter. Would you take me to her?" she asked.

"Of course, Mrs. Arnold, come this way."

Nanette led the way to the Nursery, opened the door easily and Mendy entered. The door closed with ease and she could detect a faint click. She knew the door locked.

19

The Hunters

Nathan received the map from Elaina's friend and he was ecstatic that it had only taken two days to arrive. Now, they could go forth with his plan to locate Jeffery Warren.

The captain assembled the men that would accompany Nathan to the cabin in Ackmon at the destination of the car. Nathan was in charge of the entire operation.

The men changed into civilian clothes to pose as hunters. If they encountered anyone in the woods, they could use this ruse to cover the main purpose of being in that area.

The operation had to look legitimate. They packed a cooler with beer and soda. There were the usual items of food a hunting party might eat. Hunting rifles were necessary, along with sleeping bags and a tent. A well-used propane gas grill was in the back of the van. Their hunting clothes were well worn and soiled before this trip began. Each man had a hunting license in the event he was questioned as to why he was on the property.

Two RVs were loaded with eight officers who had been briefed for this particular operation. Each man knew exactly what his job was and, win or lose, he would give it his all in hopes that this one shot would be the one to find and rescue the two girls.

There was one last serious thing Nathan said to the men. "Until we find something substantially significant, we are here to have fun and find some game. Another caution, you must not slip with your conversation. Talk about your girlfriends, wife and kids or whatever a civilian hunter would say. Is this clear?" In unison, the men answered, "Yes."

Immediately the men started telling jokes. Until told otherwise, they shut out their police lives. The men were anxious and the trip to the outskirts of Ackmon seemed pleasant enough. The lead van, that Nathan was driving, turned onto a dirt road. The men became alert and cooled the camaraderie. As was planned, Nathan stopped his van and got out. Spreading the map on the hood, he and one other man began to discuss their plans for the night, rather loudly.

"This road is not on the map, guys. Let's take it for a short way to see if it is suitable to pitch our tent," he suggested.

"It sounds good to me," one officer said.

"It can't hurt," another joined in.

"Keep your eyes open for a good clearing," Nathan said. He folded the map and got into the van.

He eased the van through the thicket. His training told him this road was used frequently. The two vans had gone about a half a mile. Nathan stopped and looked around. He did not notice any "POSTED" signs on the property, so far. He did see the top of a cabin chimney ahead.

"Look there, guys," Nathan yelled pointing to the chimney. "Let's check it out and see if anyone's home." He returned to the van and moved it slowly up in the yard of the cabin. He got out and walked up to the porch.

"Hello! Is anybody home?" He stepped to the door and knocked. There was no answer. He peeked into the window.

The men were standing around looking at Nathan.

"Can I help you gentlemen?" A gruff voice startled everyone. They all turned in his direction and Nathan spoke.   "Hi there, we are looking for a place to camp for the night. Is this your place?" he asked.

"It is," Bernie answered.

"We want to do a little hunting. Is this property available? It looks pretty heavy in there," Nathan pointed toward the woods.

"This property is POSTED. Did you not see the signs?" Bernie was getting a little annoyed.

"Sorry, I didn't see any signs. Did any of you see a sign?" Nathan asked. One man answered, "I wasn't paying much attention, but didn't notice any."

"It is posted gentlemen and we do not invite anyone to hunt or fish here. I must ask you to leave the premises." Bernie was getting impatient.

"Sure, Mr..?" Nathan hesitated, waiting for the man to reveal his name.

"My name is not important. Now, if you will leave, I'll get back to my reading."

"We have a map here," he reached into his pocket and took out a new map of the area. Then Nathan asked Bernie, "Would you show us where hunting is allowed? We were told it's in this area. We really thought it might be here. We sure don't want to intrude."

"I'm not a hunter of innocent animals, sir, and I do not have a clue where that might take place. Now, if you will excuse me, I will return to my solitude."

Bernie went into the cabin and closed the door, leaving the police team standing with their jaws hanging down.

"Let's get out of here guys. We'll stop further down the road and see what we can find." Nathan pretended he was upset. He got in his van and slammed the door. There was a "damn" and "that sucks" from someone in the crowd.

Nathan led the way out to the main road. He drove until he found a roadside space large enough for the two vans and stopped. He went back to the second van. The three officers who were with Nathan followed him. He poked his head in the window.

"You guys blew it, damn it! How in the hell did that guy sneak up on us? Wasn't anyone covering our ass?" Not one of them had a comment. Nathan was furious and he was not pretending.

"Let's get back to the station. The operation is officially scrapped," he snapped.

All four, including Nathan did not say a word the entire trip back to Atlanta. When they reached the station, Nathan ordered them to get back into their uniforms and stow the gear. "I will see you all in the captain's office in one hour," he snapped.

Nathan got into his own car and went home. He changed clothes, grabbed a sandwich and went back to the station. The captain stayed late to wait for their return.

Nathan entered the station and went directly to the coffee machine. He sure wished he had something stronger to drink but this would have to do for now. He dreaded facing the wrath of the captain.

The captain was waiting for him. He stopped his pacing when he spotted Nathan.

"Come in Nate," the captain said. "What in the hell happened out there?"

"All I can say, Capp, is nothing. A man appeared from nowhere. I mean nowhere. None of us saw him coming. All of us were scanning the area as we went in. There wasn't a swinging dick anywhere. He definitely was not in that cabin because I looked in the window. There was no sign of anything there to indicate anyone had been in there for some time. Another thing, somehow, he knew we were there. Maybe there were cameras all through the woods. We didn't detect any. I consider myself pretty sharp at what I do and I saw no cameras, unless we are talking really hi-tech stuff."

The captain suggested Nate take another look at Jeffery Warren's file. What does he do for a living? What is his field of education? Nate commented on the captain's questions.

"I have done my homework, Capp. He is well educated, has a degree in electronic engineering, a degree in architecture, a degree in accounting. My God, Capp, he's practically a genius."

"That might be the key, Nate. Maybe the grounds around the cabin were electronically rigged somehow. Find out who could have installed such a system. The man may be a genius but I doubt he would do the work himself," the captain commented.

The team was beginning to wander in. The captain was questioning each man and getting his ideas on the situation. They all were in agreement with Nathan. The captain dismissed the team and said to Nathan.

"Let's take a closer look tomorrow, Nate. I'm going home."

"Okay, Capp. I am too."

Second #7 Letter

June 15, 2003

Dear Rene,

I have not heard from you in a long time. What is the matter? I called you several times with no answer. Have you been away? I am worried sick. Please call me soon.

My dear husband has hired a secretary for me. I tell her my story and she puts it on paper. Therefore, I am sending more of the story with each letter.

Mendy cannot understand Jeffery's mild actions. She anticipates a hateful act but nothing comes. What became of his revenge plans is what she thinks about most. One minute he is nasty the other he is nice. What is she to think? How can one plan an escape when an escape might not be what one wants?

What is happening with Ken and Bridget? It appears that they will get married. It is odd that Eric has not said anything about the wedding. I believe he is in love with Bridget.

I cried when you told me of the renovation of the old homestead and Herr Seegan giving it to Bridget for a wedding gift.

Honey, I do hope you are not ill. You have to be strong to carry on. There are things you must learn before you hear that horn blow and I will tell you as much as I can under the circumstances.

As for me, I feel okay, mentally that is. Physically, I am not so good. I have my good days and bad days. I feel my good days outnumber the bad. That is not a bad thing.

I will stop for now and hope you have written. We all look forward to hearing from you.

Love,

Rosy

20

Hope

Mendy found her daughter sitting at a little table having a party with her dolls. There was music playing softly in the background. Mendy recognized the tune as one from Disney World. *Damn it,* she thought. *That lunatic has thought of everything a child could possibly want.*

"Hi, sweetheart, whatcha doing?" Mendy asked sweetly.

"Hi Mommy, we are having a party, wanta join us?"

"Okay, honey. After our party, I want to talk to you about something, okay?"

"Okay. Want some lemonade and cookies?"

"I'd love some. Baby, can you put your dollies away for a little while so we can talk?"

"Of course, it's time for their nap anyway," she replied.

Misty busied herself tucking in her dolls. Afterward, she sat down with her mother and continued to drink her lemonade.

"Sweetie, I have to talk to you like you were grown up. Do you understand how much trouble we are in here?"

"Yes, Mommy."

"You do?" Mendy was shocked as she asked the question. "You know why they are being so nice to us?"

"Sure I do. I hear them talking. They think I am just a baby and I don't know what they are saying. But I do, you know?"

"What have you heard, honey?"

"Well, I heard Jeffery say to Bernie, 'That bitch will pay for what she's done to me.'"

"Did they say who had done something to him?"

"I heard Bernie say, 'Jeffery, I think you are making a mistake with Mendy.' That's you Mommy."

"What else did you hear?"

"Jeffery got real mad at Bernie, then he said, 'Bernie, you have said this before, so don't remind me again.'"

"He said you put a razor blade in his shoe and cut off his toes and he cried in front of his friends and was embarrassed, and he wanted to get back at you. You didn't, did you Mommy?" At first Mendy did not know exactly how to answer the question.

"Well, honey, many years ago, when Jeffery and I were in school, he and some friends killed my best friend's beautiful cat. He did it just because she wouldn't go out with him. That was just plain mean. I made a promise to my best friend that I would find out who had killed her cat. Honey, it was a beautiful, loving little pet. After he killed it, he threw it up on her balcony. She walked out on her balcony and almost stepped on it. Its blood was all over the place. It made her very sick and I felt so sorry for her it made me mad that someone so cruel existed in our school. I did find out who did it and, yes, it was I who told someone to get even for my friend. I really didn't know how they would get even. When I found out, it really made me feel sad but in a way, I was glad he learned that getting even was a bad thing.

"Now, Jeffery wants to, again, get even with me, even though he knows that he will be caught eventually. Until then, he will keep us here. I really don't know how long or how long his being nice to us will continue. I don't think he will be mean to you but if he does something dreadful to me, can you be brave?"

Misty did not say anything for a while. She just stared at her mother with a serious look on her face. Then, she spoke. "Mommy,   I know what getting even means. We do it at school all the time. Grownups get even too, but meaner stuff than us kids. The teacher tells us, all the time, that getting even always leads to getting even some more and it never stops, so don't do it to begin with. It looks to me like Jeffery will never stop trying to get even with you. Yes, I can be brave. Didn't I fool you when you came for breakfast? I like to pretend. If you want me to, I will keep on pretending. Jeffery doesn't know the difference. He thinks I will do anything he tells me to just so he will keep being nice to me. Mommy, tell me what I should do and I'll do it."

Mendy almost had tears come to her eyes. When her throat began to tighten up, she curbed her desire to cry and her fury kicked in.

"Sweetheart, I'm so proud of you. You answered my questions like a grownup young lady. I was so worried about you. Now that we have had this little talk, I know you will help us get back home." Mendy put her arms around Misty and held her tight.

Misty pulled away but held on to Mendy's hands. Then, she asked.

"Mommy, remember when Debbie said that Daddy was with a woman when we were taken by those ugly men?"

"Yes."

"What did she mean?" Misty asked.

Mendy really had to come up with a good explanation, one that Misty could understand. She finally answered her daughter.

"Misty, being a grownup is really complicated, but I will try my best to explain it to you." Mendy swallowed and began.

"When two people like each other a lot, they get a feeling inside that makes them want to spend more time with each other. Sometimes this feeling gets so strong nothing will prevent them from being together. I think Daddy had that feeling and went with the woman to her house to be together. Can you understand, baby?"

"I think so, Mommy. One day at school, I wanted to sit by Tommy and Judy was sitting there. I had a feeling that I wanted to sit by Tommy, so I pushed her out of the chair and I sat next to Tommy. When I sat down, the feeling went away. Does that mean Daddy won't like us anymore?" she asked.

"I don't think so, honey. We must forget about that for now and think about what we can do to get out of here. You just keep on listening to the grownups and when we get a chance to be together again, we will talk about it. Okay?"

"Okay, Mommy."

Mendy wanted to continue talking to Misty but in walked Jeffery.

"You could have knocked, you know!" Mendy spat.

"Mendy, I have to talk to you." Jeffery turned to Misty and asked, "You don't mind if I take your mother away for awhile do you Princess?"

"Of course not, I have things to do anyway." She smiled at Jeffery.

"Mommy, will you come back to my room and play with me?"

"Of course I will, honey. You go along for now, okay?"

Misty turned with a very grownup stance and slowly strolled away.

Jeffery took Mendy into the library.

"Your friends are getting too close for their own safety. They were posing as hunters looking for a place to camp. The fools, they do not understand with whom they are dealing. Bernie took care of the situation and sent them packing. I assume they will return. We are ready for them. I told you this place is impenetrable. You could be here until you have grandchildren and even then, they still cannot get in. It is also soundproof, so yell, if it will help relieve your anxiety."

Mendy said nothing. She waited patiently until he spoke again. "They are above us as we speak. Isn't it exciting?"

"I can hardly contain myself," Mendy said calmly, although she was shaking inside and hope for escape entered her mind. Jeffery went on and on about how good he was etc.

She felt she could outdo Jeffery any day of the week if she had the proper ammunition... and she would get that ammunition, one way or another...

21

Nathan's Hunt

Nathan and his band of hunters had found Jeffery's cabin and that is as far as the operation got. His captain was upset and the mission was scrapped.

Nathan went home but he could not get the mission out of his mind. He kept wondering, how had that guy appeared out of nowhere with eight men on guard? There had to be a surveillance camera in the woods. But where?

A partially eaten sandwich was at Nathan's fingertips. He started to reach for it when the phone rang. It was Jason.

"Hello man!" Nathan said. "Whas up?" In his street talk, Jason replied.

"Saw that blonde gal again. The one with that dude you are looking for," Jason said.

"Where?" Nathan asked.

"Going in one of dem ritzy stores on Peachtree Street. Rollo went in and followed her around awhile. He copped one of her packages. We watched until she came out and my man, that's got wheels, is following her."

"Jason, you and the guys are jewels in the Queen's crown. I owe you, big time. How long ago was that?"

"Bout one or two o'clock. He is not back yet. I'll lay it on you when I hear from him."

"Okay, buddy. Take my cell phone number. I keep it with me wherever I go."

"Later, man." Jason hung up.

Nathan smiled and finished the stale sandwich. His nerves were frayed. He did not hear from Jason that night. The next morning he got on the computer to check further on Jeffery.

He found where he worked and that he was the sole owner of the firm. He had 22 employees and unlimited clients throughout the world. There was no record of a marriage. Also, Jeffery's address was listed as the same as the cabin.

Nathan thought intently. He saw no car tracks when he was there. He particularly noticed when he walked up to the cabin door. It appeared to him, even though the cabin looked clean inside, there were no personal items lying around. No personal photos of family were on the tables that he could observe from the glass in the door. *There is more to this than the eye can see*, Nathan thought. The cabin had to be just a front of some kind.

He continued to search the net for more information about Jeffery. He already knew when Jeffery and his brother Bernhard came to this country and the family that had adopted them. He also knew that the family had, at one time, lived in Bartsville. Trevor Arnold lived in Bartsville. That is not just a coincidence. There has to be a connection.

His phone rang interrupting his thoughts. Again, it was Jason.

"Jason, my man! Whatcha got for me?" Nathan asked.

"Not much, man. My man followed that chick to just outside of Ackmon. She turned into a road that didn't even look like a road. My man got caught! He hadn't been on that road no time before this dude stopped him. But, we figured he might be stopped so my man told the dude the chick had left a package at the store and he was trying to get her to stop so he could give it to her but she wouldn't. The dude thanked him, took the package and made him turn around and leave and he gave him a ten spot for his trouble. My man was happy, but where does that leave you?"

"Let's meet somewhere and you can show me on a map just where this road is, okay?"

"How about we meet at that statue where we met Janice that day?" Jason stated.

"That's good? How about making it around 11 o'clock? Can you make it then?" Nathan asked.

"You got it, man."

Nathan was getting excited. He vowed to get to bottom of this mystery. Little by little, he would chop away at the questions that were plaguing him. He phoned his captain and brought him up-to-date on what was happening, and that he would not be in for a while.

Jason and the boys were at the statue of Grant as promised. Nathan walked up to them and made the 'old Afro-American hand-shake.' He brought out his map and spread it on a bench nearby. Jason looked at it for a few minutes without saying anything. Then, he pointed.

"That's it, right there."

"Damn, you can barely see it," Nathan swore.

"It don't lead nowhere, man. That chick was going somewhere, man. A chick like that, don't go to the woods without nobody with her. My man said she's been there before and she acted like she knew exactly where she was going. But where?" Jason asked.

"I don't know the answer, buddy, but I intend to find out," Nathan replied.

"Gotta go, man. Stay cool now, ye hear?"

"Gotcha!" Jason chuckled.

Nathan folded the map, stuck it in his inside coat pocket and went back to his car. He sat there contemplating his next move. He hit on an idea as he started up the car and headed downtown. The library! He would go to the library and scan the early editions to see if there were any articles about Jeffery. An important architect like him had to have something written about his work.

He entered the library and was directed to the newspaper scan machine and was instructed on how to proceed. Nathan needed no instructions. He had done this process many times in investigating other crimes.

Nathan started as far back as the time Jeffery graduated from his first college and twelve years later, *Bingo!,* he found an article about a futuristic building that he designed and supervised its construction so it would be totally his design. The headline read "Another Ultra Modern Design by the Renowned Jeffery Warren." Nathan read the article carefully so as not to miss a single detail. It stated that Mr. Warren had the ultimate imagination in his designs. They were so "out of this world" one reporter stated. Mr. Warren was born much too soon for his designs. However, his outrageous designs were so much in demand that there was a two-year waiting list. Those who the reporter interviewed stated the two-year wait was well worth it. Since their buildings were completed, the profits had tripled. Their clients were fascinated by the concept of the buildings.

Nathan continued to scroll the papers. He hit on one article that explained an underground estate of a wealthy Japanese citizen designed by Jeffery Warren. This article enhanced an idea that Nathan had been kicking around in his head.

Somewhere in those woods was an entrance to an underground house. There had to be a surveillance system in the trees somehow. Otherwise, a security person could not know when someone was on the premises.

Nathan was mentally putting together his evidence. He had a composite of the young man that Jason said was in the truck the night Mrs. Arnold and her daughter disappeared and the same man that approached the hunting crew at the cabin. There was Jason's friend that followed the blonde woman into the woods. That was no help. He saw nothing but a dude, as Jason had put it, that gave him money and told him to get lost. He did not see where the car went that the woman was driving.

It had been a mere 9 days since Mrs. Arnold and her daughter disappeared and he was no closer to finding them than when he started. He thought he, perhaps, could get a warrant to question the man in the drawing if he could possibly be drawn out again at the cabin.

Nathan could not go again, because the man had seen him and possibly would not show himself but send someone else. That would be of no value. It was time for Nathan to bring in the big guns...

22

Mendy

Mendy was tiring of hearing how Jeffery had left no stone unturned to keep his home private. However, she listened in hope that he would tell her something that might give her the clue she was looking for, a weak spot somewhere.

He had treated Deborah badly and, just maybe, she would show Mendy where that weak spot was. Debbie was not bright enough to think before she spoke about things. Her greed for material things would be her undoing, and Mendy fully intended to make peace with her and get her to talking. If she could make Debbie think that she could have a friend in her, Mendy could turn that around to her advantage.

Mendy interrupted Jeffrey's boasting.

"Jeffrey? How is Deborah doing? I haven't seen her in a while. I would like to make peace with her. That is, if you have no objections. After all, she is my sister-in-law. There is a lot she has missed since she has been away from the family. Her mother and father loved her very much. So does Trevor. Deborah didn't give him or Elaine a chance to mend their ways after they went off to college. They loved her, in their own way. It wasn't Deborah's fault that their parents shunned the other children when she came into this world."

"You can get off your soap box now, my dear. Deborah has told me the entire story," Jeffery commented.

"But, there are two sides to every story. Aren't there Jeffery?" Mendy stated.

"As a bystander, I can see both sides. One has to place himself in the other's shoes to understand that both sides were correct in their thinking, the thinking of a child, taking place. However, the hurt still hurts, doesn't it?" Mendy said.

"I believe you are a wise person and your philosophy impresses me," Jeffery stated.

Mendy could not determine if that was a compliment or not, so she let it pass.

"Then, you have no objections to us talking?" she asked.

"No objections whatsoever, my dear. I do not believe Deborah has anything on her schedule today. How is yours?" He grinned as he asked her the question then continued.

"I have pressing business today and will be away. But, I will mention the fact that you want to solicit an audience with Deborah."

"And I suppose your slapping her in the face shows your total respect for Her Highness?" Mendy expressed her disgust for the man.

"Don't rile me, Mendy! The limit to my patience with you is reaching it summit."

"Oh! Please do excuse my manners. I am a guest in your home. Am I not?" She replied. Jeffery said nothing but glared at her when he turned and stalked off.

Jeffery joined Bernie in the security room.

"Any further activity," he asked.

"No, it was just a black kid in an older car, following Deborah. He claimed she had left a package in a department store and he was trying to flag her down to give it to her," Bernie answered.

"Did he, in fact, have her package?"

"He did give Bolton a package and he gave the kid a tip and sent him on his way. It didn't seem suspicious. The kid took the tip and high-tailed it out. I did ask Deborah if she left the package in the store. She examined the contents and confirmed the merchandise was hers."

At this last statement, Jeffery left Bernie and went to Deborah's room. He knocked lightly and heard a faint, "Come in."

"Deborah! I would like to apologize for my actions of late." He sat down on a stool in Deborah's dressing room and continued.

"As you may comprehend, I have a lot on my mind at this time and I should not have lashed out at you. Will you accept my humble apology?" he asked.

"Jeffery, sometimes I just don't understand you. Haven't I always been a good companion to you?"

"You have, indeed, my pet. I have no complaints."

"Then, tell me. Why did you bring Mendy and Misty here? They are the last people on earth I need to mess up my life. Another thing, what about your annual ball, will she mess that up too?"

"Listen to me, sweetheart, you told me you understood what I was doing and you were all for it. What happened?" He waited to see what her brilliant answer would be.

"Yes Jeffery, I was for it. It sounded to me like it would be fun to watch my sister-in-law squirm. It hasn't turned out that way. You act as if you have the Queen of England here as your guest. You built that special bedroom and nursery for them, and spent a fortune, I might add, so they would be comfortable. Why? How long do you plan to disrupt our lives? Now that she is here, do you plan to send me away? Jeffery, do you love Mendy?"

Jeffery turned red in the face and it was obvious that Deborah noticed. Then, he spoke.

"Love her? Yes, maybe I do. So much that my hatred for what she did to me is consuming my every thought. I have used that hatred in every design I ever created. That hatred has kept my designs in demand all these years. Her act has driven me to the point of ultimate fame and fortune. Love her? What do you think? As for you, you know what the score is. You have the option to stay or go. You are not a prisoner. If you do choose to go, my pet, it will only take a few minutes to change all you know about this place. You could never tell anyone where it is because you will not know. So, my lovely, you are most welcome to continue sharing my home and accept what I must do at some future point." She knew he was in a serious mode.

Deborah felt it was in her best interest to keep her mouth shut and go along with Jeffery. She had been living a luxurious and peaceful existence for some time now and by no means wanted it taken away. Finally, she spoke to Jeffery.

"I choose to stay. This is my home. The only one I have known since I left home. My support for you and what you decide to do with them will continue."

"Good. Now, Mendy wants to chat with you. Do be civil, won't you?" he asked. "I do believe she had nothing to do with your difficulty with your brother and sister."

"I will do my best, Jeffery, not to embarrass you again."

Before Jeffery departed her bedroom, he added.

"To your question, regarding the annual ball, the answer is, no. The event will be on schedule, and you will be lovely as ever." He walked out and closed the door.

Third Letter to #7

July 1, 2003

Dear Rene,

      Please, please have someone call me. I have to know if you are okay. I have had no word since March. You must be getting my letters, they haven't been returned to me.

      I will continue sending my notes with the continuing story until I hear from you.

      Nathan knew of a person that could positively make a difference in his investigation, so he arranged to meet this person.

      Deborah agreed to meet Mendy and settle their differences. Mendy can find a way out if she wants to.

      I wonder about Jeffery, Mendy is correct you know. Because of her or her actions, he did achieve fame and fortune.

      This letter will be short. However, my notes are long. As I told you, my secretary is most efficient. Without her, I just couldn't do it.

      I am hopeful that a letter from you arrives soon.

Love,

Rosy

23

TooMuch

Nathan was up a wall, so to speak, so he wracked his brain for favors he had coming to him from his street people. Jason and his boys were helping on one hand but he needed someone to work the other hand. The PIs that Mendy's parents hired were kept busy and out of his hair.

Nathan left the library and headed downtown. He knew of only one person that could pull off a deception such as he needed in this case.

TooMuch was a homeless person. He got his name from his sense of humor about the homeless. Everyone frequently said, "Man, you are too much." The name stuck like glue.

Nathan knew for sure that TooMuch had hidden money and lots of it. However, he preferred to be known as a homeless person. He had given up the rat race many years ago. He was a genius and had owned and operated many businesses but became bored. They were no longer a challenge for him. Large corporations even the law enforcement agencies, offered him a number of positions but he refused them. He dropped out of society and wandered into the streets of Atlanta and there he stayed. He was highly respected for his street smarts and it delighted him when he outsmarted the so-called best.

Nathan had obtained information from TooMuch on many occasions that assisted him in solving some of his cases.

Jason and his gang knew TooMuch very well and often conversed with each other regarding a problem.

As Nathan cruised downtown Atlanta, he could not be sure just where to find TooMuch but in the past, when he needed him, he always appeared somewhere. How TooMuch knew Nathan needed his expertise when he did was anybody's guess. He just knew and made himself visible. Sure enough, TooMuch appeared. Nathan had only circled one block several times. He pulled the car up to the curb in front of TooMuch. He did not even look at Nathan. All he had to say was, "Can you spare a cup of coffee?" Nathan replied. "Corner, two blocks, fifteen minutes, see you there."

Nathan drove off. To avert suspicions, Nathan slowly circled the block again and casually headed to the coffee shop.

Nathan entered the coffee shop and took a booth in the far left corner away from prying eyes and ears. He barely had taken a sip of his coffee when in came TooMuch.

The detective was not a familiar face in the diner, but TooMuch was a fixture. He had been around a long time and the regulars knew to leave him alone. He was forever talking someone into buying him a breakfast or lunch. His greeting to each person he passed was friendly and finally he got to Nathan.

"I'm ready for that breakfast you promised," he said to Nathan with a grin.

"Breakfast? How did an offer of a mere cup of coffee turn into a breakfast?" TooMuch slid into the booth.

"You are aware, my good man, that my services are expensive and guaranteed. Otherwise you wouldn't be here, right?"

"Oh, sit down! You should be buying my breakfast. You have more money than Howard Hughes."

TooMuch smiled and asked, "How may I be of service to you?"

"I have a delicate problem, my friend. Have you heard the name of Jeffery Warren?"

"Sure. I attended a grand opening dinner he sponsored at the time he designed and built his office building. Quite an interesting design, I might add. It is far more advanced, futuristic, than a person would believe possible in this century. Why are you interested in him?" TooMuch asked.

"We have reason to believe he is connected to the disappearance of a lady and her daughter."

"That would be Mrs. Trevor Arnold and their daughter Misty, would it not?" TooMuch added.

"How do you know about it?" Nathan asked.

"My good man, I do keep up with current events. Plus, there is talk on the streets. It's much like a puzzle; one can take bits and pieces from this one and that one and complete the puzzle."

"What have you heard? Anything I can use to find them?"

"I'd rather not say at this moment. I am formulating a plan and the final details of the plan are forthcoming. I will not give you half information. I've been interested in this case since Jason's discovery of the gentleman with the blonde, whose name happens to be Deborah Arnold, the sister of Trevor Arnold."

"My God! When I talked to Mr. Arnold, he never mentioned he had a sister named Deborah." Nathan was perplexed as he ran his hands through his hair. TooMuch spoke again.

"Your weakest link is Deborah. She is an airhead and most vulnerable."

"Do you know about a cabin outside Ackmon?" Nathan asked.
"Of course, and I might caution you, do not go there again. Your first mission was a joke on the streets. You are dealing with a highly intelligent person here. He's almost on my level, but not quite." TooMuch stated with satisfaction.

"What do you suggest?" Nathan asked.

"Busy yourself with other things, my friend. I have the situation under control. I will inform you at the proper time, as to when to make your final move. Jason and the boys are doing the legwork for me; so do not contact him either, okay?"

"Do you know about Mr. Arnold's other sister, Elaina?" "Yes! I have helped her organization on several occasions. The Miss Elaina is quite a woman. I have met her and worked with her many times." TooMuch fell silent. Nathan pondered the new developments for a few minutes, then added.

"I can't just sit on my hands until you solve the case. How do you want me to go about the investigation without looking like a stupid ass?"

"Do what you are doing now but without a vendetta to storm his private land. I will draw him out at my own time, and you will be the first to move in and make the kill." TooMuch thanked Nathan for the breakfast and walked out making his exit as dramatic as he was accustomed to doing.

Nathan sat in the booth for another thirty minutes or so going over the information mentally. He trusted TooMuch and if Jason and the boys were in on it, he had no worries. In the meantime, he would gather as much information about Jeffery and his brother Bernhard plus the airhead, Deborah, as he could so when the arrests took place and the ladies freed, he could make his case stick. Nathan admitted to himself that he was indeed working against a mastermind. The idea of TooMuch working on the case comforted him.

24

Mendy and Deborah

Deborah sat very still staring into the mirror and wondered, *is Jeffery losing interest in me now that Mendy is on the scene?* She was confused as to the relationship Jeffery had with Mendy. She could not understand why Jeffery was treating her so well. Why didn't he punish her as he had planned all these years? Deborah was confused and tears ran down her cheeks. The more she thought about it the more she became the vicious person she used to be, before she met Jeffery. He had made her soft, and at this very moment, she did not like the feeling. She looked herself in the eye and swore aloud. "I'll just have to do something about my dear sister-in-law. I will chat with her, you bet I will."

She took her own sweet time to finish her nails, hair, makeup, and then dressed to perfection. She glanced one last time in the full-length mirror before leaving her room.

Mendy and Misty were sitting at a table on the terrace putting together a puzzle when Deborah strolled up and asked if she could join them. She spoke lovingly to Misty.

"How's the puzzle coming along, little one?" Misty looked up.

"It's almost finished. Mommy helped me a little, but I did most of it."

"I knew you could. You are a smart little girl. Would you mind if Nanette took your puzzle up to your room and helped you finish it?"

"I guess that means that the grownups want to talk, right?"

"I guess so, honey. Grownup talk is sometimes very boring for a young lady such as you." Deborah rang for Nanette and Misty went off with her.

"Jeffery said you would like to speak to me. What about?" Deborah asked.

"Nothing in particular, just talk to get more acquainted. Trevor and I had been married several years and I had not met you before our arrival here. Now would be a good time to do so. Don't you think?"

"I never had the desire to meet you. What makes you think I want to get acquainted with you now?" Deborah asked.

"Why not? I do not plan to be a guest, as Jeffery so gallantly expresses, longer than absolutely necessary. Soon, either I walk out of here or be planted with the fishes in his beautiful pond. Either way will be more pleasant than listening to Jeffery boasting about his accomplishments. He deserved what he got and I am not sorry for it. It seems to me, he owes me a debt of gratitude. He turned out better than he would have had he relied on a sports career as he thought was so important. A normal man would kill his grandmother to have what Jeffery has. The man is insane, Deborah." Mendy took a sip of iced tea and waited for a reply. Deborah glared at her for a moment then said.

"You don't know what you are talking about. Jeffery is a sweet loving person and very generous. He's worked hard to get what he has and I won't let you mess it up."

"Mess it up! I would not even think of messing it up, as you say. I just want to get out of here and get on with our lives. I cannot even visualize what all this is doing to Misty. She is too young to be uprooted and kept from her father for reasons she does not understand. At this moment, she is in denial and that is not healthy. She watched as a despicable person was raping me and witnessed her mother kill two men. How do you interpret such actions for a child so young?" Mendy stated.

Deborah's eyes got very big and round as she absorbed Mendy's statement.

"My God in Heaven! No one told me that happened. That poor little angel! Jeffery just told me that Bernie grabbed you two off the street and brought you here. You are lying to me Mendy. Stop it now!" Deborah shouted.

"Think, Deborah. What would I gain by lying to you? Just who is lying to you? Can you even imagine how Trevor is feeling about now? That article you read to me from the paper, how do you think that makes me feel? I don't know what the reason is or why he was with that woman. Don't you think I would like a chance to find out? My marriage to your brother could be over. How do you think Trevor will take the news that I was raped? Will he want me back? Misty will never be the same little girl we love so much. Get the answers to these questions, Deborah, and then tell me how bad you have had it."

Deborah came over to Mendy and put her arms around her.
"Mendy, I'm so sorry this has happened. Please forgive me. I have been so wrapped up in my own survival all these years, I never though of anyone else." Deborah cried for a while; went back to her seat and wiped her eyes and blew her nose. Mendy did not cry. She just got madder and madder but she knew she had to control herself. Deborah was vulnerable and she could be an excellent ally. Careful planning has to be done so Jeffery will not blame Deborah for her escape. Mendy realized Deborah had it made with Jeffery and she surely did not want Jeffery to harm her or kick her out of his home. She was not capable of making her own way at this point of her life. Maybe, when she was younger, but certainly not now.

"Deborah, tell me about your youth with Trevor and Elaina. Was it so bad?" Mendy asked.

"It was at the time. I have thought about it a lot since I grew up and I missed the companionship of my brother and sister. But I guess it was my fault entirely. I was a little brat and I took advantage of it. Mama and Daddy pushed them aside and I thought that was neat. I got anything I wanted. I didn't care what the cost was. Poor Trevor and Elaina had to take jobs in school to save for their college expenses. Daddy had spent all his extra money on me. But I didn't care then. I cried for a week when you two got married. I wanted to be there so bad. I thought I was not welcomed, so I just didn't go. Can you understand, Mendy?"

"Yes, I do understand. I was no angel growing up as Jeffery may have told you. I was an only child and spoiled to the high heavens. There was no one around to spite. Therefore, I grew out of it. Now, it's Trevor and Misty I consider first. At least it was before this."

Deborah was feeling melancholy. "Do you think Trevor would talk to me if I went to see him?" Deborah asked.

"I think he would be delighted. He always loved you even though he didn't have a chance to show you. There were several occasions when you got into scrapes in grammar school that he took care of it so you wouldn't get into trouble. You never knew, did you? Elaina paid back the little boy whose lunch money you took. You never knew that either, did you? So, you see. They don't deserve your wrath."

They talked so long they did not realize how late the hour was. Jeffery appeared on the terrace.

"Have you ladies made your peace?" he asked as he directed his question to Mendy.

"We have discussed a few points of interest," she said. Deborah stood and said to Jeffery.

"I think we can be civil to each other while she is here." She walked into the house leaving Jeffery and Mendy alone.

25

Deborah Goes Home

Nathan decided not to tell his captain about TooMuch. He would wait until he got the okay for the arrest of Jeffery and/or Bernhard Warren or Von Seegen, whichever name they legally had.

Nathan was putting on a good show for his people and had several plans to tell his captain if he asked too many questions about the investigation. He mostly stayed away from the station. He would always tell his captain that he was off to interview this one or that one. He spent most of the time researching Jeffery's and Bernhard's activities to the best of his knowledge.

Jeffery Warren was in his office three days a week, sometimes four, but when he was not, Nathan figured he was at that mysterious place in the woods. It really irked him to stay behind the scenes, as instructed by TooMuch. He knew he had to follow the instructions if this Jeffery Warren could be trapped and lead them to Mendy and Misty. He had 100% confidence in the knowledge and skills of TooMuch.

Nathan marveled at what the street people knew and most would not even consider telling a cop. He was just thankful he had befriended people like TooMuch, Jason and his boys. Nathan's motto was "Never burn your bridges behind you if you could avoid it." However, detectives like Nathan were few. He would not arrest a street person, unless of course they had really committed a serious crime against society. He had gained numerous favors in the right places, and he felt good about himself.

Nathan went to Bartsville to talk to the sheriff again. Murphy was very receptive and glad to see him. They were sitting comfortably in Murphy's office. He asked Nathan how the case was going.

"It's moving very slowly. Is there anything new from your end?"

"I've been over and over all the details we have gathered so far and I can't even begin to connect that Warren kid to Mendy's disappearance. He left town after his graduation from high school and no one has heard from him since. His parents moved away about five years later. I guess they were too embarrassed about that cat-killing incident. We did find out that the Warren kid killed the cat and nothing could was done about it. Hell, pets were killed or died every day back then and nobody blinked an eye," Murphy stated.

"I discovered, through scanning the papers, that there was an incident that happened in the high school involving the Warren kid. Something, about getting his toes cut off. What do you know about that?" Nathan asked.

"Well, word was that Mendy's best girlfriend was the one who owned the cat and Mendy, being the most level-headed of the three that hung together, swore she would find out who killed the cat and get even. We all suspected she had something to do with the toe cutting, but we could never prove anything. Maybe this Warren fellow has done some getting even on his own. Have you checked out that possibility?" Murphy asked.

"We have some pretty good leads in the case but nothing concrete. Have you talked to Trevor Arnold or Mendy's parents lately?"

"Yeah, but nothing's changed. Arnold is still upset and yells at me every time we meet. Does he worry you to death too?"

"It's not so much Mr. Arnold but Mr. and Mrs. Parker. They are driving a wedge into every lead we get by sending those damn PIs snooping around." Nathan stood and shook Murphy's hand.

"Murphy, it's been a pleasure, but I have to get my tail back to the city and earn what little pay I hope to get on Friday. If anything good comes down, I'll be sure to let you know first hand."

"Thanks, buddy, I will surely appreciate it. I sure would like to be the one to tell the Parkers if it's good news."

"Oh, and if it's bad, I suppose you will leave that portion to me, uh?" Nathan said with a grin.

Nathan headed back to the city. Murphy could not add much to what Nathan had already accumulated. He could not tell Murphy that he had been in close contact with Trevor Arnold and his sister Elaina. They both would play an important part when the climax came to this whole business.

Elaina had finished the case she was working on and took a few days to visit Trevor. They were eating lunch on the patio at Trevor's house one afternoon when a silver Jaguar drove up the drive. They could not see who was driving the car until it came to a stop not too far from the patio.

When Deborah stepped from the car, both Trevor and Elaina were speechless. Neither had seen nor heard from their little sister since they went off to college.

"My God! Debbie, is that you?" Elaina yelled and stood up.
"It's me in the flesh," Deborah smiled as she strolled up to her siblings.

"Where on earth did you materialize from?" Elaina asked.

"Here and there," she answered.

Elaina put her arms around Deborah and when they pulled apart, there were tears in their eyes.

"Hi there little sister," Trevor said as he opened his arms and gestured to her to come to him. Deborah went willingly into his arms.

While Trevor was holding her, he whispered, "It's good to have you safe in my arms." Deborah knew he meant it.

"Break it up, you two and sit down. Have you had lunch? There is salad and sandwiches here. Let me fix you one. We have just begun our lunch. Please join us won't you?" Elaina was sincerely glad to see her sister. For once in her life, Deborah felt like she belonged with them.

"There's more to catch up on than we have time to cover." Deborah said as she began to eat her salad.

"Let's just start at the beginning," Elaina suggested.   "Trevor, I heard about Mendy and Misty. Have they found them yet?" Deborah asked.

"No. There has been no word from Mendy. The detective working on the case has given us little hope. The more time that passes the less chance they are alive. I cannot work effectively anymore, nor can I get any sleep. I have taken a leave for a month hoping my family will be back and we can get back to normal." Trevor's voice was cracking. Deborah put her hand on his.

"I'm so sorry, Trev. I'm sure it will turn out okay. Just hang in there." She attempted to console him.

"Tell us, Deb, What have you been doing all these years? You look as if you are doing okay."

"I'm fine. You tell me about you. I have missed so much of your successes. I heard you were with the FBI, Elaina. Is that so?" Deborah diverted the conversation away from herself.

"It is so, but there is little I can talk about. It is exciting and interesting and I travel a lot. My job gives me little time for socializing, except in the line of duty. Did you settle on a career?" Elaina asked.

"I have tried a lot of things. I like interior decorating. Mostly, I decorate department stores on my own. I don't work for anyone. I tried that but could never accept other people's ideas or follow their orders."

"How well we know that," Trevor added to the conversation.

"I suppose I was a little difficult to live with while growing up. I think it's time to bury the hatchet. Can you two let sleeping dogs lie and become a family again? It's a terrible feeling when I hear other people talk about their families when I had no one. Can you ever forgive me?" Deborah pleaded.

"It seems we all have some forgiving to do," Elaina said. Trevor agreed. "Lets work on it for awhile and see."

The sun was setting when Deborah said she had to leave. They said their goodbyes and made plans to meet again before Elaina returned to her duties.

Letter #8

15 July 2003
Dearest Rosy,

I am ashamed that I have not written. However, I was quite incapacitated. A severe stroke left me speechless and a bit shaken up. I arrived at my home this morning from a rehabilitation facility. I can speak now and walk some but I will not be running any races.

Jennifer, my secretary, has stood by me and I wanted to tell her to write to you but, alas, I could not until now. Do forgive an old lady.

Jennifer has typed my notes as often as I could say the words and it has been slow going. What few words I have are enclosed. They will continue the story of Ken and Bridget.

How are your treatments coming along? I am anxious to learn how you and the family are. You can tell your mailman that I am back and will finish my story.

Thank you for continuing the story of Mendy. My daughter or granddaughter has read your letters to me. They have been wonderful and patient.

There is only one more phase of my story to tell so I will stop for now and start my notes for next time.

Love,

Rene

SIXTEEN

The Tragedy

Bridget had just received her wedding gift from her father. She spent the next several weeks planning the wedding. Her gown had been finished and the invitations were ready to be sent out. The honeymoon reservations had not been made. She thought there was ample time to do that. She and Ken had set the final date. In three weeks time the event would take place, but not at Eric's estate. They had agreed to hold the wedding in her garden.

She was satisfied that everyone had done an excellent job to make the wedding a success. It was time she relaxed and gave Ken the attention he so gallantly deserved.

Ken and her father had taken a walk down the block to a little tobacco shop. Rudolf had a group of friends that congregated there for idle chitchat. Ken had nothing particular to do this sunny Saturday morning, so he asked Rudolf if he would like to take a walk. He suggested they go to the tobacco shop and meet his friends. This was okay with Ken so they set out.

Bridget was busy giving necessary instructions to the cook, when the doorbell rang. Stacy, the housekeeper, hurried to the door. There stood two uniformed police officers. She called for Bridget excitedly and asked the police officers to come in. Bridget went into the foyer, saw the officers and asked if she could be of any service to them.

"Miss Bridget Barteau?" one of the officers asked.

"Yes, I am Bridget Barteau," she answered.

"Are you acquainted with a Mr. Ken Mitchell and Herr Rudolf Von Seegan?"

"Yes I am. Ken is my fiancé and Herr Von Seegan is my father. Why do you ask?"

"Please sit down Miss Barteau. We have some rather disturbing news to report." After she sat down in the living room, the officer continued.

"Mr. Mitchell and Herr Von Seegan were seated by the front window in Adolf's Smoke Shop. A runaway truck crashed through the window. I am afraid both, along with two others, were killed. I'm so sorry I have the unfortunate task of informing you of this, Miss Barteau."

For an undetermined amount of time, she said nothing, just stared at the police officer. She was in total shock. Stacy was standing nearby. The officer asked her if Miss Barteau had someone to call. "She is in shock and needs medical attention," he said.

"Herr Von Hussen is a family friend I will call him," Stacy said. In the meantime, the officer phoned for an ambulance. Stacy made the call to Eric and he said he would go directly to the hospital.

The police officers stayed with Bridget until the ambulance arrived and had her safely on the way to the hospital. She still had not displayed any emotions to the accident.

Eric arrived at the hospital and went directly to Bridget's room. He was standing by her bedside holding her hand when the doctor entered. He urged Eric to keep talking to her but not about the accident. He started telling her about Angelica and her upcoming recital; what she would be wearing, what tune she would be dancing to and a variety of other subjects he felt would be appropriate.

Eric never left her bedside. His heart was breaking he loved her so deeply. He wanted to take her in his arms and hold her until she spoke again.

Three and a half hours had passed. Eric still had her hand in his. Without any notice at all, Bridget began crying softly at first. A tear was escaping from her closed lids. It ever so gently eased its way down her lovely cheek. Eric called her name several times. She did not open her eyes. He pushed the buzzer for the nurse. She came in and he asked her to get the doctor. He immediately came into the room.

"Any change?" he asked.

"Look!" Eric pointed to her cheek.

"That's good news," the doctor said. "She will be coming around very soon now, so be prepared for the worst. The accident is becoming a reality to her now. I will stay with her. She may need a sedative when she breaks loose. When it happens, hold her tight and let her sob it all out. If I see she's in no danger, I'll leave you to help her through it."

"Thanks doctor, I will stay here with her."

Sure enough, the tears were getting stronger but she had made no sound. The doctor said softly, "It won't be long now, just be ready." Eric and the doctor talked very low for about twenty minutes. Then it happened. Bridget opened her eyes, looked at Eric and the reality did hit her and hit her hard.

"Oh my God Eric, why?" Eric sat down on her bed, took her in his willing arms and held on. She had both of them in tears before she finished and had no more tears to shed.

Eric released her long enough to give her a damp towel for her face. Only then was she able to tell Eric what the officers had told her. She asked if they were positive that her father and Ken both were dead.

"I'm truly sorry, my dear, but it is true."

When Eric felt she could handle it, he told her she would have to identify the bodies. She asked him to go with her to the city morgue. She said she was ready to do it.

Bridget regained her composure. The doctor examined her, determined that she was ready to leave, signed her release form and she was cleared to leave the hospital.

They went directly to the morgue where Ken and her father were. She made the identifications and notified the funeral home then told the Morgue attendant to release the bodies to the funeral home.

Eric took her to his house. He did not want her to be alone this particular night. She did not object and felt she needed to be with someone at this time. She was okay on the ride home. They talked and talked about the accident as the doctor had recommended. Eric insisted that she talk about the deaths as much as possible so she could fully accept it now and later she would not suffer more than normal.

Eric learned the details of the accident from the police report and how it happened according to the witnesses.

He assisted Bridget in making the arrangements. There would be a double funeral.

The funerals took place and both her father and Ken were interred in the Von Seegan family plot. Bridget knew her father would be pleased. They were very close and he loved Ken like a son.

After the funerals, Bridget was ready to return to her own home. She had been in contact with Stacy and she was doing a good job running the household without Bridget.

Stacy was proud of the trust Bridget had placed in her. She had worked hard to reclaim the trust she lost when employed by the Von Hussen family. When the agency told her of this position, she jumped at the chance to prove herself a top-rated servant. She knew she was capable and put forth more effort than most. The education she had given herself paid off when Bridget asked her to manage the household accounts.

Bridget went home to that huge empty house. Ken and her father could be seen everywhere. She began sobbing once again. She knew it would be this way, but she had to release the pain and deal with it.

Rosy Answers Letter #8

August 12, 2003

Dear Rene,

      Your letter was a breath of fresh air to me. I am so relieved and thankful that you are okay. Girl, you scared me to death but I understand.

      I am not fairing too well these days. The cancer is getting the best of me. Thank God in Heaven that I can still think. I do urge you to hurry with your story. Mine is near to the end. My secretary will finish typing my notes this week and I will forward them to you.

      It was so tragic and sad to hear of the deaths of Ken and Herr Von Seegan. Things were beginning to look good for Bridget and Ken. Now what will she be doing? She has no family, no Ken, poor child, my heart really breaks for her.

      Deborah and Mendy have mended some fences but Jeffery cannot think of them at this time. He is more concerned about people snooping on his property.

      I won't go into it further here; it is all neatly in my notes. It is time for my rest period. Let me say once again, I am so happy you are home.

      We all will gladly receive your next letter. Write soon.

Love,

Rosy

26

The Truce

Jeffery sat down at the table with Mendy. He was curious as to what the girls had discussed.

"I assume you and Deborah have settled your differences," he stated.

"She did admit that it was not I to whom she should be directing her resentment. I have no hard feeling toward her. She was not the one who had us kidnapped. Tell me, Jeffery, what do you plan to do with us?" she asked.

"Well, my dear, in the beginning I was so filled with hate for you that I put all my energy into planning your fate. However now, after our little visit here, I have gotten to know you much better than I did back when, and your little girl is so precious. You both softened me, which is most disturbing." He rose and started pacing. Mendy had no comment at this point. She stayed quiet and listened. He continued.

"My fate is now on the line. I have put us all in jeopardy because of a childhood grudge." He sat down again and looked Mendy directly in the eye.

"Mendy, what would you have done about the affair your husband had, if you had not come here?" He asked her. Mendy thought for a few seconds.

"Oh, Jeffery, why would he destroy the union we had. I had no idea he was unhappy. Do you know if he has continued to see this woman?" she asked sadly.

"I honestly have heard nothing to indicate that he has seen her again," Jeffery answered.

"My feelings for Trevor have changed drastically. I don't know if forgiving him is a possibility. I have told Misty about it and I couldn't tell if she understood or not. The poor little thing just will not talk about the things that have happened. She hasn't even asked why we are here, not even the rape in the van. Jeffery, you bastard! She saw that brute rape me, not once but twice. He would have done the same to Misty had I not intervened. How could you allow this?" Mendy was getting madder by the minute.

The conversation had gone in the wrong direction. Jeffery intended to bare his soul and profess his love for her but now it was impossible to divert back.

"I do apologize for that. Bernie had no idea the man was so illiterate. He would have intervened, had he known at the time. It is most unfortunate, but what's done is done and we must attempt to ease the situation. As for your dilemma, my dear, the authorities have been poking around up above. They haven't figured out how to get in yet and I doubt that they will. However, you cannot stay here forever, so we must plan for what is best for all concerned. I do not plan to harm either you or Misty, but you can see the situation is not ideal. How can I allow you to go free without repercussions from the authorities?" he asked seriously. "I have too much at stake to let this destroy all I have worked for all of my adult life no matter what the reason I was so driven."

Mendy was absorbing his statements and he was getting through to her. She felt that it really was her fault that this abduction took place. She was trying to think of a suitable plan of her own. Hate was not in her at this moment and vulnerability consumed her. Then she spoke.

"Jeffery, is it possible for us to work out an agreement between us, one that we both can live with? Perhaps Bernie could have hired the two men to do some odd jobs for you, maybe on the cabin and they knew it was deserted most of the time. They didn't know about your surveillance cameras. That fellow Jeeter and his brother happened to see Misty and me walking down the street; temptation consumed them, and brought us to the cabin for their own little pleasures. When they were through with their adventure, they left Misty and me in the forest to fend for ourselves. Your camera detected us and Bernie went to the cabin to investigate. He rescued us and brought us here. I can easily fake amnesia and Misty is already in denial. When or if the authorities reach us the rest of the story is up to you. What do you think?"

Jeffery drew a hearty breath and let it out.

"That's a brilliant idea. However, it is full of holes. First, Deborah knows you are her sister-in-law, even though she only met you when you came here. The possibility of pulling this scheme off is slim to none. Deborah could easily deny knowing you. Because of your amnesia, we didn't know your names. But, how can I trust you to go along with it?" he asked.

"Jeffery, you all have been marvelous to us. You have treated us very well. Although that man accosted me, there is no real harm done to me. But I am positive Misty will require medical attention," she answered.

Mendy was not about to lay all her cards on the table just yet. It just might be interesting to continue the ruse. When they are safely home, she could see if Trevor would tell her of his affair. Her thoughts were running wild. Jeffery startled her when he spoke.

"We will have to put some careful thought into this madness and discuss it thoroughly." Jeffery excused himself and Mendy went to Misty's room.

Bernie was in the surveillance room when Jeffery entered. He conveyed the story Mendy had concocted and waited for Bernie's response. He ran his fingers through his hair then smiled.

"That's quite a plan. My question is how do we account for the fact that Mendy killed the two brothers?"

"I thought about that. They do have a reckless reputation. Anyone could have done them in. There is no evidence that they were killed here or thrown into the river. Is there?" Jeffery asked concerned.

"No absolutely none," Bernie answered with confidence.

"Where is Deborah?" Jeffery asked.

"She went into the city. She said she would talk to the manager of Zilo's Department Store about decorating. She's due back soon."

"Tell her to see me the moment she returns."

"Okay." They said nothing further and Jeffery departed.

Some time later Deborah strolled into Jeffery's study.

"Hello, Jeffery, Bernie said you wanted to see me," she stated.

"Yes, we have urgent business to discuss which concerns us all. Where were you all day?" He asked

"I went to visit Trevor today."

"You did what?" He asked excitedly.

"Yes, and Elaina happened to be taking a vacation and she was at Trevor's house."

"What prompted your sudden family reunion?"

"Well, Mendy got me to thinking. She told me some things I never realized happened when I was at home tormenting Trevor and Elaina. I feel so much better now. I am glad I decided to make amends."

"You didn't happen to mention that Mendy and her daughter were here, did you?"

"Of course not, I may be a little shallow, but I'm not stupid. They tried to pry personal information from me, but I changed the subject and we started laughing about incidents that happened when we were children. I think things are okay with us. We plan to meet again sometime."

"That prompts me to tell you something," said Jeffery. "I am confident I can trust you."

"What is it?" she asked with interest.

"You realize what a sticky situation we are in at present. Mendy and I were discussing it today. She came up with an excellent plan that will benefit all of us."

He recounted the entire conversation to Deborah and he asked her to express her views. She was totally surprised and pleased that he wanted her opinion on something more important than what she bought while shopping. She hesitated in answering. What she said would have to hold some merit or she would feel inadequate to converse with him. Finally, she said.

"It sounds good to me. I could be the key that unlocks the mystery."

"How's that?" he asked with peaked interest.

"Well, actually I didn't know what Mendy looked like before I saw her here. When they were married, there were no pictures in the papers, the ones that I read anyway. When I go back to Trevor's house, I can look to see if there are any pictures anywhere and I can act surprised and tell them I know where Mendy and Misty are. Then, tell them the amnesia story. Wouldn't that work, Jeffery?"

"Could you actually pull it off?" he asked her.

"Yes I certainly can. I had some training when I enrolled in acting school. That's when I ran away from home and they couldn't find me. I visualized becoming a great actress so they would be envious of me. Oh, how immature I was then."

"Let's get together with the others and go over the plan. Do you think we can trust Mendy to stick with the plan and not change her mind and press charges against us?" he asked her.

"I think we can. After all, you haven't mistreated either of them and it could have turned out worse for her after she found out Trevor was cheating on her. Let's ask her," she suggested.

Letter #9

9 September 2003

Dear Rosy,

 This letter will conclude my story of Ken and Bridget. I trust you, your husband and your mailman were amazed. However, the story is true to the best of my recollection.

 It is sad that our lives are ending and so much time lapsed before we reconnected.

 My memories of our childhood are wonderful and those I do not want to erase. They will remain until I breathe my last breath.

 As for you dear Rosy, enjoy what time you have left and remember the blessings not the shortcomings.

 Take care of yourself my friend.

Love,

Rene

SEVENTEEN

Finale

After Bridget settled in, she phoned both attorneys regarding the wills. She put off the readings as long as she could. The time had come to face it. She felt she could not do this alone. Again, she called on Eric. Naturally, he willingly agreed to accompany her to the attorney's office.

Ken's attorney was due to fly into Berlin within the week. She dreaded the thoughts of having to do this all over again when Ken's attorney arrived.

As planned, Eric was prompt in coming for Bridget. They were at the attorney's office exactly at the agreed upon time. He had everything ready upon their arrival.

Her father's will was extensive, explaining that there were no other heirs. Bridget inherited the entire estate. She was astonished at how vast his holdings were.

The attorney had been a friend to Herr Von Seegan for many years. He explained what her father had to go through in order to regain his property after the war. The search for his children was relentless. He was so relieved and happy that the good Lord had brought his Bridget back into his life.

It took very little time in the reading of Ken's will. Bridget was, again, sole heir to his entire estate, which consisted mostly of investments and his bank accounts. It was substantial. She realized that she was indeed a wealthy woman.

On the way home, Eric suggested they take a holiday to the Canary Islands, to get away from things for a while. She was pleased that he had suggested it. The thought of taking a trip was already on her mind but she hesitated to go alone.

Eric very seldom traveled without Angelica, his mother or Jacco. This trip would be no exception. Bridget was pleased. His family was an added reward as she loved them very much, especially Angelica. The enthusiasm she displayed indicated to Eric that it was time they all moved on with their lives.

During the next few months, Eric and Bridget became the focus of attention and became "an item." Eric refused to let her sink into the trap of becoming that poor thing that lost her fiancé just weeks before her wedding.

The two were together constantly. Eric had no time to start another book. However, he knew he would have to settle down and write another book as he had promised his publisher.

Angelica was approaching her graduation from high school. She had been accepted and preparing for college.

The comings and goings were frantic around the Von Hussen house. The Senior Prom, the graduation, getting Angelica established in the college dorm, had everyone's nerves on edge. Frau Von Hussen had organized and given instructions, which she insisted be followed to the letter. No single detail went astray. Eric and Jacco were ready to throw up their hands in defeat.

As expected, Eric had thoroughly checked out the young man who was to take his daughter to the prom without a chaperone. His thoughts raced back to his own youth. Many handkerchiefs were soaked from perspiration. He knew he had to clip the apron strings just a little, but he was not quite ready to cut them completely.

Throughout this period, Bridget took the opportunity to spend some time alone at her own home. She seemed to be adjusting well. Less time now was spent thinking of Ken and her father.

The next few days she spent pampering, shopping trips, the hairdresser and the spa, which she needed desperately. She did a lot of thinking about herself and Eric. She was madly in love with him. She believed with all her heart that he had the same feelings for her.

The relationship she and Ken experienced was not true love but more of trusting and loyal friends. She realized the marriage would not have lasted and a good friendship wasted. She did not try to understand why Ken had to die, but the realization of his death was there and it was very hard to accept.

Angelica's prom was of a dream setting. A night she would cherish for many years to come. She was the center of attention throughout the evening. She and her date were crowned King and Queen of the prom.

Eric was so proud when he saw her pictures. His excitement prompted his call to Bridget. He rattled on and on about Angelica. Such a doting father, Bridget thought. It will be so hard for him when she goes off to college.

Bridget was experiencing similar feelings. After all, she was thoroughly familiar with Angelica's life.

In his enthusiasm of the moment, he blurted out the question.

"Will you marry me, my love?"

Bridget was so astonished she was silent for a few seconds. Did she really hear what she thought she heard? He repeated the question and waited.

"Of course I will, darling. I thought you would never ask." He apologized for the abrupt way he had asked her. It just popped out. But he was not sorry that it happened. He told her he had loved her since his first glimpse of her on the cruise. Bridget expressed her feelings for him also. She told him she knew she loved him when they were dancing at his party.

Angelica's graduation and departure to college took place under Frau Von Hussen's expert direction. They all were sad and glad at the same time. They each admitted to themselves that Angelica was now a young woman who would seek her own destiny, rise or fall. However, there were no doubts that she would rise to the highest level.

The main event, the wedding, was the talk of Eric's social circle. His family and friends were pleased and excited to be a part of this perfect union between Eric and Bridget.

Neither had ever been married, therefore, the nuptials would be formal to the hilt. The extravaganza took place. Angelica was Bridget's maid of honor. Frau Von Hussen wept throughout the entire service.

The celebration after the wedding was one never seen before no expense spared. Bridget was in her glory moment. After the priest pronounced them man and wife, the kiss Eric gave her sealed her fate. She was, willingly, trapped in a life of sheer bliss.

Rosy Answers Letter #9

September 30, 2003
Dearest Rene,

     Your letters have portrayed such a beautiful but tragic story. It is difficult to believe it was true.

     Did you know Bridget personally? Is she still happy with Eric and his family?

     Please continue to write to me. I need to know you are still there.

     The doctors have put a time limit on my existence. Three months is not a long time. I will not let a single moment pass and not make the most of it.

     I have enclosed the finale of my story and I trust you will, if you have not already, contact Mendy. She would be ecstatic to hear from you.

     I am not dead yet so keep those letters coming.

Love,
Rosy

27

Finale

Mendy was in the playroom and she and Misty were discussing the plan. Mendy explained in simple words so she could understand what she had to do when the time came.

Misty was excited as she listened to the story her mother was telling her. When Mendy had explained what was to happen and would continue to happen even when they returned home. Misty clapped her hands.

"Mommy, this will be so much fun. I can pretend and no one can tell me it isn't real."

"When we are absolutely alone, you and I will talk about it, okay?"

"Yes, I know just what to do," she said and giggled.

"Now, we must go down and tell the grownups that we understand." Mendy took her daughter's hand and went down to the dining room.

Jeffery, Bernie, Deborah and the entire household staff were there. They entered the room and sat down. Everyone was silent then, Jeffery calmly addressed the assembly.

"If we succeed with this plan, first, we have to take a picture of Mendy and Misty. Second, I will take it to the authorities and explain how it came to be that you two have been here and we have done nothing to attempt to find out your identities."

Bernie had the Polaroid camera ready and when Jeffery paused in his instructions, he took the photo of Mendy and Misty.

Misty was delighting over the entire scenario. She interrupted and gleefully added.

"Oh, Jeffery, all of us will be in a play. We all will be pretending. I do that with my dolls," she said with a smile.

"Princess, you will do fine. After this is all over, we will get together and go to some enchanting place. Would you like that?" He asked.

"Oh yes. You will be so proud of me."

"I'm sure I will, honey."

The group continued to discuss the plan, even the minute details. They were so engrossed in the plan that they were surprised when Jeffery looked toward the entrance to the dining room and saw a hoard of police officers entering the dining room. He was speechless and it took a few moments for him to believe an intruder was successful in penetrating his home.

"Jeffery Warren, Bernhard Warren, you are under arrest for the kidnapping of Mendy and Misty Arnold." Nathan read them the Miranda Rights. Jeffery had regained his senses and spoke directly to Nathan.

"What's the charge again, officer?"

"Kidnapping, you heard me the first time," Nathan snapped.

Elaina rushed over to Mendy.

"Mendy, are you alright?" She looked puzzled at Elaina and said nothing.

"Mendy, it's Elaina, your sister-in-law. Don't you know me?"
Then Mendy spoke, "I'm afraid I don't know you Miss. What name did you call me?"

"Mendy, Mendy Sue Arnold and this is your daughter, Misty Arnold." Elaina was beginning to get concerned. Mendy looked directly into Elaina's eyes and stated.

"I am sorry Miss; I am not familiar with the person you speak of," Mendy stated with a puzzled look on her face.

Elaina turned to Misty.

"Misty I'm your Aunt Elaina. Your father sent me to bring you home." Misty did not change her expression. She just starred at Elaina.

"What have you done to them?" She screamed at Jeffery.
"Madam, would you tell me what in Hell this is all about, perhaps I could supply some answers," Jeffery stated.

"Don't act like these two here are just casual friends of yours," Nathan added.

"At this very moment, these two, as you put it, are indeed my friends," Jeffery replied.

"Don't give me that crap, Warren. These two disappeared more than two weeks ago and we have been looking for them until now."

"My dear fellow, please ask the lady and the child how they happened to be here," Jeffery demanded.

Both, Mendy and Misty had this blank look. Nathan directed his question to Mendy.

"Mrs. Arnold, could you tell me what you are doing here?"
"Of course I can, officer. Mr. Warren was kind enough to take us into his

home after an unpleasant encounter with two wretched beings. Mr. Warren's physician determined we both have been horribly abused." Nathan's astonished look implied he halfway was swallowing her story.

Jeffery spoke up.

"We were discussing this dilemma when you so rudely invaded my home. By the way, may I see your warrant for such an intrusion?" Nathan handed Jeffery the warrant.

"We all have to go to the station and sort this whole thing out," he said.

"Unless you have reasonable cause to do so, officer, I suggest you prove, without a doubt, that a crime has been committed here," Jeffery calmly stated. Nathan turned to Elaina and she shrugged her shoulders as if saying, "He's got you there."

"The lady and the child are free to go at their discretion. As you can see, it is a clear case of amnesia. They have not been able to tell us who they are." Jeffery picked up the picture Bernie had laid on the table.

"I was in the process of taking the picture to the authorities. Now, if these are the females you are looking for, it will answer the questions that have been plaguing us. We would have come forward sooner, but they have been recovering from their ordeal. Your agency will have a full report from my physician."

Elaina asked Mendy if she would come with her. She would introduce her to the man to whom she is married. Mendy looked at Jeffery and he assured her that it was the proper thing to do.

"What about the child. Is she my daughter?" Mendy asked innocently.

"Yes dear and your husband is anxious for your return." Elaina answered.

Mendy went to Jeffery. She put her arms around him and he responded.

"Jeffery, thank you for all you have done to assist us. I felt so safe here. Do we really have to go?" She asked.

"Yes, my dear, for now you must go with the lady and the officers," Jeffery said.

"You will keep in touch won't you?" Mendy asked.

"My dear, a team of horses couldn't detain me." Misty also approached him and said she would see him soon.

"Mr. Warren, I'm rather glad this turned out on the better side. Normally it doesn't. You will be hearing from us." Nathan shook his hand and started to leave.

"Officer, do you mind telling me just how you penetrated my home? It would be most beneficial for my future security." Nathan grinned and answered him.

"All I can say is your security is lacking. You should change the code on the shed door. Too many people might have it."

With that statement, he tipped his finger to his hat and asked Mendy if she was ready to go.

There were no grounds for the arrest of Jeffery so the best Nathan could do was order his men to withdraw from the premises. Nathan was so fascinated with the underground structure he asked Jeffery if he could return and take a more thorough look. Jeffery agreed to give him a tour at any time he was available.   Elaina and Nathan took the girls home. They were in the back seat of Nathan's car. Mendy stole a glance at Misty and winked. Misty didn't even blink. She turned her head and peered out the window.

They drove up to Mendy's house. Trevor was waiting for them on the terrace. Elaina had called and informed him that they had found his wife and daughter but something was terribly wrong. They did not remember who they were. Trevor refused to believe it. He had not ever encountered someone with amnesia. How was he supposed to act? Elaina encouraged him to take one step at a time until Mendy adjusted. Time probably would be the answer.

Mendy and Misty walked onto the terrace and began looking around as if they were in a strange place. Misty went over to the railing and saw her cherished swans. She said nothing as she watch them gliding over the surface of the lake.

Trevor spoke to Mendy.

"Hello, Mendy how are you?" Mendy did not change the expression on her face.

"I have been told you are my husband and the little girl is our daughter. This is difficult for me to comprehend just now. I ask you to have patience with us." Trevor didn't know what to say.

"Do you need to freshen up before dinner? I'll show you and Misty to your rooms."

Trevor was shaking with the desire to hold her in his arms and he dreaded the fact that he and his beautiful wife would be in separate bedrooms. Elaina had already explained that separate bedrooms would be appropriate for now. He was so relieved to have them back with him. He led them to the rooms they would be occupying and left them to get accustomed to their surroundings.

Trevor went back down and joined Elaina on the terrace. His heart was racing and he was at a loss to understand Mendy's indifference to him and Misty, she was his angel before this happened. His thoughts were running wild. Will they ever come out of it?

"Trev?" Elaina asked as she put her hand on his arm. "Are you okay?"

"No, I'm not okay. My wife does not recognize me and my daughter acts as if I am a total stranger. How can we live like this? Does the doctor have any idea when or if they will snap out of it?" Elaina had no answer for him. He started sobbing and she could not comfort him. She left him alone and went to see if she could help Mendy. She knew Trevor had to be alone to deal with it.

She knocked on Mendy's door then heard a faint, "Come in." Mendy was standing at her closet as if looking to see what clothes were there.

"Is there anything I can help you with Mendy?" Elaina asked.

"No, I don't believe so. Are all these clothes mine?" she asked.

"Yes they are. Don't you remember anything?"

"This room seems to be familiar somehow. I feel comfortable in it. Do you live here Miss?" Mendy asked.

"Oh no, I'm just visiting. Trevor is my brother. I won't be here much longer. I have to get back to work. I took a mini vacation to be with him while you were away. He has missed you very much and he does love you and Misty."

Mendy almost blew it. She wanted to say, "Of course he does. He runs to another woman at the first opportunity that comes along." However, she held her tongue and wished Elaina would leave soon. She could handle Trevor but Elaina was another story.

"Miss, do you mind, I would like to be alone for awhile with the little girl. We should be getting acquainted if she's my daughter," Mendy said.

"That's a great idea. It will be good for you both." Elaina hugged Mendy and left the room.

Mendy waited for a little while before going to Misty's room. Then she entered the hallway and searched up and down to make sure no one was near by and then entered Misty's room.

When she saw Misty, she put her finger to her lips as if to say, "be very quiet."

"Hi, Sweetheart, you were terrific. You acted like you didn't even know Daddy. Does it hurt not to give Daddy a big hug?" she asked Misty.

"It does a little and I did miss Daddy a whole lot, but Jeffery is nice too. When can we see him again?" she asked.   "Not for awhile, honey. We have to play act a little longer. Can you do it?"

"I don't know Mommy, I'll try very hard." Mendy put her arms around Misty held her tight and whispered into her ear. "Baby, I'll let you know when we can stop pretending, okay?" Misty thought the game was fun and did not mind playing her part a little while longer.

They talked and played together and Mendy helped Misty bathe and dress. She also had freshened up and changed clothing. They both were beginning to wish they were back in their paradise with Jeffery where they no longer had to pretend. They had lived well with Trevor, but since learning of his infidelities, Mendy's attitude had changed drastically. She had changed. Why? Did she ever love Trevor as she imagined she did? He was no longer her knight in shining armor.

Misty entered her thoughts. She was only playing a game. However, Mendy's game was real. She wanted Jeffery. The thought amazed her but she was certain that she had fallen in love with him. She had to end this ruse soon, not only for Misty but also for her. Jeffery had made no indication that he could love her after all she had done to him; however, she would take that chance. She and Misty could have a new life with or without either Trevor or Jeffery. Then her thoughts switched to the beginning, she was not sure she could make love to anyone after the rape. That memory was fading but she knew she would have to deal with it when Misty decided to ask her about it.

Her thoughts vanished as she and Misty strolled onto the terrace. Trevor and Elaina were sitting at the table and saw the girls were heading in their direction.

"Well, aren't you two looking fresh and beautiful?" Trevor complimented them and invited them to join him and Elaina.

Mendy and Misty played their deadly game for another week. Mendy decided she could not put Misty through this any longer. She asked Misty if she would rather stay at Trevor's house or go back to Jeffery. Misty did not hesitate to say she wanted to live with Jeffery.

Her mind was made up; Mendy approached Trevor one morning before Misty had gotten up.

"Trevor? It's of no use to continue and make believe we are a family. Misty and I have to leave here. You are entitled to a life of your own. Please make arrangements for a divorce." She did not wait for a reply from him. She went directly to the phone and called Jeffery.

Letter #10

15 October 2003

Dear Rosy,

I have a confession to make. At last, I can finish my story. Yes dear my story. It started a long time ago. Ken and I met when he and his family were in France. His father was an ambassador from the United States.

Ken was only 16 at that time and I at 15 and foolishly believed I was a woman. Can you imagine two children roaming the streets of Paris? My girlfriend and I had the false confidence to handle any situation. She had a great influence over me, more than I care to admit now.

One afternoon our parents were in a meeting and we two girls were bored out of our minds. We decided to take a little stroll down-town. We stopped at a quaint little sidewalk café. There were two handsome teens giving us the once-over. Naturally, we were thrilled to get the slightest attention, especially from two handsome older guys who were expressing an interest in us.

We adjusted the chairs, so we would be facing in their direction. One glance, one wink or a slight rise of an eyebrow led to, eventually, them joining our table.

We got so desperate we were sneaking out at every opportunity to meet these boys. On the other hand, the boys had their own devious plans for us. One thing led to another and my girl friend, fortunately escaped damage. I was not so lucky; hence, I got pregnant with Ken's child, Sasha.

Ken was so gallant; he wanted to approach his parents to obtain permission to get married. He did express his feelings for me.

The idea was simply out of the question. Well, to make a painful story short, I confessed to my parents and keeping the baby was not an option. The scandal would weigh heavily on our reputation in our social circle.

As soon as time would permit, my family sent me away, supposedly to a finishing school in the States. My parents joined me just before the baby was born. Afterwards, we moved to Bartsville, Georgia. That is when I entered school there and met you.

Unknown to my parents, Ken and I stayed in touch. I told Ken what adoption agency had our little girl and where it was located. He never forgot.

As time passed, my interests shifted to other things and people. As you know, my father's job took us away from Bartsville. The communication between Ken and I fell by the wayside.

Ken met Marsha, fell in love and they were married. As it happened, Marsha was from Bartsville and that is where they decided to settle.

Ken and Marsha could not have children and after many attempts and failures to conceive, they decided to adopt. Ken knew just where to go. It was a miracle; Sasha was still there and Ken was pleased to get his little girl back. Marsha fell in love with Sasha the moment she laid eyes on her.

After the disappearance of Sasha and Marsha's death, Ken was on his way to destruction, as I told you in the story. When he recovered, he contacted me.

At that time, my parents were gone, leaving me free and financially able to do whatever I wanted. I told Ken about my sailing to Germany. He liked the idea and said he would go along if I had no objections.

Now, you know the entire story as it happened. I know you are disappointed that I kept this from you but please understand it was necessary for all concerned.

Eric and I had a great marriage. We had Angelica, and I firmly believe, without a doubt that somehow Eric rescued my Sasha from that creek bank before Ken's search party reached her. As for the white angelic hair, only God knows.

I have enjoyed her as my own. Her beautiful children, my grandchildren, have made our life together complete. Eric passed away and all my regrets passed with him. I now have no secrets in my closet.

I continue to enjoy Angelica and her children, which to them I am their Nana, as it should be.

To learn that Jeffery and Bernie are my brothers and they are alive and well makes this story worth bringing to a close.

Honey, if I do not hear from you again you can rest assured I will meet you soon at a far better place.

Good-bye my dear friend.

Love,
Rene/aka Bridget

Rosy's Final Answer

November 2, 2003

Rene, My Dear Friend,

I have enjoyed your letters and I am grateful you allowed me the perfect chance to confess. Yes, my dear, it was not Mendy's story. It was mine. Mendy is fine and happy.

My daughter and I did indeed go back to Jeffery. Jeffery was in love with me all along. When Bernie took us to his place, he did have some horrible fate planned for me. He couldn't carry out his plan. He realized that he loved me too much and wanted a life with me, and at the time I agreed to the amnesia plan, he knew I was in love with him.

As for Deborah, Jeffery was just an ornament to her. She and Bernie approached Jeffery and confessed that they had been in love for many years. He gave them his blessings and told them about Misty and me coming to live there permanently.

When I spoke to you on the telephone about Jeffery and Bernie being a Von Seegan, then I knew. However, I wanted to hear it from you.

As I have a date with the Angel of Death, I won't be able to make the trip to Germany but afterward, my dear Jeffery and Bernie will make the trip to see you.

Love you forever,

Rosy

THE END

LaVergne, TN USA
09 April 2010
178753LV00001B/14/P